Reflection Pond

ଈଓ ◆ ଓଃ

Kacey Vanderkarr

This book is a work of fiction. Names, characters, places, and incidents either are products of the author's imagination or are used fictitiously. Any resemblance to actual persons, living or dead, events, or locales is entirely coincidental.

Reflection Pond
Copyright © 2014 Kacey Vanderkarr
All rights reserved.

Cover design by Bioblossom Creative
www.bioblossomcreative.com
Book design by Kacey Vanderkarr

Visit www.KaceyVanderkarr.com

First Printing: April 2014
Urban Fey Press

ISBN-13 978-0615966236

Also in this Series

Also Available from Kacey Vanderkarr

Short Fiction

For MB and RLL,
who give me courage.

෯ ✦ ෮

Reflection Pond

৪৩ ◆ ৫৪

✎ One ✎

HIS HAND SLID under Callie's shirt, branded skin, slipped into places she tried to keep hidden.

"No," she said, shoving his fingers away. "No."

Nate froze and made a disgusted sound. "Callie…"

She tugged her shirt down.

He sighed. "This has to stop. Do you expect me to wait forever?"

Callie climbed off the bed and curled her trembling hands into fists. She hated the wash of his breath on her neck, the smell of his skin, soap and cheap cologne. She'd never loved him, only hoped that if she tried hard enough, she'd miraculously transform into a puzzle that still had all its pieces. *Fake it until you make it,* she thought bitterly.

"Callie…" He stood now, came two steps closer as she shrank away. "We can work this out."

Behind Nate, the bed lay disheveled and made a mockery of her inadequacy. She added to the list of things she hated—the ten by eight foot space of Nate's room, the bed, the way he said her name, his refusal to give up.

"I said *I can't,* Nate." His name slid between clenched teeth. Callie backed up further, until the cold roundness of the doorknob pressed into her back. Her heartbeat thundered everywhere, chest, fingertips, and scalp.

Nate scraped his hands through unruly curls. He was attractive enough, she supposed, muscular from playing football. But he was right; she couldn't expect him to wait forever, just as he couldn't expect her to ever be ready.

The hard ball of the doorknob filled her hand. She bolted, leaving Nate standing dumbfounded, surrounded by the dirty clothes that lined his floor and the sparkling football trophies on his shelves.

She didn't stop to see if he was chasing her. It didn't matter if he was because every part of her body screamed to run faster. Out the front door, across the patchy lawn, past her foster home next door where the screen gaped open and the shutters hung crooked.

Callie pushed harder, wondering if she could run fast enough to dissipate like smoke, to *un-become*.

She couldn't go home—if she could call it home—where the stench of her foster mother's cancer seeped into the walls, where she was expected to play parent to the younger foster kids. She couldn't return to Nate—not ever—not with the humiliation clawing at her chest. Callie knew she'd never be ready. Not in a week, a month…a year.

Never.

The thought of Nate's skin on hers made Callie gag as she steered her legs toward the park. She gasped for air around the bile burning her throat. She knew she looked crazy but couldn't bring herself to care. She blew past the old man walking his dog and the girl drawing a hopscotch board on broken concrete. It was as though seventeen years of needing to escape had finally caught up with her.

The sun shone bright, but to Callie, it was shadows.

Struggling trees surrounding a mucky pond came into view—the park. She registered the change from hard, unforgiving sidewalk to scratchy, dry grass, and didn't slow. She ran around empty benches where bums slept at night, under the swing set, clattering the chains that dangled without seats. She ran with a singular vision—freedom.

Callie didn't see the motorbike or hear the shouts that intruded upon the desolate wasteland of her life. She didn't see the man as he fell from his bike or the look of horror on his face. She saw the sky, impossibly blue, as she flew into the air. Callie saw the dank, clouded surface of the reflection pond, too dirty to have ever served as a mirror, and she saw her life—a short, inconsequential blip on the grand map of existence.

And then, she broke the surface.

The blue sky smudged gray like a painting and the splash echoed in her ears, muffled by the suffocating sound of being underwater. The reflection pond felt wrong—warm, silky, like the lining of a winter coat—and it made her remember.

She opened her mouth to scream, tasting imaginary, pink bubbles, but nothing happened. No stagnant pond water rushed into her throat.

She didn't drown. She didn't even choke.

Callie fell through the water and hit a solid, freezing cold floor with the force of a two-story drop. Her lungs paralyzed from the impact and she rolled onto her back, eyes widening. Above her, floating as though suspended by magic, was the pond. She could make out the bottom, clogged with weeds. Sand swirled around the spot she'd fallen through, hitting an invisible barrier and bouncing back. Humid, floral scented air rushed into her lungs and she sat up, surprised to find her clothes and hair dry.

Heart hammering, she dragged herself to her feet and rubbed the sore spots on her elbows. The fear of suffocation faded, replaced with curiosity and the unmistakable relief of escaping Nate.

Pale light filtered through the pond and cast dancing beams onto the walls. The only other illumination came from small rocks that lined the floor. There was a word for that in the back of her mind—bioluminescent. Dark stone walls dripped with humidity. In the distance, water gurgled. Bright flowers in blues, purples, and pinks hung from vines, their heavy heads as large as dinner plates, bowed to the ground.

It was like something from a painting, too beautiful to be real.

"We have stairs you know," a male voice said.

Callie whirled to find two guys.

They were as alike as they were different, around her age or a little older. They held an identical posture as they stood staring at her, arms crossed over their chests, legs wide, feet bare and dirty. There was a lightness about them and Callie imagined they could move very fast if they wanted. The taller one had wavy, jet black hair that hung to his shoulders, and intense, light blue eyes. His lips twisted into a smirk. The second boy was shorter than the first, very pale, with green eyes and ginger hair that bordered on strawberry blond. His features were small and fine, pretty for a boy; and he smiled, amused.

"What message have you brought us?" the dark-haired boy asked, smirk turning into a grimace.

Callie stared, wondering if she'd hit her head and this was just a wacky, concussion-induced vision. The boy's eyes narrowed. She looked up; the pond was still there, swirling with absolute benevolence. She searched for an exit. Stone walls. Stone floor. The pond. The three of them with no doors. A new fear fizzled in her stomach.

"I don't—" she started, voice breathy and uncertain. Her gaze returned to the pond. "How?"

The dark haired boy snorted, drawing her gaze. "This is the antechamber; you know your charms are stripped here."

"Don't be rude," the redhead spoke up. He took a step forward, holding his forearm out. "I'm Ash," he nodded his head towards the other boy, "this is Rowan."

"How—did I just...how did I get here?" Despite falling through the pond, Callie's mouth was dry. She stared at his offered arm, confused. Where did he intend to escort her? "Did you fall through too? Are we trapped?"

The dark-haired one, Rowan, took a step closer, a curious expression on his face. "She doesn't know," he said, fascinated, glancing at Ash. "She has no idea."

Ash looked between Rowan and Callie, his face a question mark. "That's not possible."

"It is," Rowan insisted. He pushed the ends of Callie's sweaty hair off of her chest, and she was too frozen with terror to stop him. "Look," he pointed to her pale skin, "she doesn't have an imprint." Rowan glowered furiously at Callie, as though she had any idea what he meant.

She glanced down at the purple tank top she wore. Loose strands of hair clung to her skin. She backed away, gasping when her shoulders hit the warm foliage that covered the walls. "What is going on?" She gestured to the ceiling. "I just fell through…" Callie cleared her throat, voice hoarse and high with borderline hysteria. "I just fell through the pond." She shook her arms. "I'm not even wet." When Ash didn't answer, she turned to Rowan. "Please. What's going on?"

Ash glanced at Rowan, incredulous, ignoring Callie. "*You* don't have an imprint yet."

Rowan's dark eyebrows lowered. "Like I could forget. So nice of you to remind me." He shook his head and jabbed his finger at Callie again. "Look at her, Ash. She could be related to Sapphire's line. Look at her eyes. They're the same blue." He took another step closer, which she reciprocated by pressing her spine into the wall.

"I think you're freaking her out," Ash said.

Callie lifted her chin in a last-ditch effort not to cry. She was trapped. Her hands curled into stubborn fists. "How did I fall through there?" Something moved in the pond now, something big and solid, wearing a red t-shirt—the guy who'd caused her to plunge into the water.

"Hey!" She waved her arms and followed him from one end of the pond to the other on shaky legs. "I'm right here. Hey!" Panic bubbled in Callie's chest as she watched his head whip from side to side, looking for her.

"Hey!" Rowan said, raising his voice to match hers.

"I'm here." She flailed her arms around some more. The guy kicked his feet, traveling from one end of the small pond to the other. Tears leaked onto Callie's cheeks. She wiped them away. "Why can't you hear me?"

"Knock that off." Rowan batted her arms down. "He's not gonna answer. What's your name, anyway?"

"*Rowan!*" Ash admonished.

They'd cornered her against a wall and stood before her, expressions perplexed. She'd have to get through both of them if she wanted to run. *If* she could evade them in a room with no doors. *Think,* she ordered herself.

"It's Cal—" she started to answer, searching over their shoulders for a way out. The panic in her chest was rising, an ocean constricted to a jar. She would burst under the pressure.

Ash covered her mouth with his hand. "Shh!"

She tried to bite his palm. His hand tasted sweet, floral.

Ash pulled away and grinned. "You don't need to tell us your name," he said, wiping his hand on his pants. "You can't just ask people that, Row. You know better."

"She's not really one of us," Rowan said.

"She came through the ward. She *is*."

"I am what?" Callie asked, realizing the only way out was to be the way she came in—the pond. But how was she supposed to get herself back up through it? Even if she jumped, her fingertips would be several feet away from the water. It would have to work. Maybe she could climb on one of their shoulders. She eyed the taller one.

"Maybe we should take her to Hazel. She'll know what to do," Rowan said.

"That's probably a good idea," Ash hesitated, "but..."

"But *what?*" Irritation tinged Rowan's words. "You want to keep her trapped here as a plaything?"

"No. You're right." Ash held out his arm again. "Come along then."

Callie didn't move. Did he think she would go with them without a fight? Above her, the guy had climbed out of the pond. He'd probably already given up on finding her. What would they tell her foster family? *She fell into the pond and just disappeared. I swear.*

Typical.

"Clearly there's been some kind of misunderstanding," Callie said, forcing her voice to remain reasonable. "I just need to get back up there, and we can forget this ever happened." She nodded. She'd read somewhere that nodding helped convince people to agree with you.

Rowan sighed. "You can come on your own, or we can force you. I'm trained in torture techniques that make ax murderers cringe."

"You don't have to be dramatic," Ash said. He pushed his arm closer to Callie, insistent, it nearly touched her nose. "Once Hazel sees you, we can figure out what you're doing here and get you on your way." He waited. "Come on. Don't be rude."

Callie didn't get it and she didn't like it—she'd somehow fallen through water and remained dry. These two guys were weird. She *especially* didn't like that the guy had left her for dead in the pond.

Ass.

She lifted her arms to shove the guys away and make a run for it—to where, she didn't know—but Rowan caught her wrists.

"Don't bother. Ash—get the rope."

Callie couldn't tell if he was joking. Fear stabbed at her throat.

"For the love—. Row, shut up." Ash tried to pry Rowan's hands off, but he held tight.

"Let me go." Callie jabbed her elbow at his face and missed by a lot. Being a foster for most of her life had given her street smarts, but Callie didn't know the first thing about fighting, unless she counted evading Nate's advances, which she didn't. Callie didn't count on Nate for much. Rowan's fingers tightened on the soft inside of her wrist and she flinched, not because it hurt, but because it tingled, as if it'd fallen asleep.

"Be nice," Ash said, knocking Rowan's hand away. "It's okay." He smiled and presented his arm again like a father waiting to accompany his daughter down the aisle.

The gesture made Callie slightly nauseous. She rubbed her wrist. Her fear gave way to annoyance. Maybe this Hazel person could get her back...*up?* She had to get out of this room. If there was one thing Callie couldn't stand, it was being trapped, caged in like an animal, held down. She needed doors. She needed windows. She needed a sky above her.

"And I can't leave until I meet Hazel?" she asked. Her instincts said to humor them until she could escape.

"You can't leave," Rowan said. *"Ever."* A slow, irritating smile spread across his mouth.

"If you don't shut up, I'm going to set you on fire," Ash said, but he was smiling at the other boy. Maybe here, under the pond, setting people on fire was a normal thing to do.

"Hazel will help you," Ash said to Callie. "Besides, it's not like we can just throw you up through the pond." He made a dismissive gesture as if it was a ridiculous notion.

"You can leave if you die," Rowan said thoughtfully.

"Fire," Ash reminded.

Rowan made a gesture that said *lead the way.*

"Fine," Callie conceded, looping her arm through Ash's, cringing once again at the strange sensation she got when they touched her. "Take me to Hazel." *Get me out of this room.*

Ash beamed and pulled her toward the wall. Rowan trailed behind, muttering something about the *"idiocy of mere mortals."*

"Wait," she said as Ash tried to drag her into the stone. "that's a *rock* wall." The room had no exits, no doors, not even a hole large enough to crawl through.

Rowan snickered. "Well, of course it is." He gave her a hard shove and she shut her eyes as her face careened toward the stone, knowing that she'd made a terrible mistake.

ℰ✦ℭ

Rowan watched the girl disappear and tried to ignore the tightness in his chest.

It wasn't because she was pretty—of course she was, beauty was a given in *Eirensae.* Sometimes he longed for the diversity of the human world, where no one was glamoured to perfection. He wanted scars to map out a history that actually meant something. Flawlessness turned his stomach.

The humid, overheated air shifted as he stepped through the portal and into the common space of the tunnels, turning cooler, though the suffocating scent of flowers remained. He supposed he should enjoy the scent, associate it with home, but *home* was an elusive word.

The city was beautiful. Rowan had never gotten used to it. He'd thought that over time the magnificence would grow on him and one day he'd wake up and think, *Oh, I fit here.*

In a couple months, it'd be two years since he'd crossed the portal into the city, and it still felt just as foreign as the first day. Besides, beauty was fragile. Take the blooms that dripped from every surface here, easily plucked. Rowan was fire and *Eirensae* was a flower. No good could come of that combination.

The girl's arched mouth fell into a gasp as she looked up at the glamoured ceiling. A blond cascade of hair skimmed over her shoulders as she leaned farther backwards, trying to take it all in.

Rowan didn't believe a single word that came out of her mouth. *He* couldn't lie, but he didn't think she was like him. It didn't matter if she looked like Sapphire. Lots of girls had blond hair and blue eyes. Lots of girls were beautiful. It didn't mean she belonged here. No one *fell* through the pond by accident.

Tearing his gaze from the curve of her throat, Rowan tried to scrape away the cynicism and see the room through new eyes. The walls were similar to those in the antechamber, made of solid, knobby gray rock. Deep green vines snaked across them, weaving in and out of each other, sometimes creating great leaves as long as his legs. Flowers of every shape and color dripped in a kaleidoscope, their petals huge, each color brighter and more impossible than the last. Rowan curled his toes against the cool, compressed dirt floor and glanced up.

Millions of stars dotted what should've been a stone ceiling. It was vast and velvet, the sky over an ocean, away from lights and people, and as magical as it was fake. The glamour was lovely but not as impressive to those who knew its true form. Rowan focused on the sky until it dissolved into the rock ceiling underneath. The presence of the ordinary stone satisfied him for some reason and he let the glamoured night sky slide back into place.

Ash tugged on the girl's arm.

"That's impossible," she murmured transfixed, eyes wide.

A cluster of shooting stars flashed across the darkness, brightening the room for a few seconds. They fizzled on the opposite end, just above the tunnel that lead to the library, Rowan's favorite place in *Eirensae*. Even now—*especially* now—Rowan longed to hide in the books, devour the information, immerse himself in the one thing that had never let him down.

"Stop showing off," he said, fighting the urge to scowl at Ash. He pushed around them and entered the far passageway that led to Hazel's hideaway, anxious to get rid of the girl and spend the afternoon with his quarterstaff, beating the hell out of something.

"You'll soon learn that nothing is impossible here," Ash said, voice skipping through the tunnels.

Rowan quickened his steps, not caring whether they followed or not.

ℬ◆ℛ

"What have you brought me?" Hazel asked Rowan, turning her violet gaze on the girl, who fidgeted from one foot to the other and crossed her arms.

Though she was the leader of the city, Hazel was a small, compact woman, with long, wavy hair the color of copper. Her arms and legs were bare and milky pale as though she'd never seen the sun. She lazed on a mound of turquoise pillows suspended on a lush dais over a small koi pond. Hazel trailed her fingers through the water and lifted one eyebrow.

"She fell through the pond," Rowan said, bored. He picked at his fingernails and evaded Hazel's eyes. He'd never trusted her much and she'd never done anything to make him feel otherwise. If anything, she went out of her way to avoid him.

"Fell?" Hazel's eyebrow rose higher, interested now.

"She's one of us, isn't she?" Ash said, excited. "She couldn't have come through the—"

Hazel held up a hand and Ash's mouth snapped shut.

"Why are you here?" Hazel's words weren't angry, but commanding, as though choosing silence could never be an option.

The girl spoke immediately. "I don't know."

"Hmm," Hazel said, swirling her index finger through the water again. "Come here."

She seemed to move on autopilot, stumbling toward Hazel with an unwilling gait. She glanced over her shoulder at Rowan and Ash, gaze pleading, before turning back to Hazel.

When Hazel sat up, long strands of her hair slid off the dais and fell into the water. They floated like fiery snakes. Rowan liked the comparison; Hazel was a bit like Medusa. He tilted his head, considering.

"Give me your hands," Hazel ordered.

A test, to see if the girl was one of them. Rowan didn't want to think it possible.

Heavy stillness settled over the room—even Rowan held his breath. The girl pushed her hands, palms up, toward Hazel; her fingers shook. Hazel lifted her hands, contemplating, before lowering them.

The room dimmed when their skin touched, the orbs losing power. Rowan cursed. He knew what the girl was experiencing, the heightened senses, a sizzling rush of pure power.

Hazel pulled her hands away, and as though a switch had flipped, the orbs brightened.

The girl was breathing hard and pressed her hands to her chest. "What *was* that?"

"That's what I'd like to know," Rowan said, reexamining her. She looked ordinary, like any other human, but the display of power said otherwise. The knowledge was bitter on his tongue and felt like betrayal. How many more would return? How many more would prove Rowan a failure?

"Take her to the city. Prepare her for the welcome ceremony." With that, Hazel settled back on the pillows and shut her eyes, as though bored with the new girl.

"What? No. I'm not staying here," the girl protested.

Hazel remained silent, feigning sleep.

The girl's voice gathered strength with every word. "Who are you? Where are we?" Then belatedly, when no one answered, "What's a welcome ceremony?"

Rowan almost respected her courage. He'd known he was coming to the city, and he'd still been terrified.

Hazel lifted a dismissive hand and flicked it in their direction. She covered her face with her arm. Rowan wasted no time. He clamped a hand on the girl's shoulder and steered her away from Hazel. If she was staying, fine, he didn't want to spend another second looking at her.

She yanked out of his grasp. "I'm not going with you. What *was* that? What's happening? Who are you?" Her small hands curled into fists.

He hoped she would try to hit him. He liked a challenge.

Rowan narrowed his eyes until they were nothing more than furious slashes. "We already explained this to you. I'm Rowan. That's Ash. What more do you need to know?"

"Um, I have a list of questions. Where should I start? How about take me back?" she demanded.

"No."

"Take. Me. Back."

"No." Rowan gritted his teeth.

"Rowan," Ash chastised. He held out his arm again. "It'll be easier for everyone if you just do what Hazel wants." *Trust me,* he mouthed.

"Screw you!" The tiny ball of her right fist barreled toward Ash but Rowan stepped forward and took the weak brunt of her punch in his shoulder.

"That's all you got? Oh, come on!" Rowan encircled her upper arm with his fingers. "My grandmother hits harder than you."

Ash chuckled. "Your grandmother?"

"Figure of speech," Rowan said, wrenching the girl toward the door.

"Let me go," she screeched again, dragging her feet. Her heels skidded across the floor.

Rowan smiled, glad that she was angry. He didn't want her here. She didn't want to be here. Maybe if she were lucky, he'd help her back to the human world where she belonged. He pulled harder.

"Oh, Ash," Hazel called, "make sure she chooses a suitable name as well."

"What does that mean?" she demanded as they left the room, speaking through her teeth. She kept tossing angry glances at Rowan.

Her entire body vibrated beneath his fingers sending hot spikes of energy up his arm. He refused to believe she was fae, but damn, she was strong.

Ash led the way toward the portal to the city. "I'm sure your name is lovely, but we all choose other names here. It protects us."

She stopped. Rowan crashed into her and swore.

"Us? What do you mean by *us?*" she asked.

"What do you mean by us?" Rowan mocked, feeling resentment burn in his gut.

She whirled out of his grasp and stuck her face close to his. He took a surprised step back. Their bodies were inches apart. Her fingers quaked like leaves in a windstorm.

Go ahead, hit me, he thought.

"I don't like this any more than you do," she said. Her sweet scented breath clouded Rowan's face. "I have no idea what's going on here, and frankly, I'm kind of freaking out. So if you're going to be an ass, why don't you just shut up?"

Rowan's eyes widened and his mouth opened and shut like a fish. "Fine." Without looking at Ash, Rowan stalked off in the direction they'd come, seething.

80 ♦ CR

"Good riddance," Callie muttered, relieved now that he was gone. If Ash and Hazel unnerved her with their cryptic speeches, Rowan downright unraveled her. She didn't think she'd ever met someone who she disliked so much so immediately.

"Like I was saying," Ash continued as though nothing had happened, "We choose new names once we get here. Trees or plants, usually, though flowers are acceptable." He shrugged and pushed through some hanging vines, revealing yet another stone passageway. "Think about it. You don't have to decide right this second."

Rowan was forgotten as a name rose from the depths of Callie's mind, as though it was waiting there all along. It should've disturbed her, but it settled over Callie like a warm blanket.

Calla Lily.

They passed a cluster of glowing orbs. "And what are these things?" she asked. "And what was that when Hazel touched me? Who are you people? Why am I here?" She glanced up, relieved to see a plain stone ceiling, and not something that boggled her mind. "Where the hell are we?"

"One question at a time. I'm not allowed to say too much. You'll have to wait to speak to the Elders."

"Elders?" Callie parroted.

"It'll get easier. I promise."

Fat chance, Callie thought. They'd told her that every time she was placed with a new foster family. It was a lie. Every. Time.

"You do realize that I'm not staying here...right? I have a house and a family..." she trailed off, reaching the point where things always got awkward.

"Fosters?" Ash asked with a knowing smile. "Most of us come from fosters. It's just how things are done."

"What *things?*" she said. An orb hung next to Callie's face and she poked it with her index finger. It felt like an ordinary old rock, hard, gritty, and cool to the touch. The light brightened and then fizzled out. "Seriously. Is this like Wonderland? Am I dreaming?"

"Alice in Wonderland? No—nothing like that."

Ash pulled Callie's arm, dragging her toward a stone archway. From it, brilliant green light spilled into the caves, brightening the gray stone walls and illuminating the blooms like scattered gemstones. They passed through the opening and Callie gasped.

"It's better than Wonderland," Ash whispered. "So much better. Welcome to *Eirensae.*"

ഇ♦ഇ

Hazel still sat on her dais. *Lording over the city,* Rowan thought.

Her eyes remained closed when she spoke. "Rowan? Is there something further you need from me?" Her tone was dismissive.

Rowan ignored it. "That girl doesn't belong here."

"That's not really your decision."

"And what about the Elders?" he challenged.

Hazel opened her eyes now, caught Rowan in them as one might trap a butterfly with a pin. "Of course I will address this with them."

"When?"

"Not your concern, *child,*" she said the word like an expletive.

Almost two years and still she thought nothing of him. Rowan tamped down the fury inside of him. "I am not a child."

"But not yet a member of the city. You have no power here."

"But the girl," he said again.

"Is not your concern."

Lights flashed behind Rowan's eyes and his mind fogged with Hazel's power. He clenched his jaw, trying to fight it, but Rowan held no defensive energy. His body gave up long before he did.

Hazel gasped and his head cleared. "I apologize," she said, her face a mask of feigned disbelief.

Rowan didn't buy any of it. He'd seen Hazel manipulate an entire city with her mock innocence. His jaw clicked as he released the pressure. "As you wish," he said, snubbing her apology. He turned on his heel and left Hazel to gloat over her power.

৪১ ♦ ৫৪

Callie went from the humid shelter of the caves to a wonderland as picturesque as an Irish countryside. The city was beautiful, from the gentle rolling hills blanketed in bright grass to the cottages with their thatch roofs and smoke pouring from their chimneys. To Callie's right, multistory, statuesque buildings stretched toward the sky, their bases blending into the earth. Vines heavy with fruit and flowers crossed over their fronts, jamming the roofs and obscuring the structure underneath. There were trees everywhere, huge weeping willows, Japanese maples in a riot of shades including violet, pink, and blue, oaks, pines, ash, and

15

a multitude of flowering trees. Flowers lined the compacted dirt path that wound through the city. A river wove between the cottages. The sky was a perfect blue, cloudless and uniform from skyline to skyline. A cheery yellow sun warmed her.

The residents of the city gaped as she and Ash wound between the cottages and eventually reached the larger buildings that faced them, following the dirt path. Callie stared back, unable to stop herself. It seemed that all the women had long, flowing hair and pretty, oval faces. Several male heads turned in her direction and Callie face flushed at the attention. Their dress ranged from jeans to tunics to t-shirts.

"Who are you people?" she whispered.

Ash ignored Callie's mutterings and led her between the buildings that blotted out the sun. The temperature dropped and Callie rubbed her arms.

"Who lives here?"

"Elders, mostly. Some staff, other important people." Ash said.

Most of structures looked identical, soaring facades covered with greenery and blooms. Callie knew she'd never find her way out unassisted. From a distance, the city didn't look big, but once inside it, the buildings blocked any view of the surrounding fields, forest, and cottages.

Ash stopped in front of a towering building, gesturing grandly. Cobblestone steps adorned the front of a spacious porch. An inlaid gem tree sparkled from the arched double doors.

"This," Ash said with reverence, "is the palace."

It was four stories, every inch covered in ivy. A sprawling second floor balcony spilling with flowers obscured most of the jutting turrets that reached toward the sky, windows glittering in the afternoon sun.

A noisy huddle of people waited just inside.

Excitement weighed heavy in the air and the voices quieted as Callie and Ash entered. The gazes of the gathered crowd were warm as sunlight on bare skin, their faces curious and beautiful. It reminded Callie of the time she'd traveled with a friend to a fashion show where all the models had flawless, airbrushed skin. The women here looked perfect with bright, gem colored eyes and flowing hair. The men were immaculate in dark tunics and pants, their eyes just as bright as the women's were. There was a wrongness about it that Callie couldn't quite place. The beauty was lovely but unnatural, too smooth, like the beveled edge of colored glass.

Callie looked away, up to the gilt ceiling. A forest of trees, their leaves glimmering jewels, decorated the walls. The city's permanent scent of flowers enveloped Callie as the door shut behind her. *Eirensae,* Ash had called it.

"Good morning," a warm voice greeted, and a blond woman with blue eyes folded her into a hug.

Callie stayed stiff, unsure of what she was supposed to do. But this woman was soft and warm. She radiated safety. Callie inhaled the lilac scent of her hair and relaxed a fraction. The voices rose around her again like the gurgling of a river.

"We're so glad you came back to us," the woman said. She looked very young, with just a few wrinkles at the corners of her eyes. Her hair was pulled into a braid that hung long and straight over one shoulder. A tattoo peeked from beneath it, spanning the flat part of her chest above her breasts. The swirling lines matched the blue of the woman's dress.

She looped her arm through Callie's and drew her through the throng. The tingle that radiated from the woman was mellow, comforting, and Callie found herself leaning closer to her. Ash fell behind, speaking to a girl with bright red curls that matched the shade of his hair exactly. *His sister,* Callie realized with a twinge of jealousy.

"The tailor is here to take your sizes. We'll have everything ready for this evening. I'm Cypress, by the way," the woman said.

"Calla Lily," Callie said, trying on the new name. "Callie," she amended.

"Hm," Cypress said, thoughtful. "Calla Lily. Most people think it is a flower of purity, but it actually stands for resurrection. It's a wonderful choice for your new life."

"I don't know you. I don't even know where we are. I have zero intention of staying here no matter what you say."

Cypress paused, drawing Callie to the side. "I want you to think about something," she said, eyes serious. "Were you happy there?"

Callie thought about Nate and her foster mother's cancer. Sickness. Despair. Always running but never escaping. "Not really," she said eventually, nauseous with the realization.

"Here, you will have an entire city of family. You will be happy. You don't trust us, but we haven't had the chance to earn it. Just say you'll give us the chance."

Callie frowned as Cypress pulled her further into the palace without waiting for a response. They crossed into a pristine kitchen with modern appliances. It looked like something from a gourmet restaurant, four double ovens, a twelve-foot flat-face stovetop, four side-by-side refrigerators and two chest style deep freezers dominated the room. After seeing the cottages at the edge of the city, the opulence surprised her.

"What's your favorite color?" Cypress asked.

"Um…blue?" Callie answered, watching groups of people open the refrigerators and ovens. The sweet smell of cooking pastries filled the room.

"Ah, perfect. That will bring out your eyes." They exited the kitchen, entering a soaring hallway lined with gilded doors. At the end, an archway opened into a great room.

Callie mapped the palace in her head for escape routes, but unless she jumped out a window, she'd only seen the front doors, and she'd have to cross an ocean of people to get there. They reached the end of the hallway and stepped through the arched frame.

"This is the ballroom where your ceremony will be held," Cypress said, opening her arms wide and executing a half turn.

Ballroom was an understatement. The room was humongous, at least a football field long. People milled about, carrying in tables and chairs. A stage stood half-assembled in the center. Cypress stopped a young girl as she passed. "Callie would like the decorations to be blue."

"Of course," the girl replied, hurrying off, skirt billowing behind her.

"What exactly is a welcome ceremony?" Callie asked. "And how did you know I was here? It's been what, ten minutes…and already there's chairs—" she broke off as two men slid by her carrying a heavy wooden table.

"The ceremony welcomes you back to the arms of nature, your rightful home," a scathing voice from behind them said.

Rowan.

Callie felt the wonder of the palace fade with his presence. She turned to find him leaning against a table, expression dripping with sarcasm. His dark hair was pushed behind his ears. He scowled at Callie as though he wished to be anywhere else.

Before Callie could make a derisive comment about Rowan's presence, Cypress cleared her throat and touched Callie's shoulder, gesturing to the red haired girl Callie had seen Ash talking with. "I'll leave you in Willow's capable hands. I trust you'll clean up your attitude before this evening, Rowan. You know your responsibility here." She gave him a pointed look before exiting the room in a cloud of lilac scented air.

Callie smirked at the reprimand.

"I'm Willow," the girl said, bumping Callie's arm in a casual, haphazard way. When she tilted her head, curls fell over one shoulder. "You," she pointed at Rowan, "go away. She won't need you until later."

"What exactly do you mean by *need?*" Callie asked, coming alert. If they thought she was going anywhere with him, they were crazy. As it was, she planned on finding a way to escape as soon as they left her alone. Cypress's speech about giving them a chance was nice, but it wasn't enough to eclipse the creepy feeling in her stomach.

"Rowan will escort you tonight," Willow said.

"You're kidding me. That's not happening. I'd rather have rusty spikes shoved under my fingernails." They'd have to drug her to get her to agree. "I'm not staying. Just show me the door, and I'll be on my way."

Rowan, keeping his eyes on Callie, did a small bow. "It would be my pleasure to escort you to the ceremony tonight. Also, I have an excellent supply of both rusted and non-rusted spikes, which we can peruse at your leisure."

"Great." Willow slapped her hands together and ignored their snarky remarks. "Now *go away.*" She turned her back on Rowan.

Callie resisted the urge to glare at him as they walked away. Still, she felt his gaze prickle the back of her neck.

Willow threw both arms around Callie. "I'm so glad you're here. I've been waiting *forever.*" She jumped up and down awkwardly since Callie didn't move.

"Um," Callie said, spitting out a mouthful of Willow's hair. "You have?"

Willow leaned back, keeping hold of Callie's shoulders. "You are going to love it here. The food, the dancing," Willow gave a longing sigh, "the *boys*. It's like…like, a dream come true. Like winning the life lottery or suddenly learning you're rich. Except better." She squeezed Callie's shoulders and widened her eyes, serious. "You'll see," she promised. "By tomorrow, you'll forget all about the human world."

✌ Two ✍

"WHAT IS YOUR problem, Rowan?" Ash demanded. "You don't have to act like that."

They were in the middle of Rowan's cottage. Rowan stood in the front corner, rifling through his collection of weapons. He didn't have to look behind him to know that Ash had sat on the edge of the handmade table and propped his feet on a chair. It was the stance he took whenever he wanted to lecture Rowan, which happened frequently enough.

"I have no idea what you're talking about," Rowan said, finding his heaviest quarterstaff and testing the weight. It was the one he used when he needed to exhaust himself, usually whenever he had too much anger to keep inside.

"The girl, Rowan. The girl is gorgeous. She clearly belongs here."

Rowan propped the staff on his shoulder but didn't turn to face Ash. "If you hadn't noticed, everyone here is gorgeous. It's called glamour. You should try it sometime."

"Callie is one of us—family—isn't that the point?" Ash said, unaffected by Rowan's meanness.

"Callie," Rowan said, letting the name settle like melted candy on his tongue. It fit her. *"Family,"* he scoffed, finally turning. Ash was the closest thing Rowan had to family, and half the time he wasn't even sure Ash *liked* him.

Ash eased off the table and crossed his arms. "Why are you being like this? Is it because she wasn't brought back by trackers?"

Rowan sighed and stalked to the door.

"What is it then? Why don't you just tell me why you're acting like such an ass?" Ash followed him into the approaching twilight, shutting the door behind them.

Rowan whirled, quarterstaff in front of him, inches from Ash's face. "I'm not acting. I *am* an ass." He backed away from Ash and crouched into an attack position. Then he let his mind go blank.

ဆ◆Ო

Music and voices from the ballroom traveled up the stairs and rumbled through the floor, giving a lively heartbeat to the palace. Rowan had trained, showered, and dressed for the party, dreading it the entire time. He remembered his welcome ceremony clearly—the lights, the music, the mystery of the oblivion that followed. He'd been terrified, sure, but curiosity and the strong desire to finally have a home won out over everything. Rowan had jumped headfirst into this new life, fully expecting it to fit like a well-tailored suit.

He'd never been more wrong.

He looked like them, wore his glamour just as well, but he'd spent enough time in *Eirensae* to know that he didn't belong here. His missing imprint reminded everyone around him daily. He'd tried so hard he'd nearly lost himself. Effort didn't give him a free pass to the in-crowd. You could only get that with an amulet and an imprint. Skills were meaningless, desire useless, even dumb luck wouldn't help him.

His time filtered down like sand in an hourglass, and far more sand filled the bottom of the glass than what remained in the top.

He paused, hand on the doorknob, ready to enter without knocking. He sighed and knocked politely, pushing the door open only when he didn't get a response. His heart rate quickened as he scanned the room and found it empty.

She'd left—he couldn't understand why that bothered him so much. It wasn't as though they knew each other, or even that he liked

22

her. Maybe it irritated him that she'd taken her discomfort with her, and he'd thoroughly enjoyed her discomfort.

A soft cry drew his gaze to the open window. Bone-white fingers clutched the edge. He found himself leaning out the window, meeting Callie's wide eyes as she dangled above a two-story drop.

"I know what you're doing," he said, voice bored. "You'll probably break your ankle." He knew what Callie saw as she looked up at him; a guy in black jeans and a black t-shirt, a bad boy who didn't belong and didn't care. He'd cultivated that image so carefully that sometimes even he believed it. He'd turned so many people away with his hostility that they'd stopped trying to befriend him. Rowan preferred it that way, no obligations, no expectations.

"Not that you care," Callie said. Her fingers curled into the wood and tried to find purchase.

"I've seen open fractures, you know, where the bone rips through the skin." He shuddered. "Nasty."

"You're not helping," she said through clenched teeth.

"Oh, sorry. Would you prefer I help the process along, throw you out the window and lament over your corpse? Wax poetic about how your life ended so soon and so tragically? It's a bit dramatic though, falling to your death just to evade a party. Rude, too, if you ask me, considering all of this is to welcome you back to your rightful home and all that bullshit."

Callie groaned. Tension leaked into her words. "I didn't ask for a party. I didn't ask for any of this. I just want to go home."

"What's your master plan here?" A pause. He used the break to inspect his nails. "Have you considered how you're going to get back through the pond? I suggest *go go gadget arms* or *abracadabra*." He held up a finger. "I know. Click your heels." Rowan frowned as though deep in thought. "Wait—that might not work considering we don't wear shoes."

"Maybe I'll just die and save myself the trouble."

"Well, good luck with that." Rowan turned away as though to leave. He never would've let her fall—that's what he told himself—but she pissed him off *so much*. When her hand slipped and she screamed, he was there in an instant, fingers curled around her wrist, adrenaline thundering through his veins.

She swung beneath him like the pendulum in a grandfather clock. Despite the strain on his muscles, he couldn't resist getting in one more jab.

"Last chance to change your mind. I mean, if I were in this situation, I'd clearly pick the fall. Parties are such a yawn around here, with all the drinking and debauchery." He nodded to the city behind her before leaning on the ledge as though the extra weight was nothing to him. His shoulder ached and the window ledge bit painfully into the back of his arm.

To Callie's credit, she scowled. Rowan towed her upward and they crashed onto the carpet. She stumbled to her feet and smoothed the hem of her skirt over the pale curve of her legs.

"Should I thank you, or would that expand your already enormous ego?" She frowned at the angry scrapes on her arms as Rowan stood.

"I think you're insulting me. I should've let you fall." He went to the window and slammed it shut. Locks were unnecessary in the city, so he pulled the curtains with finality.

"Guess so." She turned away, but not before he saw the tears in her eyes.

He was being an ass. Ash was sure to have a lecture waiting.

"What are you really doing here? It's obvious you don't want me here just as much as I don't want to be here," she said quietly.

He heard what she wasn't saying. *What am I really doing here?* He wished he had an answer, but Rowan didn't even know why he was in *Eirensae.*

"I'm here to escort you to the ceremony, of course. I *always* choose debauchery over death. It's my basic nature. Remember that." *Still* being an ass. If there was a switch to turn it off, Rowan sure hadn't located it.

Callie huffed and pulled her gown off the hanger. It was the shimmering blue of a sunlit ocean and matched the blooms still pinned in the waving fall of her hair despite her recent suspension from the window. She was the most beautiful thing he'd ever seen.

Her shoulders quaked as she gave him her back. "This has been really great," she said, voice hitching. "I mean—look at this," she shook the dress, "I've never seen anything so pretty. I don't even know what to think. I just—I don't understand how I got here, or *why* I'm here. Or why you hate me so much. Everyone keeps acting like they know me, but they don't. And most of all, I'm scared, okay? I'm scared." Her shoulders quivered again.

He hoped he hadn't made her cry. There was nothing worse than making a girl cry. He stepped closer, hand hovering uncertain between them.

Surprise lit Callie's face when she turned. Rowan was close enough to draw her into his arms if he wished. Instead, he caught her wrists. The dress slithered to pool at their feet. The scrapes on her elbows were shallow, rug burns more than cuts. To Rowan, they were badges that ate away his insides.

"What do you want?" she growled, cheeks flushing pink.

Rowan almost smiled. He deserved her animosity, probably much more than she was giving. She tried to pull out of his grasp, but he held firm, turning her arms over, careful to keep his fingers gentle.

He took one of her arms in both of his hands. Healing energy pulsed at his core, fathomless and dark. He closed his eyes. Rowan's power was like a sixth sense to him. Just as one didn't have to think to smell or hear or see, Rowan didn't have to think to heal. It simply happened. He felt energy charge his fingers and disperse into Callie's skin, warming his hands and her arm. With it came the knowledge that she'd fallen against the carpet and scraped her elbows. It was always that way, the simple revelation of what or who caused the injury—even if he hadn't witnessed it. He saw other things too—injuries that weren't visible, things she'd hidden deep within herself. They clawed at his energy and Rowan struggled to keep his face blank against the debilitating pain. There was darkness in Callie, and darkness was something he understood.

When he completed one arm, he healed the second. Callie remained silent the entire time. She twisted her arms the second he finished and inspected her newly pink elbows.

"We're not all bad," Rowan said, turning away. "Get dressed." He headed out the door before she could respond.

ℰ✦ℛ

"This is crazy," Callie said, swiveling her arms one way and then the other as though the wounds might reappear. Who were these people—*what* were they?

The injuries were gone. An unblemished expanse of skin covered Callie's arms, interrupted by a few stubborn freckles and faint scars. She ran her fingertips over her elbows, impressed. Rowan's touch lingered there, warm and tingling, like static electricity waiting to discharge.

Callie thought of her foster mother's cancer and the chemo that ate away her insides. The agony that seeped into the walls of her house, bitter with the scent of impending death.

Rowan had healed Callie with a touch. Without medicine.

Without pain.

Curiosity rose inside of her.

Callie picked up the discarded gown on the floor. *One night,* she promised herself. She could play the role, buy into whatever crazy thing they wanted her to believe, and then she'd sneak away. *And go back to your awesome life?* her mind whispered.

"One night," she said.

Callie undressed and stepped into the silken fabric. It hugged her skin. *The tailor is good,* she thought, distracted by the reflection in the mirror. The color, ocean blue, brought out the highlights in her eyes, which were rimmed perfectly with kohl, the expert work of Willow. The girl staring from the mirror looked dark and mysterious, *radiant.* Callie's heart hammered against her ribs.

Magical.

She chuckled away the errant thought.

She must be crazy, going through with this party. Callie pressed her fingertips to the mirror, half expecting her hand to disappear through it as she saw in the movies. Maybe she was dreaming. Maybe she'd fallen asleep in Nate's bed and created another reality so she wouldn't have to face the real one.

When she was little, back before she'd realized that the world was an awful, cruel place, Callie had dreamed that her mother was a princess. She'd drawn pictures of castles sparkling with jewels and white knights on horses. She convinced herself that one day a carriage would come for her and she'd never look back. Then she'd been placed with the Johnson's and Callie had lost all hope.

And maybe she was crazy, but was it so wrong of her to be curious? To ask, *what if?* She glanced again at her reflection. They'd pinned flowers in her hair and covered her eyelids with glitter. Maybe she wanted this.

Maybe this was the most excited she'd been.

Ever.

A soft knock drew her from the mirror to the door. A woman smiled from the hallway, her blond hair falling in soft waves around her face, drawing a snap of memory from Callie, like seeing a photograph of someone she knew years ago.

The woman wore a shimmering golden gown that showed the intricate, curving tattoo on her chest. "Calla Lily," she whispered, drawing Callie into a soft, fragrant hug. "I can't believe you're finally here. You don't know how long I've been waiting."

Callie pulled away from the awkward hug and the woman laughed, a light, bell sound. Her dress swooshed as she led Callie deeper into the room. "Of course you wouldn't recognize me. I'm Sapphire."

But Callie did recognize her, or at least, she *thought* she did. Something prickled at the back of her mind, and eventually bloomed into realization. "You look like me."

Sapphire's smile stretched into a grin.

"Yes." She draped an arm over Callie's shoulders and led her to the mirror. Their eyes stared back, identically slanted. Their hairlines arched into the same peak, just slightly off center. The same bow lips, the same dusting of freckles.

"Sisters," Sapphire said softly. "Not that I'm supposed to tell you that. Family is hard to find around here, but I have an advantage. I saw you coming."

"You did?" Callie murmured, still transfixed on the mirror. *Sister,* she thought. Someone to hold her hand, someone to share secrets with, someone to love. She wanted that, didn't she? Tears filled her eyes and she shook her head. "You're lying." If this was some kind of joke, it was the worst kind of cruel.

Sapphire laughed again, squeezing Callie's shoulders, warming them. "If only you knew how funny that is." She withdrew and moved toward the door, dress glistening like a jar of fireflies. "I just wanted to say hello before the ceremony. We'll have plenty of time to catch up now that you're home."

The door shut behind Sapphire, leaving Callie alone. She leaned over, putting her hands on her knees. "When I open my eyes," she whispered, "this will all disappear." Squeezing her eyes shut, she took three deep breaths.

One.

Two.

Three...

🙠✦🙢

Rowan felt Callie shiver. Her arm was delicate against his, as though any force might take her down. The pulse at her wrist fluttered erratically and the vessels at her throat jumped just as fast.

The people spread before him like a sea of twinkling colors. Rowan knew all their names and faces, how long they'd lived in *Eirensae,* what their powers were, but he could think of less than ten whom he actually cared for.

Callie's fingers pushed into his arm and he snuck a sideways glance at her. She'd lifted her chin, but her free hand trembled against the banister. An uncertain smile tugged at the corners of her lips. Rowan wished he had a camera to record this moment, one of the few he might like to take with him when he left. He settled for memorizing the graceful slope of her neck, the slant of her cheekbones, the way her scent—lilacs and chamomile—made him dizzy. He should've told her she looked beautiful, she was, after all, a girl, and they liked that sort of thing.

When they reached the final steps, the crowd broke into applause.

"People of *Eirensae*," Hazel cried. She stood on the stage in the center of the room, her tiny body swathed in gold fabric, a crown of red curls around her head. "I present to you, Calla Lily, a child of *Eirensae* returned to her rightful home."

Cheers resounded through the crowd. Rowan clapped along with the rest of them. Callie's cheeks flamed bright pink and she stared at the gold-flecked floor.

Hazel lifted her arms and the glowing orbs that hung suspended above them flickered. "Join me in welcoming her." She said a few more words in Gaelic, which were repeated by the crowd, and then the band behind her started playing. Hazel stepped off the stage and disappeared into the throng of people.

"What did she say?" Callie asked, angling toward Rowan.

"The Gaelic? It's an ancient incantation. It means welcome home."

"Oh," she said. Her expression remained perplexed. "Can I ask you something?" she murmured, gazing over his shoulder.

He shrugged.

"Is it weird…or maybe wrong, that all of this…it feels—I feel," her words drifted away.

"Like home?" he supplied, feeling his throat close around the word.

Callie bit her lip. "Never mind."

Rowan kept Callie firmly in his grasp as she was passed from person to person. Some of them hugged her and whispered, "Welcome home," while others touched her forearm, her face, her hair. The sweet scent of flowers and honey with an earthy undertone enveloped them. He knew the welcome ceremony was overwhelming Callie, but for some reason, the gentle return pressure of her fingers on his relieved him.

Callie inspected the palace with a silly, half-smile on her lips. The room rose two stories above them. Glowing orbs danced like a million stars in the space—so many that he couldn't make out the ceiling beyond them. Blue fabric that matched Callie's dress lined the walls. It spilled onto the floor and ended in a waterfall of azure flowers that people crushed underfoot. A five-piece string band played on the stage. Already several people danced to the haunting music, twirling around the golden wood floor.

Willow sashayed up, flinging her hair over her shoulder. "Can I get you something to drink?" She gave Rowan a pointed look.

"I—uh...sure," Callie said finally. "Is there soda, or something?"

Rowan smirked and let the dancers swallow him up. Across the room, he leaned against the bar and grinned at the faerie bartender. He didn't have to get drunk to see her unglamoured. She smiled back, showing him teeth that tapered into sharp points.

"Rowan." She shook her hair, blinked, and her eyes changed from vivid green to sunshine yellow. "I saw you with the girl."

"Mmm?" He said, noncommittal, leaning in close to hear her over the party.

She blinked again. Yellow to florescent pink. "Pick your poison. I'm sure Callie will be amicable to our...selection."

Rowan felt laughter rumble in his chest. "Just give me whatever."

The bartender disappeared for a moment and returned with two champagne flutes, one filled with a deep blue fizzing drink that puffed violet smoke, the other was a dark shade of indigo that swirled and sparkled. She winked at Rowan, one eye teal, the other pitch black, iris-less. "Have a good time," she cooed, trailing her tongue over the sharp daggers in her mouth.

Rowan thanked her and pushed his way to the crowd, shuddering over thoughts of the faerie's teeth and the rending they could deliver.

When Rowan neared the group, he saw Callie fidgeting with her hands, scanning the crowd. He let himself think she was looking for him. He crept up from behind and whispered in her ear. "Looking for someone?"

She jumped and spun, nearly knocking the drinks from his hands.

"Ooh!" Willow exclaimed. "Drink the blue. It makes you—" Ash shushed her. "It's good," she amended.

Callie inspected the drinks, skepticism all over her face. "What is it?"

"Oblivion," Ash said with a grin.

Rowan handed her the blue drink, giving the other to Willow, who thanked him and downed the flute in one swallow. Callie was slower, pressing the glass to her lips and inhaling before tipping it back. If it tasted strange, she didn't comment. She took another sip of the wine and Rowan wondered how long it would take the drink to affect her.

"Shall we dance?" Ash asked, nodding to the dance floor, making Rowan regret not being the first to ask.

"Um…no. Not really." She took a few steps back, distancing herself from them as if she thought they might drag her on the floor against her will.

Ash frowned. "You have to dance, it's your ceremony."

"It's like the law or something," Willow chimed in, looping her arm through Ash's. Standing side by side, their features were nearly identical, down to the way they tilted their heads and waited for Callie to answer.

"I don't dance," she said. "Besides, there's tons of people out there. No one is going to notice me standing over here, drinking my…oblivion."

Ash and Willow shared a look.

"She says that now," Ash said. "Dancing is like breathing around here. We dance for *everything.*"

"Birth," Willow said, "dance, death, dance, sunrise, dance, sunset, dance—"

"She gets it," Rowan interrupted.

"The same rule applies to drinking," Ash said. He pushed the bottom of Callie's glass back to her lips. "Drink up, gorgeous."

Hazel found them before anyone managed to get Callie away from the wall. "I trust you are well?" she asked, inspecting Callie with open curiosity. There was something else in her gaze that turned Rowan's insides to stone. *Want.*

Rowan had a strong urge to step between them.

31

Callie nodded, gaze going to Ash who'd stepped away slowly like a child trying to evade his parents. He disappeared into the churning swarm of people.

Rowan frowned—of course they'd all abandon Callie if Hazel was involved. He moved closer to Callie and fixed his sour expression on Hazel, but she ignored him, gesturing to the mass of moving bodies.

"It pleases *Eirensae* to have our children return home. We are glad to welcome you back." Her eyes shifted to Rowan and her mouth furrowed as though she'd been sucking a lemon. "We'll meet with the Elders to discuss your living arrangements in the morning. Be sure to keep her safe," she said, turning back to Callie.

Callie lifted her chin. "I think I should go home."

Hazel laughed. It was the sound of branches scraping across a frozen lake. "Child…you *are* home." She brushed Callie's cheek before disappearing into the throng.

"You should mingle. Everyone's here for you," Rowan said after Hazel retreated.

Callie gazed at the spot where Hazel had been, her expression a mixture of worry and curiosity. "I just keep thinking I'll wake up," she said, bringing a hand to her face where Hazel had touched her. "This doesn't happen. There just…there isn't—" she broke off and tossed Rowan a glance. Her cheeks turned red.

"Welcome to the never-ending dream," Rowan said bitterly. "Let's dance."

℘♦℆

Everything was surreal and cloudy. It felt good to let loose and move and embrace the blankness at the edges of her mind. Her limbs felt electric against Rowan's, *free*. His body was fluid, his motions in perfect time with the music. Callie didn't even have to think about what would come next, everything just *flowed*. It was as though they'd bottled the pure essence of life in the drinks they kept handing her. They pulsed in her veins and rippled in her mind. She was *alive*.

Callie spun away from Rowan straight into Ash's arms. She felt him laugh and then Ash dipped her until her hair swept the floor, dropping flowers all the way. Ash danced more carefully than Rowan, each step measured and planned, but dancing with Rowan was a lot like falling, and she thought that was the best part.

"What'll it be?" the bartender asked.

Callie looked up, blinking to clear the dizziness. She didn't remember walking to the bar. A giggle fell from her lips before she could stop it. The woman's hair was blue, not the crayon blue that turned green when you washed it, but iridescent blue, as though the strands were made from tissue lamé. When she grinned, she revealed a mouth full of sharp teeth, pointed like a cat. The bartender's eyes flashed from green to violet.

Callie pressed her fingers into her eyes. They felt numb, much like her thoughts. There was something she was supposed to do, somewhere to be, but whenever she tried to pull up the thought, she had the strangest urge to dance. She giggled more.

A man stepped up to the bar. Green, spiky leaves grew from his head and hung down his shoulders like bizarre dreadlocks. He asked for a Poplar Pixie, which turned out to be a green drink with yellow chunks floating in it.

Callie covered her eyes.

"Are you okay?"

She dropped her hands only to wish she hadn't. Black antennae sprouted from a man's forehead and ended in tiny balls. When he moved, they danced above his head like a New Year's Eve headband.

"I've got it from here," Rowan said, catching Callie around the waist as she tried to stumble away.

"She's unwell," the man said, concerned.

"I said *I've got it,*" Rowan barked. His fingers gripped her elbow in a steel vice, forcing her thoughts to clear.

"I think I'm hallucinating." Callie leaned her weight on Rowan to stay upright, certain she was dreaming or dying. Maybe she'd already died. She thought of the pond. *Suffocating.*

Then they were in another room, and when Rowan shut the door, it became blissfully silent. Callie collapsed on the first flat surface she found—a coffee table. Rowan took the couch across from her.

"The bartender—she had these teeth..." She curled her fingers into claws to demonstrate. "And that man—he had leaves...and that other man..."

"Is a giant, man-eating ant," he finished.

Callie's eyes widened. She *knew* what she saw, but even now, the memory felt hazy, soft at the edges.

"It's the drinks. They allow you to see us in our true form," he said.

She squinted at Rowan. Though his face wavered along with the room, he still looked normal. Too-long black hair curled just above his shoulder, wary blue eyes watched her. The front of his tunic gaped open, showing Callie his bare chest.

"You look fine," she mumbled.

"Of course I do," he said. "It's because I have clothes on."

Callie frowned.

"I can take them off if you prefer..."

Her face emptied of blood. "No...*no.*"

"Really? It's no big deal..." He undid two buttons of his tunic.

Lifting a hand, she gestured to his chest and attempted to change the subject. "Why don't you have a tattoo?" She'd seen so many tonight, trees, flowers, plants, all intricate and looping graceful lines.

Rowan's laughter died instantly and his expression turned dark. "First of all, it's an imprint. If you're going to live here, at least learn the language."

"Who said I *wanted* to live here?" She threw at him. She pressed her hands to her head. Her body felt insignificant, as though her mass wasn't enough to root her in place. "I *tried* to go home, but *you,*" she jabbed a finger at him, "y*ou*—"

"You don't have a choice. You belong here...it's your home." He said the word *home* as though it burned the inside of his mouth.

"I don't know you."

"I don't know you, either," Rowan said. He whispered something else, but it was too low for Callie to hear.

34

"This is your fault," she accused. "You did this. What did you give me? Why am I seeing things?" She swayed, her body wanting to dance, even when she told it no.

Rowan stood, leaving a trail of blue footprints across the white carpet. "Come on. Hazel will worry if you don't enjoy your party."

"I don't care. Take me home."

"Haven't you heard the stories? Once you come to faerie you *can't* go home."

"Faerie? You're joking, right?" Her gaze sharpened suddenly on Rowan's shoulders. "What's that?" She lifted a finger and poked the subtle protrusion that rose from his back.

Rowan caught both her hands and smiled tightly. "Maybe I'll show you sometime."

Callie ignored his hand and shoved to her feet, keeping one hand out to catch herself. "Why don't you show me now?"

Rowan smirked and opened the door. String music exploded through the doorway and vibrated the bottoms of Callie's feet. Rowan tugged her into the hallway where a woman with skin as green and bumpy as an alligator was kissing a man—or at least Callie thought it was a man—with gray fur.

She froze and stared for so long that she didn't hear Rowan calling her name. Eventually, he came back for her and caught her arms, talking softly as though to an injured animal.

"Come on, Callie…maybe you're not drunk enough yet."

"No…no more," she protested.

As soon as they reentered the ballroom, he handed Callie another drink. This one was thick pink and smelled of berries.

The woman with alligator green skin waltzed by in the arms of a man with gills. A girl with fire red hair stopped in front of Callie, her skin alabaster white and smooth as stones washed for centuries by a river. She took the glass from Callie's hand and swallowed down the frothy pink liquid, clutching the flute with webbed fingers.

"Willow?" Callie blurted.

Ash appeared at her side. He too, had pale skin and webbed fingers. Callie gaped at them.

"You need to drink more," Willow insisted, snatching a glass from a waiter's tray as he passed.

"Oh my God." Callie took the glass from Willow's waiting fingers. She didn't want to drink it, did she? By the time she decided not to, the glass was already empty. "Who are you?" Callie squinted at them. "*What* are you?"

Willow didn't answer, just procured another glass. "You're too coherent for this conversation," she declared. "Drink that and then go dance. You need to worry less and have more fun. You'll have plenty of time to panic when the celebration is over."

Callie looked to Rowan. He lifted a shoulder.

Ash held out his webbed hand.

Then—

৪০ Three ৪৩

LIGHTS FLICKERED THROUGH the window, illuminating Callie's face. She lifted one eyelid and groaned. Her shoulder blades and tailbone ached as though she'd fallen asleep on a sharp rock. *Why* was she on the floor? A steady beat throbbed at the base of her skull, like someone taking an ax to her brain and chopping it into tiny pieces. She pressed a palm to her forehead in hope of drowning out the world. A rumble shook the floor, vibrating up through Callie's body.

She forced both eyes open. A gilt ceiling rose over her. Lightning turned the gold into knives that stabbed at her eyeballs. Her clothes felt damp and sticky. Her mouth tasted like rotten fruit. She rolled onto her side, cringing the entire way.

…and blinked.

…and blinked.

A woman lay next to Callie, hair spilling across the floor in a dark, silken waterfall. Her eyes were open, a startling blue that reminded Callie of an endless sky, bright against the china pale of her iridescent skin. She looked like stone, so smooth, so cold. A single scarlet droplet dangled from the woman's dry lips.

Wine, Callie thought, but the idea had no roots.

Where was she?

Callie couldn't remember.

As she watched, the dark bit of liquid grew heavier and heavier, finally falling into a large puddle of—

Wine?

She was so still. So pale. So—

Dead.

Callie scrambled to her feet, her hands slipping and fumbling. Her mouth rounded, but no sound came out. The woman was wreathed in red. It splattered her face and trailed her neck. It spread beneath her like a blanket.

*Help—someone—*where was she? Callie lifted her hands in front of her face, horrified. Her arms were streaked with blood, an abstract painting of death.

"Help me," she said. "Help me!" Her voice gained strength and she screamed. She ran for the closed door, her heels sliding in blood. She crashed into the frame, leaving bright, damning handprints. "Help me, help me, help me."

She left smudges on the doorknob and on the golden walls of the never-ending hallway. She threw open doors to empty rooms, still screaming. "Help me!" *Nobody, nobody.* She yelled at the hallway, the doors, the windows.

Finally, *footsteps.* Callie ran toward them, the swirl of her dress flinging blood onto the floor. She crashed into a blond woman. She knew her…knew her…

"Sapphire!" Callie shrieked. "There's a—and she's—"

Sapphire's hands were all over Callie. "Where is it? I don't see any—"

A dark-haired boy emerged from a far doorway. "What's all this screaming?" he growled, then he saw Callie and his face went pale. "Let me heal her," he said, rushing to them and pushing Sapphire away.

"She's not hurt," Sapphire said.

"Then what—"

Callie grabbed a fistful of each of their shirts. Sapphire and Rowan. She knew them now. "She's dead. She's dead."

Rowan's expression went from worried to confused to horrified, and then he was running away from them, into the room where Callie had been. Sapphire went after him. Callie followed, her stomach twisting. She reached the doorway as Rowan said, "She's gone." He was knelt over the woman, hands pressed to her face.

Callie could see the wounds now, how they tore at her flesh, jagged slices in her arms, her legs, her neck. Callie's gaze traveled over the pooled blood to Rowan. His lips were moving.

"What happened?" he said. "What happened?"

Sapphire was on her knees now, the woman's head cradled in her lap. "Orchid," she whispered, saying the name over and over again like a prayer.

Callie swallowed the bile at the back of her tongue. "I don't know. I don't—"

"What happened?"

She backed away, his words sliced through her skull. She tried to remember, but there was nothing.

Nothing.

ॐ◆ॐ

"Take Callie back to your cottage," Sapphire said, gathering the prophetess against her. When she closed her eyes, fat tears dripped onto her cheeks and fell from her chin. The prophetess's head lolled, her mouth hung open.

For a moment, Rowan was speechless. "To my cottage? She did this, Sapphire. I'm not going to house—"

"She is *innocent*," Sapphire said through clenched teeth.

Rowan gestured to Callie. She stood in the doorway, blood soaked arms splayed, eyes wild. "She literally has blood all over her hands." When he glanced back, instead of the prophetess, Rowan saw the broken body of his foster mother. Nausea turned his stomach and guilt burned in his throat. When he blinked, the prophetess's face returned.

"She is my *sister*, Rowan. It's the prophecy. It's happening."

"We need to—wait. What?"

"Rowan," Sapphire snapped. "Orchid is gone, that means it's my place now, and I order you to take Callie back and get her cleaned up. You will speak of this to no one."

39

The blood drained from Rowan's face. What Sapphire asked was impossible. He was a master at evasion, twisting the truth until it bordered on falsehood, but those tricks only took him so far. "You know I can't lie."

Sapphire closed her eyes and Rowan watched her throat work. "Come closer," she said, drawing him down to her. She pressed her lips to his ear and spoke his true name. Rowan's body vibrated beneath the weight of the command. "You may speak only to Callie and myself about finding Orchid like this. Your story is that you took Callie back to your cottage when the party disbanded." When she pulled away, her eyes were full of pleading and tinged with remorse. "I'm sorry," she said, voice breaking. "Hazel will believe that she didn't do it. But the rest of them..." she trailed off. "We have to protect her. Please, Rowan."

Rowan nodded and stepped away from Sapphire, chest full of horror. His feet trailed blood. Callie still filled the open door, dress stark against pale skin. Wraith-like. Her hands trembled, leaves caught in the wind. A growing outline of crimson rounded her feet like the makings of a pagan circle.

He took her arm. The sudden burst of energy from the girl surprised him. He should've been used to it by now, but he'd never felt such a unique energy. It was as though it ran in torrents inside her veins. Every cell, every pore. Pure, untapped energy.

"I didn't do it," Callie whispered as he led her into the hallway.

Rowan used glamour to hide the blood stains and pinked her cheeks so she looked drunk, not devastated. Her eyes were twin oceans at midnight, wide with terror. If anyone looked too hard, they were screwed.

"I believe you," he said. And because he couldn't lie, it must've been true. If Callie had killed the prophetess, then Rowan was just as much to blame because he was the last person to see them together.

He'd taken Callie to a room while the party was still in full swing. She was stumbling, cheeks bright, tongue loose. She'd laughed and danced—and she was beautiful in faerie form, with her golden hair and iridescent blue skin. He'd spun her around the dance floor and she'd clung to him, uninhibited.

He'd envied that freedom—the release of who you were to who you *are*.

But eventually her eyes grew tired and Rowan led her away where she could sleep it off. Orchid was waiting inside for them and Rowan had gone into the next room to give them privacy at Orchid's request. He must've fallen asleep, because the next thing he remembered was Callie shrieking in the hallway. He was supposed to keep Callie safe— that was his duty as escort—and he'd let her down. If he'd stayed, the prophetess would still be alive. Callie wouldn't be scared and soaked with blood.

He was just as much to blame as anyone. Perhaps more.

It wasn't the first time he'd let someone die.

They crept through the silent palace, passing rooms full of sleeping fae, just splashes of bright color lit by lightning. The storm rumbled again and Callie gripped his arm tighter. Her heartbeat pounded in her fingertips and rattled against his skin.

"I didn't do it," she said again. And then quieter, "Why can't I remember?"

Rowan didn't have a good answer for her. He could tell her the truth—that faerie wine leaves your mind riddled with holes, a block of Swiss cheese. He didn't think it sounded reassuring.

They were in the foyer now. The ceiling stretched above them, carved with gold leaves. The storm flickered against the windows, casting dancing shadows on the floor and walls. They'd almost made it outside, but then the heavy double doors opened and Ash stumbled in, soaking wet and shivering. His gaze went to Rowan and then to Callie, back to Rowan.

Rowan saw the other boy's mind trying to piece it together. "Where have you been?" he asked, heading off Ash's inevitable questions.

"The wards were breached. I heard Jack and Hawthorne answer the alarm and—why is she covered in blood?"

Rowan's mouth moved, but no words came out. This was the effect of Sapphire using his true name. He could have all the good intentions he wanted, but he couldn't break her order. Rowan frowned and rubbed his forehead—it was the last thing he needed. If it weren't Sapphire, he would be pissed. She had not used his name lightly. The prophetess was the ruler's last mode of control over the city. The fae had free will, to a point, but the final word always came from the leader.

In their case, Hazel.

"I didn't do it," Callie said.

"I took Callie back to my cottage when the party disbanded," Rowan said. Verbatim. *Damn faerie law.*

Ash gave Rowan a withering glare and turned to Callie. "Are you hurt? Do you need a healer?" He reached for her hand but she flinched away.

"Why don't I remember?" Callie asked. "Oh god, oh god." She hid her face in Rowan's shoulder.

"I took Callie back to my cottage when the party disbanded." This time, Rowan met Ash's gaze and held it. "You should find Sapphire." He tugged on Callie, leading her to the entrance.

"Rowan," Ash said, but Rowan didn't stop. Through the doors. Into the storm.

80♦Q3

Callie sat at Rowan's table, shivering in her wet clothes. They'd waded through the whipping wind and pellets of stinging rain, sticking to the shadows. Rowan muttered the entire way, but he hadn't let go of her hand until they reached his cottage, a tiny two-room wooden structure. Candles lit the inside and a warm, cheery fire burned in one corner.

Every time she closed her eyes, she saw the vacant stare of the woman—the prophetess, they'd called her—and the blood dripping from her lips. Though it wasn't same as the last time she'd experienced a tragedy, Callie felt helpless and small, a leaf in a raging river.

Rowan handed her a mug of tea. The warmth seeped into her fingers as she frowned into it.

"You should change," he said. He'd already taken off his shirt and hung it by the fire. Rainwater clung to his eyelashes and dripped onto his shoulders. The dark hair at the nape of his neck curled.

Callie pressed the mug to her face, warming her cheeks. She kept trying to remember the night before, but her mind was blank as a sheet of paper. There were no hints, no flashes. She swallowed hard and set the tea on the table.

The *what if* was the worst part.

"Did I kill her?" She looked up then, catching annoyance on Rowan's face.

Instead of answering, he went to a closet and returned with a towel and change of clothes. "They'll probably be too big, but at least they're dry." When she didn't take them, he dropped them next to the tea.

"Why won't you answer me?" She picked up the towel and wiped her face.

"Because I don't know, and I can't lie." He slumped in the chair across from her and ran a hand over his face. "No, I don't think you killed her, but I can't say for certain. Hazel isn't careful. She thinks she has *Eirensae* on lockdown, but—"

"What was that, yesterday? You healed me with your hands—with *magic*. What are you?" Callie's heart thumped in her throat. She had a massive headache and her fingers were frozen. She'd never wanted to go home more in her life. She missed the tiny room she shared with her foster sisters and the knowing she was safe—sort of. She even missed Nate. The consistency of disappointment was comforting.

"We're fae—faeries."

Callie's gaze flew to his face. "Faeries?"

He smirked. It wasn't a cocky expression, more self-deprecating. He sat back in the chair and picked up her discarded towel, pulling at the threads. "We're just one big happy family beneath the reflection pond."

His tone made Callie shiver.

"You should change," he said again, pushing the clothes to her.

The rain had washed away the stains, but Callie could still smell the blood—floral, sweet. Wrong. Her pulse picked up again. "You'll tell them I didn't do it, right? I didn't. I mean, I can't remember and if I killed someone—"

"Sapphire thinks you didn't do it. You can trust her judgment."

Callie tried to distance herself from the situation. It was too unbelievable for her to wrap her head around it. *Faeries, murder, magic.* How the hell did she end up in the middle of it?

"I still don't understand why...or what...what you are."

"What *we* are," Rowan said. "You're fae, too."

"Oh, god." Callie shook her head. She closed her eyes. *Wake up, wake up, wake up!* "I don't believe you." She cracked one eyelid.

Rowan lifted a shoulder. "Believe it, don't believe, doesn't really matter. It's still true. Besides, you've got Sapphire. If you can't believe that she's your sister, then you're stupider than I thought."

There was *that*. Callie picked up the clothes but didn't move to change. For as long as she could remember, she'd wanted a sibling. A *sister*. She'd had foster siblings, so many she'd lost count, but there was an unspoken rule amongst fosters. They never got too close because you never knew what tomorrow would bring.

It was easier being alone, not *feeling*. Because feelings always led to hurt.

Callie had her future all planned out. She had exactly eleven months and twenty-three days until her eighteenth birthday, the day she would be tossed into the world as a legal adult.

She'd longed for that day since she was little, right about the time she'd started elementary school and realized that not all children had stand-in parents. Not all kids were fosters—some had parents who loved them.

Callie had tried to love her foster parents, but with eleven homes in seventeen years, it was hard to grow attached to anyone. Even harder after her third home. She was the one who was abused, yet her record stated that she was a "problem case," as though those two words could sum up the horrid scars.

At eighteen, she could change her name, change her *everything*. She could move to New York or California, become a new person. And maybe eventually, she would believe it, too.

If Rowan was telling the truth, *if*—and it was a *big* if—she belonged in *Eirensae*, then how had she ended up as a foster? Her file was sealed. Callie had always assumed she'd come from a rape victim or a maybe a prisoner. She'd wanted to think that her birth mother had loved her, and that's why she'd given Callie up, because life as a foster was better than what Callie's life would've been.

Her mother had been wrong, of course, but the best intentions didn't always yield the best results.

"If I'm a faerie, or fae, or whatever, then why am I just now finding out about it?" Callie asked.

Rowan stared at her for a long time. "How old are you?"

"Seventeen."

"Holy shit." He sat back hard, gaze never leaving her face.

"What?" she said, glancing at the door, certain that someone would come bursting through it, ready to charge her with murder. Did they have police in faerieland?

"Get changed," Rowan said. "We need to see Sapphire."

୫୭✦୪୰

"Callie is seventeen," Rowan said to Ash as soon as Callie and Sapphire were out of earshot.

Ash shrugged. "So what? Is that too young for you?"

Rowan held open the door to one of the many unused bedrooms in the palace and the two boys stepped inside. "She's still a child, vulnerable to the Fallen. The last thing we need is another Immortal wandering around."

"That's unheard of, Row. There hasn't been an Immortal in decades. Not since before the fae diverged into the four cities."

Rowan went to the window. The city was awake now. The message of the prophetess's murder had spread like a disease. The fae rushed to the palace in the rain, clutching each other, crying. Rowan knew it would rain for days.

He flattened a hand over his stomach, remembering. It was like seeing his life through someone else's eyes. It wasn't Rowan who laid on the floor bleeding out, but some weaker, lesser being. Rowan would've known better, *should've* known better. He would've saved a life instead of taken one. Seeing the prophetess had sharpened the edges of his memory until the cuts were fresh again. "It's not as unlikely as you think," he said.

"I've researched Immortals and the Fallen. Their numbers are few."

"Immortals are immensely powerful, Ash. Just because they aren't in the recorded history doesn't mean they don't exist. Regardless, Callie is a target, here inside the city and now in the human world. She's not safe anywhere."

"But Hazel—"

"Is useless," Rowan said. He watched two unglamoured faeries kiss before entering the palace. The man tangled his fingers into the woman's thistle hair. Blood stained his hands, her hair, the ruins of their clothes. Rowan wondered what it would be like to be in love so deeply that you wouldn't notice the pain.

"Why the change of heart? Yesterday you wanted to ship her back to the humans...and suddenly you care?" Ash stood now, joined Rowan at the window. The two lovers had entered into the palace, holding hands.

"I don't—" *care,* he wanted to say, but the lie lodged in Rowan's throat and choked him. "I just don't think it's fair," he amended. Life would be so much easier if he could lie. It was exhausting to plot every word into truth. Now he had Sapphire's command hanging over his head like a sword.

"So we'll talk to Hazel."

Rowan could see Ash's concerned face in the window's reflection. It pissed him off. "That'll be great," he said with a sneer. "The unimprinted non-member and a *teacher.* Maybe you can teach Hazel the ways of our past, too, counsel her on how a faerie leader is *supposed* to act because you're certainly not going to defend the city against the Fallen."

Ash flinched.

"I didn't mean—" Rowan said, regretting his words, but they both knew he *had* meant it. Ash's imprint made him an educator, and much like in the human world, it was a thankless job. He taught the incoming fae the histories and how to control their powers. But Ash really wanted to be a warrior. Ash had tried to learn after Rowan had returned to *Eirensae*.

Rowan could fight, both with weapons and his bare hands, but no matter how many times Rowan went over a block or a kick or patiently explained how to hold a quarterstaff, Ash never got it right. He was always too slow, too uncoordinated. Eventually Ash had abandoned fighting, and the two boys had focused on their mutual love of information. But it hadn't taken long for Rowan's knowledge to surpass Ash's.

"You know what? You're right." Ash said, heading for the door. He paused, hand on the knob. "I'll never be like you," he said softly, not looking at his friend, "but you'll never be like me, either."

Even though Rowan could fight, Ash still had one thing up on him. One, giant, unequivocally important thing. Ash was imprinted. A full, permanent member of the city, whereas Rowan, without his amulet or imprint, was nothing more than a meaningless child, voiceless, *worthless*.

Ash slammed the door and it was Rowan's turn to flinch. It was the first time Ash had thrown Rowan's status back in his face.

∞✦ℭℜ

Callie leaned into Sapphire's embrace, letting her eyes close, and for the first time, she didn't see the dead face of the prophetess. Sapphire smelled of blood and despair, but also something soft and familiar. Callie didn't trust any of them, but she mistrusted Sapphire the least. The memories were heavy, not of the murder, but of the past. They filled up Callie's head, struggling to break free and bring her to her knees. In this moment, she needed Sapphire. She needed anyone.

They were in a rambling office, complete with a sprawling desk covered with yellowed papers and scrolls. Shelves filled with heavy, bound pages lined the walls.

"I'm so sorry this happened to you on your first night," Sapphire said. "I assure you, murder is not commonplace in *Eirensae*. The prophetess—" her voice broke, "she was a beautiful, peaceful woman. She'd protected the city for many years."

Callie pulled away. Sapphire's face was pale and damp with tears. "Rowan seems to think she died because I'm seventeen, but I don't see what my age has—"

Sapphire paled further. "Seventeen? Oh, Callie. Of course. I guess I knew, but I didn't think... The wounds—they're ceremonial." She moved away from Callie to the desk in the corner of the room. She pushed aside papers and sat on the surface, eyes far away. "But if it's the Fallen, it doesn't make sense why they would kill her and leave you sleeping nearby. Maybe..." She rubbed her forehead. "Maybe...oh, I don't know. The visions never work like I need them to. But the Fallen..." she trailed off.

"The Fallen?" Callie prompted. She sat on the back of a couch, hands twisted in her lap. Her headache hadn't receded at all. It hunkered at the center of her skull, insistent and demanding. Her eyes felt overcooked and gritty.

Sapphire buried her face in her hands. "We haven't even had time to explain everything to you. You're supposed to have a meeting with the Elders today, but I suppose that'll be postponed until everything is cleaned up and investigated. The Fallen are—"

"Murderer!" The accusation came from the doorway and was followed by a murmuring crowd of people. Cypress and Hazel were at the end of the group. Callie sank lower, trying to become invisible.

The man who'd yelled took several steps toward her, hands raised. He backhanded Callie before she had a chance to react. "You dare come here?"

Sapphire was there in an instant, filling the space between him and Callie, who was cradling her cheek on the floor. Callie's eyes watered. She couldn't breathe enough to tell him that she didn't kill the prophetess. Or at least, she didn't *think* she did.

"You will control yourself," Sapphire said through clenched teeth, but the man shoved her away and caught Callie by the arm, dragging her upwards.

He spat hot, rancid breath over Callie's face. "I will execute you myself."

Callie cringed away from his narrowed eyes and curled lips. His dark hair reminded her of another man and she fought to keep the memory buried. Her hands curled into shaking fists and bile burned the back of her tongue.

Hazel's voice rose over the noise, "Release her, Elm."

"Release her?" he bellowed, spittle flying onto Callie's cheeks.

Sapphire was up again, fingers wrapped around Elm's wrists.

He snarled at her. "You planned this, didn't you, *prophetess?* You bring this *child* into our home to destroy us. And *you,"* he turned to Hazel. "You will lead us to our deaths." His free hand curled around Callie's throat despite Sapphire's attempts to stop him. The faces around Callie blurred to smudges. She wondered why no one stopped him, why they all stood by, frozen.

"I will rid us of this stain before she can be used to lead us to war."

Callie's pulse thundered against his fingers. Her eyes felt like grapes sucked through a straw, struggling for freedom. She couldn't breathe. The edges of her vision closed inward.

She panicked, kicking her feet and flailing, but he was too strong. *Let me go,* she screamed, but the words couldn't choke their way from her lips. Sapphire drew deep gouges in Elm's arms, but he didn't relent.

"Please," Sapphire sobbed, "please."

Let me go, Callie screamed again.

To her surprise, she found herself on the floor, gasping. Sweet air filled her lungs and she gulped it, grateful. In front of her, Elm was on his knees, hands covering his ears. Blood seeped between his fingers, staining the shoulders of his tunic crimson.

The room went eerily silent. Sapphire helped Callie to her feet, touching her hair, her cheeks, her shoulders. "You're okay," she said, "you're okay."

Callie glanced at the gathering. Their faces ranged from shocked, impassive, and curious. Except for Hazel. She looked victorious.

"Everybody out," Hazel ordered, pushing Sapphire away and sliding an arm around Callie's waist, holding her upright. "Out, now," she said when they didn't move fast enough.

"Hazel," Sapphire said, reaching once again for Callie, "let me—"

"Get out," Hazel ordered. Sapphire backed away, eyes lowered, joining the others. A woman helped Elm up and away. He glared at Hazel the entire time.

From the doorway, Sapphire mouthed, *I'm sorry*, before retreating and shutting the door softly.

Hazel led Callie to the cushy desk chair and helped her into it. The older woman sat on the desk, facing Callie. The silk of her dress whooshed as she pulled her legs into its skirts. Callie thought she looked more like a teenager than a ruler of a faerie city.

"I apologize for our lack of decorum, but I'm afraid the murder has thrown the city into chaos." Hazel settled her hand on Callie's shoulder. Her violet eyes were earnest. "I sincerely apologize for the greeting you've received. I want you to know that you are welcome here, and I will answer any questions you have." She touched Callie's throat where Elm's fingers had cut into her flesh. The ache there eased. "Our children are so precious to us, and you, Callie, are even more special because you found your way home early. I know the others are nervous about your presence here, but I see it for what it is. It's a sign of the good things to come. Your power is meant to lead our city to greatness. The prophetess foresaw it before she—" Hazel broke off.

She caught Callie's hand in both of hers, spilling warmth and energy. Did Hazel had the power to heal as Rowan did? She seemed kinder now, gentler than when Callie had met her the day before. The comfort kept the panic at bay. At least for now.

"I know this must be very confusing, and I hate to add to your worries, but until you find your amulet, you're in mortal danger from the Fallen. The prophetess's murder is a warning we cannot overlook. The sooner you don your amulet and accept your bindings to *Eirensae*, the sooner you will be safe."

Safe, Callie scoffed, thinking of the prophetess's empty eyes and of Elm's hands around her neck. Of all the things she felt, safe wasn't one of them. "I want to go home," she said. "Why won't you let me go?"

Hazel smiled. "I know you're scared, but you have to understand. The Fallen know you exist."

"I don't even know what that means." Callie heard the high sound of panic in her voice. She wished she were stronger. Fiercer. She wished she could wake up from this nightmare.

"The Fallen used to be faeries, beings with power and centuries to live. But sometimes they choose to betray their cities or not accept their place, and when that happens, they are stripped of their magic and longevity, and cast back into the human world to live and work amongst lesser creatures. Taking the life of a faerie child can grant these beings immortality and impossible strength, which is why we hide all of our children. If you return to the human world, they will never stop hunting you."

An icy finger of dread slid down Callie's neck and she shuddered. "And what's to stop them from coming here?"

Hazel squeezed Callie's hand. "We have wards that will keep them out and trained warriors as back up. We will put you under guard until you find your amulet. As a precaution, I'd like to bind you to the city. It'll prevent anyone from taking you outside the city walls."

"So I'll be a prisoner?" Callie said.

"Not a prisoner, *safe.* You'll have free run of the city. We'll protect you, I promise. In time, this will just become an awful memory. There is nothing for you to fear from us." She rubbed warmth into Callie's arms. "Besides, it's time for you to learn your true place on this earth, not as a human, but as a powerful, magical creature. Ash will teach you faerie history and help cultivate your magic."

Callie snorted. "I'm far from magical."

"I'm not the one who took Elm down—you did that all on your own. Your power is immense, Callie. I can help you learn how to defend and protect yourself."

Callie had caused blood to drip from Elm's ears? She was horrified. "I don't want this...power. I don't want any of it." She met Hazel's gaze. "Take it away. I don't want it."

Hazel pressed a gentle hand to Callie's shoulder, leaning down so she could search her face. "It doesn't work like that. You're fae. Magic is in your blood, your very makeup. I can't just make it go away." She drew Callie into a soft, scented hug.

Callie closed her eyes, wanting to believe Hazel. She didn't fully understand how this whole faerie thing worked, or really believe that she'd somehow made Elm's ears bleed, but the thought of someone wanting to kill her made Callie shiver.

"I know you're scared and uncertain, but you can trust that I will protect you." Hazel pulled away. "You are a daughter of *Eirensae*. It is my duty to defend you with my life."

Callie felt herself wavering. She'd never been more confused. She didn't know what to believe anymore. "And what about Elm?"

"He will learn to behave himself, or he will be banished. Either way, you let me worry about that."

"But he thinks I killed the prophetess."

"Yes, but I don't. And I assure you, my word goes a lot farther than his. Now, give me your palm and I'll do the binding spell. It'll only take a moment and then we'll get you set up somewhere you can sleep. You must be exhausted."

On cue, Callie yawned. When she finished, Hazel clutched a glittering knife and had a welling pool of blood cupped in her opposite hand.

"What are you going to do with that?" Callie yelled, skittering away from Hazel.

"It's for your protection," Hazel reminded. "It'll prevent anyone from taking you outside the city. It'll only hurt for a moment. Give me your hand."

Callie's fingers trembled and she couldn't bring herself to lift them.

"Callie," Hazel said softly, "trust me."

Callie blinked, her mind growing foggy.

"Trust me."

The knife burned across Callie's flesh and she drew a sharp breath. Hazel's lips moved with silent words as she pressed their palms together, mingling their blood. Heat fused their hands, hotter and hotter until Callie was certain they'd catch fire.

And then it was over. Hazel curled Callie's hand into a fist. "You'll be happy here, you'll see."

Dread exploded in Callie's stomach. She pressed her bleeding hand there.

What had she done?

ℰᴏ Four ᴄᴙ

CALLIE FELT THE hulking monstrosity of the palace watching her as she stepped into the late-morning sun. She squinted at the windows nestled between the stones, but the second floor balcony restricted her view. The sun warmed her shoulders and face and she stayed for a moment, drinking it in, letting it chase away the chill.

She was trapped.

Hazel had wrapped a strip of cloth around the cut, but Callie's hand throbbed beneath it. She couldn't even begin to make sense of it. If what Hazel said was true, then Callie was stuck under the pond. And worse, she had some kind of freak power.

Then there was the prophetess.

Cold…dead.

She shook her head to dislodge the image.

In the distance, cottages guarded the hills, smoke rising from their chimneys. All the tiny houses looked the same, round, tan stucco walls, thatch roofs. Sapphire lived in one—but Callie wasn't sure which, and didn't know if she wanted company anyway. To her left, not quite as far as the cottages, was the stone she'd come through into the city. A river ran to her right, and dense woods surrounded the entire city like the walls of a safe haven.

Questions slithered through Callie's head—a pit of restless snakes, but one remained at the forefront.

Fae.

Faerie.

That's what Rowan had told her. If he hadn't healed her, she could've convinced herself this was all an elaborate hoax, maybe a reality television show complete with costumes and computer graphics.

Callie had felt the magic on and in her skin.

Without conscious decision, she started up the path, lost in thought.

She tried to remember everything she'd learned about faeries. It wasn't much, aside from children's movies. They were magical, fickle…mischievous. And if Hollywood had it right, about six inches tall…with wings.

Believing she had any part of this world was ridiculous. Callie felt a little crazy just for buying into it, as though the cameramen would jump out from the trees at any moment and point at her.

But if it were true—if she'd done that horrible thing Hazel had accused her of, then she couldn't go home. She was safer here. Everyone else was safer, too. Callie lifted her hands in front of her face. Had she done that to Elm? Sure, she'd been scared, but it wasn't as though she ran around hemorrhaging brains.

The giant rock rose up to her left and she steered towards it, certain it was where they'd emerged from the caves. It stood over fifteen feet high, its surface riddled with crags and sharp points.

But there wasn't a door, an entranceway, or even an archway to guide her, just solid stone. Callie pressed her hands against a smooth spot to stretch the kinks in her back and fell through to the other side.

The warm humidity of the caves settled over her shoulders and she stumbled to catch her balance. The glowing orbs, which were dim when she first entered, brightened as though sensing her presence. The perfect expanse of starry night sky spread overhead, dwarfing Callie with its vastness. Through the archway behind her, she could see the rolling hills of *Eirensae* bathed in sunlight. Before her, dim, vine clogged passageways branched off in every direction. One of them would lead her to the reflection pond, but much like the cottages, Callie had no idea which.

She took the middle opening at random. The warm passage was only a couple of feet taller than her. Callie trailed her fingers over vines and flowers as she walked. The glowing orbs lit the path, brightening as she came closer.

Several minutes passed and the air grew cool. The space had shrunk and the dangling plants brushed Callie's cheeks and shoulders. Finally, she came to the end. The tunnel opened into a small room. Orbs ringed the floor, casting the walls in blue. At the heart, resting on a white pedestal, was a golden cauldron. The object was no larger than Callie's head and had tiny feet that ended in brilliant green gemstones. Soft light emitted from the top and danced on the ceiling. Callie was drawn to it like a moth to flame.

The doorway was just wide enough for one person to pass through. She stepped forward only to have her face bounce off of an invisible wall. Callie pressed her hands there like a mime. There was no glass, only air. She followed the obscure barrier all the way to the ground and then above her head.

"What the hell," she murmured.

"Callie?"

She whirled to find Ash behind her, smiling sheepishly. "You scared the crap out of me," she said, pressing a hand to her heart.

Ash shoved his hands into the pockets of his jeans and shrugged. His hair was darker than usual, damp. "Sorry."

"What is that thing?" Callie jabbed a thumb toward the room.

Ash's eyes slid past her. "The cauldron of Dagda."

"The what?"

"It was a gift to our people. It connects all of us, combines our energy. It's where we store all our magic." He reached out a hand. "Never mind that." His eyes met Callie's and then lowered to his offered palm, an invitation.

She hesitated before setting her fingers in his.

"Come on, Sapphire was worried when you didn't return from the palace."

"I didn't know *how* to get back." They all seemed to think she held some repressed knowledge of this place or the ability to magically disappear. The thought gave her pause. Maybe she *did* have that ability.

"I'm sorry—I assumed someone would show you the way." Ash slowed to walk beside her as the passageway widened. He searched her face. "I'm guessing you have tons of questions."

"This power I have," she said, feeling ridiculous, "what can I do with it?" She conveniently didn't mention the situation with Elm.

"Hmm," he said, holding up their intertwined hands. "You'll figure that out in training. I can tell you that you're very strong—maybe the strongest here."

Callie glanced at him, surprised, but Ash wasn't looking at her. She'd never been particularly strong at anything. She hadn't even been able to bench press the bar in gym. The image of Elm, hands pressed over his bleeding ears, flashed through her mind. She hadn't done that…had she?

They reached the main room. Ash caught and lifted both of Callie's hands, leading her to the flowers hanging from the walls. The spicy scent increased to intoxicating. "We all have a connection to all living things, even though our powers are different."

"You know that sounds crazy, right? I've never done a single *magical* thing in my life," Callie said, echoing her earlier thoughts. All she could think of was Rowan's hands as he healed the scrapes and the pleasant numbness that chased away the pain.

Ash plucked a huge purple bud from its stem. The sealed bloom was larger than Callie's hands. He set it carefully in her cupped palms; the petals were velvet soft and warm.

"Shut your eyes," he instructed.

She obeyed, letting her eyelids flutter closed. Her stomach gave an uneasy zing at Ash's proximity, near enough that she could feel his breath sweep her cheeks. He covered the backs of Callie's hands with his. Her heart rate increased.

"What do I do now?" Her words were breathless. Did she really believe she had some secret magical powers? Stupid, *stupid,* she scoffed.

"Do you feel the heat in our hands?" Ash said, pressing tighter.

She nodded.

"Focus on that energy. It comes from within you, your core. You should feel it build there and expand until it flows into your fingertips, into the flower."

Callie tried to do what he said, imagining the energy bursting within her, but nothing happened. "It's not working," she grumbled, pulling away from him and dropping the flower. This was stupid. She *felt* stupid, if only for wanting it so badly.

"You're not trying," he said, picking up the discarded bud. "You have to feel it here." He touched the center of Callie's chest, pressing against her sternum. "Try again." He held out the flower until she sighed and took it.

Callie closed her eyes again and focused on the spot where Ash's touch lingered on her skin. Was it her imagination or did it grow warmer? Ash's hands cradled hers.

"Push that energy into your shoulders, let it flow down your arms, into your fingertips. Feel it enclose the flower, connect to it," he instructed. Heat rose from his hands and seeped into Callie's flesh, as though they held them over a fire. A moment passed while Callie focused everything she had on the energy inside of her. "Callie," Ash whispered, "look."

The flower was opening, peeling away layer by long layer, its diameter over a foot wide. The violet petals revealed a fuchsia core, with a round, vibrant orange center. Callie laughed.

Ash laughed too, throwing his head back and holding the flower over them so all she saw was the dark bloom and the star scattered sky. The petals curled and fell around them like snowflakes, bursting into tiny flowers no bigger than Callie's fingertip with glowing orange centers. They dusted the floor, opening as they fell, scattering like fireflies at their feet.

Ash's smile faded as his gaze met hers. They dropped to her mouth. The remaining petals fell to the floor with muted, papery thuds. When his fingertips touched Callie's face and left a warm trail across her cheeks, she closed her eyes. They found the tender spots on her neck where Elm had strangled her.

She sucked in a breath, eyes popping open.

"Well, isn't this romantic?" Rowan snarled, suddenly appearing through the entrance.

Color rose in Callie's cheeks and she stared at the floor, unable to meet Rowan's eye. Her heart pounded against her ribs, and bile burned the back of her throat.

"Sapphire is looking for you," Rowan said. "Ash was supposed to bring you back, but I see you two are otherwise engaged."

"Oh shut up, Rowan." Ash brushed past him. "Come on, Callie. Let's go find Sapphire."

Callie followed Ash toward the archway where she could see the hills of *Eirensae* waiting. She chanced one last look at Rowan. He stared at the spot she'd been standing with Ash, expression a mix of distaste and disbelief. One of his hands clenched into a fist, and then they were on the other side and all Callie could see was stone.

As soon as Sapphire saw them coming up the path she rushed from her house and pulled Callie into a hug. Ash let go of her hand and she hugged Sapphire back, relieved to see her familiar face.

"I thought for sure we were too late," she said, pulling away to touch Callie's face. "I saw you leave."

Callie frowned. "Really? Did you see a way for me to get back through the pond?" She thought of the binding spell that still burned her hand. She should tell Sapphire, but it felt like a secret and lodged in her throat.

Sapphire clucked and slung an arm over Callie's shoulder, leading her toward the cottage and through the door.

"There are good things here for you, Callie. I know a lot has happened, but things will settle down now, you'll see. Besides, we have so much catching up to do," Sapphire said, easing Callie into a wooden chair at the butcher-block kitchen table. Sapphire sat in the opposite seat. "I want to know everything—what you like, what you don't like." She raised an eyebrow. "The kind of boys you like…"

Callie's eyes narrowed.

"Or girls," Sapphire amended.

A smile tugged at Callie's lips. Here was the sister she'd always wanted. She could've wept. "Where should I start?"

Sapphire leaned forward, crossing her arms on the table. "The beginning. Don't leave anything out."

ℬ◆ℭ

Rowan exhaled as he crossed into the cool, crisp air of the library. It was dusk and the fading sunlight slanted through the glass ceiling, creating prisms of light on the floor and shelves.

He couldn't stop thinking about Callie.

Her memories were bitter on the back of his tongue as he withdrew a heavy, leather bound book from the shelf and settled himself at the table. He lit a candle and closed his eyes, letting her emotions wash over him. *Terror, hopelessness, pain.*

There were flashes that he couldn't quite piece together. The color pink, cold, the feeling of sinking. He could ask her what terrible thing had happened to her, but part of him was certain he didn't want to know. The familiar scars on his back itched. Rowan rolled his shoulders.

He didn't have time to worry about it now, not with the city at risk.

Rowan flipped open the cover and pulled the candle closer. *Fraeburdh,* The City of War. He scanned the pages, nausea roiling in his gut.

"Research again?" Ash interrupted, appearing in the doorway.

Rowan sighed and shoved the book away. "I don't know where else to look. The forest, the river, the palace, the caves. Where else could my amulet be?"

"Not in *Fraeburdh,*" Ash said, sitting across from Rowan and closing the book. He folded his arms. "So…"

"If you're here to lecture me about Callie, save your breath." Rowan held his hand over the flame until it hurt.

"Actually, I'm here to apologize for earlier." He scrunched up his face and knocked Rowan's hand away from the candle.

60

"Yeah," Rowan said, knowing he should apologize, too, but also knowing that Ash wouldn't make him.

"Yeah. So who do you think murdered the prophetess?"

Rowan lifted a shoulder. "The Fallen? *Fraeburdh?* I don't know. I'm not exactly high on the information list around here." He picked at a bit of left over wax on the table. "It feels like a set up. We haven't had a breach in—"

"Ever," Ash supplied.

"So, what? Someone on the inside then? You don't mean Callie."

"Of course I don't mean Callie."

"Then who? Cypress? Sapphire? What are you getting at?"

"I don't know," Ash huffed. "You're the knowledge guru."

"You're the teacher. I'm just playing at something I'll never be." Rowan licked his fingers and extinguished the flame, casting the library into deep blue shadow.

"Aren't we all," Ash agreed. He was quiet for a moment. "Did you hear what Callie did to Elm? She has some sort of destructive power. She almost killed him. Made his ears bleed when he tried to strangle her."

Rowan went cold all over. "Strangle?"

"I guess he blamed her for the prophetess."

"Who told you this?" Rowan demanded.

Ash shrugged. "Hazel. I get to train Callie. She wanted me to be prepared."

"Mm," Rowan agreed, thinking back to what Sapphire had said about a prophecy. He needed more information, especially if they were to keep Callie safe.

ℴ◆∞

Ash set a small, round rock in the center of dirt floor and glanced at Callie. "Move this."

Save the stone and a cabinet pushed against the wall, the training room was empty. Callie stooped, picked up the rock, and set it a few feet away, ignoring the sting where Hazel had sliced through her palm.

The wound had scabbed over, the puckered, red line a constant reminder that Callie could no longer leave *Eirensae*. Two days had passed, and still, Callie felt lost.

She'd tried hoping and praying and willing herself home.

No such luck. They were half-hearted attempts, anyway. Now that she had Sapphire, she wasn't sure she wanted to give her up. At least she hadn't run into Elm again.

Ash made a rude noise. "With your *mind.*"

Standing, Callie stared at him until she felt her face fall into a frown. "My mind?" She hadn't known what to expect when Ash had given her the choice between school and training, and now that it was happening, she *still* wasn't sure.

Everything around her seemed routine. The sun rose in the morning. The fae had chores and work. They hardly glanced in Callie's direction, but she couldn't help feeling out of place.

"You know, telekinesis? With your mind."

"You're joking." She searched Ash's face, waiting for the punch line.

"Not joking." Ash picked up the rock, held it in his flattened palm. "Our powers vary. Some can move objects, control minds, heal, others can influence the elements, water, fire, and so on. Just like the different powers, the strength varies, as well." He lifted the stone to eye level. "So we test until we figure out what you can do."

Callie felt ridiculous. "I can't move the rock." She'd played sleepover games just like most teenagers, light as feather, stiff as a board, trying to lift a person with just her fingertips. It'd never worked.

"You can't if you don't try," he said, but he returned to the cabinet and put the rock inside. He took a small ball of paper from his pocket and dropped it where the rock had sat. "Light this on fire."

Callie threw up her arms. "This is stupid. I don't have magical powers. I know you people think that I belong here or whatever, but I'm not a faerie."

Ash smiled, his eyes going to the paper. A few seconds passed and the little ball burst into green flames. Callie made a sound between a squeal and a gag and covered her mouth.

"How?" she said between her fingers as the ball disintegrated black ash.

"I control fire." He found another little piece of paper in his pocket. "Your turn." When Callie didn't move, Ash put his hands on her arms; the energy tingled into her shoulders. "What are you so afraid of? That it won't work…or that it *will?*"

Callie stepped away from Ash, staring hard at the paper. *Could she?* Controlling fire seemed a lot better than whatever brain-exploding thing had happened to Elm. "What do I do?"

"Clear your mind," Ash said. "Focus on nothing but the paper. Visualize it catching fire."

She took a breath, crouching. She memorized the crumpled paper, how one side was bigger than the other, where the edges curled back. She brought up a passable vision of the paper burning in her mind, but nothing happened. Callie tried and tried, circling the paper as though another angle might work. She focused so hard that her eyes went cross and a headache formed at the bridge of her nose, but the paper did not light.

സ◆രു

Rowan slid silently into Callie's training session. With both of their backs to him, neither Ash nor Callie heard him approach. He'd just had a meeting with Hazel about the prophetess's murder. He'd been nearly sick with the thought of being caught in a lie, but Hazel had already pinned the prophetess's murder on someone else. She hardly seemed to care if Callie had been there at all. She'd dismissed him after asking only a few questions.

He couldn't believe his luck.

Callie sat back on her heels, frustration evident in the tightness of her shoulders. "I can't," she said. She pushed to her feet, lifted a foot and crushed the paper.

"Ah, the old fire trick," Rowan said. "Maybe I can help."

They whirled.

"There's nothing to help," Callie muttered.

63

"You're just giving up too easily," he said.

It'd started raining and Rowan's tunic hadn't done much to stave off the chill. When he reached for Callie's hand, their energy collided like molten lava, leaving him breathless. He tried not to show it.

Ash leaned against the wall, watching them with crossed arms. Usually, Rowan read Ash's face easily, but his friend's expression was impassive. Rowan could guess how the other boy felt, though, probably the same way Rowan felt whenever he saw Callie with Ash. He tried to convince himself he didn't care if Callie was interested in Ash, but he couldn't lie, not even to himself.

Rowan released Callie and picked up the paper, holding it in his flattened palm. "Look at me," he said, focusing on her eyes. They were blue, bright and honest, with a dark rim of green in the center. His throat tightened. "Don't blink." He couldn't help his smile as her eyes widened. "Follow my breathing."

From the edge of his vision, he saw Callie swallow. Her breathing slowed, eventually matching his. The cave around them disappeared. Rowan saw nothing but Callie, her eyes, her cheekbones, the way her hair fluttered with his breaths. She smelled of chamomile and lilacs, the scent mixed with the rain that clung to him, and he decided he liked the combination very much.

"Clear every thought except for the paper."

Callie's eyes flickered downward.

"Look at me," he whispered. Rowan waited until he felt their connection again. Even though they weren't touching, he could taste Callie's energy, feel it thrum in the air around him. She was powerful, he knew, but he suspected much *more* powerful than anyone realized. "See the fire," he continued, voice hardly a whisper, "feel it on your face. Taste the smoke."

Heat consumed him, smoky, heavy with energy. The scent of it burned the back of his tongue.

"Rowan," Ash yelped. "You're on fire!"

Rowan looked down. The paper had long since burned to fragile ash. The flames, hungry for fodder hand traveled up his arm, consuming the sleeve of his tunic. Callie launched herself at him, slapping at the flames and taking both of them to the floor. She continued to batter him until the flames died.

Then, as though for comic relief, a cool splash of water doused them.

"What was that?" Callie said with a shaky breath. She held up her palms, red and raw, and stared at them in wonder.

Rowan felt everything around him go still as the scent of Callie's blood and scorched flesh filled his nose. "Let me see."

"Your arm," Callie said with a squeak instead. Her hands were on him, gently peeling away the singed remains of his tunic.

"I'm fine." Rowan's heart pounded hard in his temples.

Ash knelt next to them, watching with a mix of horror and amazement, his knees dark with water and mud. "It's bad."

Rowan tugged his hand from Callie's grasp. "Let me see your hands."

She frowned, but obeyed, holding out her hands for his inspection.

"Do you know what you just did?" Ash asked, excited.

"I burned Rowan." She flinched at her admission.

"Forget it. I'm fine," Rowan said.

"You summoned fire," Ash said.

She finally looked at Ash, her mouth rounded with surprise. "I did?"

"And you summoned water to put it out."

Rowan used her moment of distraction to start healing her wounds.

"But your arm," she murmured.

"Shh," Rowan said, not breaking concentration. He saw the fire— how it burned her hands, and then he watched Hazel slice Callie's palm open and complete a binding spell. The knowledge surprised him so much that he almost dropped her hands. What did Hazel want from Callie? It wasn't typical for the fae to put restrictions on the members of the city. He knew she was a risk because of her age, but that didn't mean she deserved to be stuck, either. Then he went higher, easing the pain in her throat from Elm's hands.

Rowan had to swallow down rage. He wanted to kill Elm after witnessing the entire scene in his mind.

"Thanks," Callie said, standing. Her hands trembled. She reached for Rowan but he pulled away. "Can't you heal yourself?"

"Not exactly, but I'll find someone who can. You should keep practicing." He backed out of the training room before Callie could protest further. His hand felt as if he'd held it in a bucket of acid, but he'd had worse. He'd lain under a blanket of blood and watched his life flicker. In a moment of weakness, he'd allowed himself to take energy.

Rowan gritted his teeth against the pain. *This* he could handle.

He found Cypress at Sapphire's cabin and waited patiently while she healed his hand.

"Callie did this?" Cypress asked. Sapphire stood over them, watching Rowan's flesh turn from mottled red to pink.

Rowan nodded. "Then she summoned water. Do you know how strong she is? Having two powers is rare." He played dumb, wanting to see how much Sapphire would tell him.

Sapphire frowned and poked at Rowan's healed skin. "She has three. Hazel said Callie gave Elm a brain hemorrhage. He had to be healed or he would've died."

"That would've been a great loss," Rowan said with a snort, pulling at the singed sleeve of his tunic. It ended just below his elbow in shredded ruin.

Elm reminded Rowan of his foster father. Too angry, too power hungry. They'd never gotten along.

Sapphire moved to the kitchen and dropped into a wooden chair at the table. "I just can't figure it out. There are all these flashes, but it's like I'm seeing them through pond water. Everything is dark and muted, and when I see people, I'm not sure who they are." She buried her face in her hands. "It's so frustrating."

Rowan and Cypress followed Sapphire into the kitchen. Cypress sat while Rowan leaned against the table. "Did she tell you about the binding spell?" he asked. Sapphire looked up sharply. "I healed her after she tried to burn my hand off. Hazel bound her to the city."

Sapphire rubbed the space between her eyes, grimacing. "I'm expected to serve Hazel as prophetess when I don't even *trust* her."

Cypress covered Sapphire's hand. "This has been a long time coming."

Rowan scanned the two women. Blond hair, endless blue eyes, they both looked like Callie. "Is someone going to tell me what's going on?"

"Before Callie came home, I had this vision. Initially I dismissed it because it was so impossible, but now that she's here—I can't ignore it. How familiar are you with *Fraeburdh?*" Sapphire asked.

"It's the City of War. Led by King Arol."

"And do you know what Arol's power is?"

"It's not in the books—"

"Arol's abilities are unique in that he technically has none of his own, but he can absorb the power of anyone he touches. It's a close quarter kind of thing, which is why he surrounds himself with trained warriors and doesn't venture outside on his own city. He waits for the fae to come to him." Sapphire bit her lip and looked up at Rowan. "I saw Callie with him."

"And with her growing power, she'd be an asset to Arol," Cypress said.

"So that's why Hazel bound Callie to the city? To prevent *Fraeburdh* from getting her?" Rowan asked, trying to put all the pieces together.

Sapphire shook her head and leaned back in her chair. She looked tired. "No. I think Hazel wants to use Callie for herself, as a weapon. Hazel's been lying in wait for the day she had someone strong enough to take on Arol. It's a double-edged sword. We have to keep Callie from Arol, and the best place to do that is here, where he can't break through the wards. But how do we keep Hazel from using Callie? As prophetess, I'll have some pull, but Hazel will control me completely."

"We should tell her," Rowan suggested. If someone wanted to use him as a weapon, he'd sure like someone to let him in on the secret.

"And scare her away? Callie already doesn't trust us, and who can blame her? She woke up next to a dead woman she doesn't remember meeting," Sapphire said. "And that's the other thing. The prophetess's murder was a warning. She told me of the prophecy long ago. Her death will precede the fall of *Eirensae* and coincide with the return of the one who can save it."

Rowan went cold all over. "Callie," Rowan said, feeling his throat close around her name.

"Callie," Sapphire agreed.

✂ Five ✂

CALLIE LAY AWAKE, listening to the quiet sounds of Sapphire sleeping in the next bed and the incessant rain pounding against the roof. She'd started to figure things out, not that the knowledge made her feel any saner.

Sapphire saw the future. Sometimes just flashes, other times, she had long, detailed visions that she used to guide her decisions. Ash controlled fire. He could make anything burn, no matter what it was. Rowan was a healer, as was Cypress, a woman who reminded Callie a lot of Sapphire. Willow, Ash's sister, was gifted with art. She could create music, paintings, words. If it was creative, she could do it. Hazel had the ability to cloud and influence minds to her will.

There were other powers, too. Controlling the weather, the ability to read minds. So far, Callie had three powers. Fire, water, and the thing she'd done to Elm. Ash told her not to worry about it, but she couldn't stop looking at her hands as if they belonged to somebody else. He said her powers would continue to grow now that she was in *Eirensae*. He'd sounded so excited about it. Callie was less so.

Being here was a whirlwind. She'd finally stopped expecting to wake up, though she still wished for it. Longing for the place that'd never really been a home festered in her gut. She hadn't really wanted her foster home, but now that she couldn't have it, she couldn't help thinking about her foster siblings, her foster mother.

Even Nate, the boy she couldn't love.

Silently, Callie pushed the blankets away and slid from the mattress. Sapphire continued to breathe slowly with sleep. The floor was cold beneath her bare feet. Callie slipped into a robe that hung by the door, belting it tight over her sleep clothes.

She had to get out of here.

The hinges on the door didn't creak as she swung it open. Still, she hesitated, certain that Sapphire would catch her. It wasn't until she was splashing up the washed out path that she allowed herself to breathe.

The air was cool and smelled of damp, green things. Rain pelted her shoulders and slid along the curve of her scalp to sneak beneath her clothes and make her shiver. Mud squelched between her toes.

Even with the rain, *Eirensae* was beautiful. It reminded Callie of the cities she'd seen in an ad for Mexico, a combination of beautiful architecture and quaint, comfy huts.

The giant rock that led to the caves seemed farther away than she remembered, but soon she slipped through the portal. She stood dripping in the entranceway, the rainwater creating a circle around her feet. Callie inhaled the scents of the flowers and vines spanning the walls.

"Gonna try to run for it?" Rowan's voice came from behind her before she made it five steps into the passageway.

Callie froze. Her heart sank. "Can you blame me? I want to go home."

"You *are* home," he said. She heard his footsteps as he moved toward her. "Besides, it's not safe for you to out alone. Especially on a night like this." He caught her elbow.

Callie pulled away. "Why do you even care?" Tears burned behind her eyes. She turned to face him.

Rowan folded his arms. Raindrops collected on his eyelashes and ran in rivulets over his cheeks. He lifted a shoulder.

"Please," she begged. "Help me go back. I don't want this life...I just want to be—"

"Human?"

She nodded. She was a stranger in her own body. When she closed her eyes, she saw the dead prophetess, blood seeping from Elm's ears, and Rowan, his skin melting away.

"Sorry. You know I can't do that. Not even if I wanted to. You let Hazel do a binding spell."

Callie opened her mouth to protest, but Rowan held up his hand.

"Don't try to deny it. I healed the cut. I can see how each wound was created."

She glanced down at her now-smooth palm. That was admission enough. "But—" It was fear, Callie realized. This new life was out of her hands. Her powers were too vast to control.

"I can't help you leave."

"I hate you!" she screamed.

The rush of anger was short-lived and intense. To Callie's surprise, Rowan clutched his head and groaned. He doubled over, grasping fistfuls of hair. A guttural sound erupted from his throat, something terrifying enough that Callie hoped she never heard it again.

"Rowan?"

He lowered his hands, puzzled. Blood trickled from his nose and he wiped it away. "I think you tried to explode my brain."

Callie's eyes went to her fingers. She held them away from her body as though they might suddenly transform into malicious creatures of destruction.

Rowan's expression remained confused. "I have an unbelievable headache."

"I didn't…are you okay?" She reached out, tentative, afraid to touch him. Her hand looked ordinary. Pale scars dotted the back from where she'd rollerbladed through a glass window.

"You can't go anywhere," he muttered. "Not with that demon hiding beneath your skin. Come on." He waved a hand and turned back the way she'd come.

"I'll be okay," he said to Callie, who hadn't moved. "Callie," he called from the entranceway.

She snapped from the trance, keeping her palms pointed skyward as though trying to catch invisible raindrops. The look of horror remained plastered on her face as she came toward him.

The library was cold without a fire to warm it. Callie stood in the doorway, watching him. A puddle formed beneath her and she crossed her arms, shivering. He found an old blanket tucked on a shelf and tossed it over her shoulders. While she pulled it around herself, Rowan lit a few tallow candles and set them on the main table at the heart of the library.

Rowan sat and rested his head in his hands. He closed his eyes. "I knew you were powerful, but…" The implications hung between them. Rowan knew *exactly* what had happened. With energy that strong, she could take someone down with just her thoughts. Sapphire was right. Callie would be a powerful weapon.

"Does it still hurt?" She lowered herself into the chair across from Rowan, clouding him with the scent of rainwater and chamomile and smoke. "Maybe you should find Cypress. Get it healed."

"No."

"Why not? I could've killed you—you could still die. We don't know what I'm capable of." Callie pressed the edge of her blanket to Rowan's face, catching the blood that still dribbled from his nose. He heard the concern in her voice. It made him feel weak.

Rowan pushed her hands away. "I'm not leaving you alone. You'll just try to escape again."

"Then I'll come with you. We can go back to Sapphire's."

"No," he repeated.

"Rowan…"

He looked up. Something about her expression bothered him. She was afraid for him. And she could only feel that way if she cared for him.

Everything inside of him went still.

How long had it been since another person had willingly shown him compassion? It's been longer still since he'd accepted it.

Rowan felt his hand open like a flower, palm up on the scarred table, as though his muscles were surprised at what he was about to do. "Give me your hand," he said.

A thousand worst-case scenarios wound through his mind. He knew what it felt like to share this kind of energy, to be this close—and yet, he was doing it anyway. He'd never had a *damn the consequences* attitude, each move was usually calculated. Except this—except with *her*. He remembered how his heart had stopped when he'd seen her covered with blood. How he'd been terrified that he'd lost his chance.

Her fingers were freezing and pruned from standing in the rain too long, but the underlying power was pulsating and warm. "Close your eyes," he said.

Her eyelids lowered, fanning a shadow across her cheeks. "What are you doing?"

"Healing myself."

"But—"

"Would you just shut up and let me do this? My head is *killing* me."

Her mouth snapped shut. She frowned.

Rowan willed his body to relax. Callie's touch made every nerve in his body pull tight. "Empty your mind," he said, more to himself than her. There was something about Callie that made him ache all over. He'd felt it when she dangled beneath him outside the palace window. He'd felt it when he healed her. Both times.

She was special.

Rowan let his energy drain into Callie's skin. Her body offered no resistance and their power swirled together like the strands of a double helix. Callie's energy was the blue of the summer sky in August, and as viscous as honey. Rowan's was darker, *much* darker, but just as thick.

The farther he went, the more aware he was of Callie. First, her fingertips, warming from their contact, and then her arms. He slid across her chest, feeling her pulse pound against his as though they were in a race to finish first. He entered her mind, letting the disorienting feeling of seeing himself wash over him.

Her life played in fast forward, like flipping the pages of a picture book. There was water and hurt, suffocation. Pain. Memories crashed into him—swirling and swelling until Rowan was nauseous. His throat closed. He couldn't breathe. With a gasp, he threw up a wall to Callie's memory. Their energy moved along it and into her other arm, finally reaching her fingertips. It poured back into Rowan.

He breathed in relief, shocked by the absolute horror inside of Callie's mind. His heart slammed against his ribs. His energy pulsed to the tune of panic. Rowan forced himself to relax and let himself heal.

From there, his mind went into autopilot, seeking out imperfection. He saw Callie's anger attack his brain, creating weak spots in his vessels. If the attack had lasted one second longer, he'd likely be dead. As it was, Rowan was lucky he'd chosen to heal himself. Without it, he would've lived only hours.

He didn't tell Callie any of this, just let his energy traverse her body and spill into his. His head went numb, then warm.

All too soon, it was over.

Rowan pulled away, their hands disconnecting like two magnets determined to hold on. He hid his in his lap. "Thanks," he murmured, still reeling. *What* happened to her? He wanted to pull her into his arms but refused to believe he could heal her pain. Heartbreak like that was more than skin deep. It infected every cell like poison.

Callie watched him curiously.

Drops of water fell from his hair onto the table. He had to say something. "I can't heal myself, only direct the energy through someone else. It's inconvenient, but it works." His heart slowed to a normal rhythm.

Callie shivered. Did she feel the chill in her bones as he did—the frigidness that came with the severed connection? Rowan tried not to get close to too many people—especially when it came to sharing power. It was too intimate, but with Callie he found he didn't mind as much. He trusted her in a way he didn't fully understand.

"We should go back." He stood, unable to continue sharing the tiny, three-foot space without touching her.

Callie blinked and finally looked around. "Where are we?"

Rowan smiled, watching curiosity play across her face. He should've known she'd like this place. "The library."

He picked up a candle and handed her another, gesturing for her to follow.

He led her through the stacks, watching her expression brighten as she took in the thick, leather bound tomes tucked between living branches.

"It's better in the daylight," he said. "Are you familiar with the art of bonsai?"

She shook her head, lips moving as she read the titles silently.

"The library was designed when the trees were saplings, hundreds and hundreds of years ago." He stood, came closer to her, sliding his fingers over the places she'd touched. "These ridges are where the trees were shaped using wire."

"It's beautiful," she said, drawing a volume off the shelf. The cover was worn tan leather, the gold lettering faded in places.

"*Amhrán an Chroí,*" Rowan read, slipping easily into Gaelic. "Song of the Heart." He took the book from her and replaced it gently on the shelf, feeling warmth in his chest. Callie loved the library as much as he did. The fact made him happier than it should have. So what, she liked books—that didn't mean they had anything in common.

She hesitated, inspected her fingernails. Finally, she mirrored his posture, leaning on the shelf opposite him and crossing her arms. "Who are my parents?"

Rowan couldn't hide his shock. Usually it took new members of the city longer to put the pieces together. "I don't know." He lifted a shoulder, feeling regret bite at his gut. She was no different from any other faerie here—*no one* knew their parents, no matter how badly they wanted it. "We aren't *allowed* to know." Bitterness crept into his words. "The purpose of the city is to unite the children of the fae. We are to be as one. *Live mar aon ní amháin.*" He could tell by her expression that she didn't know what the words meant, joining a legion of fae who'd forgotten their native language. Now they resorted to English mostly, just like the rest of the world.

Callie fingered the tie on her robe, twisting it around her index finger. "So you all live here together, but you never know who your parents are? How is that fair?" She looked past him to the shelves beyond, eyes far away in the candlelight. "My entire life I thought my parents were dead. And now I find out they're alive—but I'll never know they're *mine?*"

The pain in the last word fell over Rowan like a sodden blanket and he took a moment to gain his composure. Hadn't he thought the exact same things?

"Long ago," he said finally, "there was war between our people. The Elders formulated a plan based on the idea of binding us together. Everyone is family, and therefore we fight for each other as family, because potentially every one of us could be related." He felt the edges of his mouth tighten. "We're one big, happy family."

Callie's face dissolved into horror. "But what about incest? I mean—if you don't know..."

Rowan chuckled. "It's chemistry. We're creatures of nature, close to the earth, all living things. It would feel inherently wrong, not that it would specifically matter." He leaned close to her, enjoying the way her eyes widened. "Trust me—we're not related. Nothing to worry about."

She snorted—actually *snorted*—and walked away from him. "Believe me, I'm not concerned about being related to you."

She went to the pillows stacked in the corner, touching random surfaces as she went—the shelves, the book that lay open on the table, a cluster of dangling orbs. He wanted to go behind her, feel each item from inside her skin.

She sat, studied him, her blue eyes shuttered. Rowan wished he'd been gifted with the ability to mind read.

"Why are you being so nice, anyway?"

Rowan sat across from her, stretching out his legs. "I don't know."

"I never said thank you—for when the prophetess died. Thanks for taking care of me and for...for not blaming me."

Rowan said nothing.

"What will happen to her? Do you...bury them? Is there a cemetery?"

"We burn our dead," he said. "They'll be a ceremony soon."

Callie nodded and the silence became awkward. "So...what's with this imprint business?"

"I already explained this to you, but maybe you were too hopped up on faerie wine to remember." She opened her mouth but Rowan held up his hand. "It's fine." Callie sat back and waited for him to continue. "An imprint shows your rank amongst the fae. Your amulet, which the Elders will explain to you, gives you this rank. When you're born, the prophet, or in our case, prophetess, divines your future. The amulet is spelled and hidden in the city. Finding it is kind of like your initiation. Choosing to put it on means you accept *Eirensae* as your home. It binds you and your magic to the city." His words became quieter. "You can't become a full member until you have it." A fact that Rowan knew all too well.

"How do I know where to look?"

"You don't—that's the thing. You're given no information about it at all. No clues. From what I understand, it's a gut feeling, some magical connection that leads you to the correct path."

"Sounds like a load of bull to me," Callie said.

"Yeah. And you only get two years."

"How long have you been here?" she asked.

Rowan answered her real question. "I have a little over two months to find my amulet. Sixty-seven days, if you care." He tried to sound blasé, but wasn't sure he pulled it off. He knew he would leave. He just didn't want anyone to know how much it bothered him. He could survive anywhere, inside a fae city or outside in the human world. All he had to do was scrape out an existence. Besides, if he were banished, he'd lose his longevity, so at least it'd be a *short* existence.

"Doesn't anyone help?" Callie asked, finally looking up.

What he saw in her eyes was more than curiosity, it was compassion, *pity*.

"Have you even started searching for yours yet? Better hurry. And don't expect help—you won't get it." He forced his expression to remain blank. "I've searched every inch of *Eirensae,* my amulet isn't here. The Elders don't believe me." Hazel had been the most adamant that he "keep searching," but offered no explanation why it was so easy for every other fae. *Days,* usually, not weeks or months, certainly not years. To them the two-year search time was laughable. Who needed that much time when the amulet's placement was so obvious?

Either he didn't belong here, or the prophetess foresaw he'd bring destruction to the city. Neither option sat well with Rowan. If he didn't belong here, that meant he *did* belong to another city. As for the second possibility, he failed to see how one fae could ruin a city, especially one without offensive power. What was he going to do? Heal them to death?

"And if you don't find it?" Callie was really paying attention now. Rowan could see the shiny flecks in her irises, smell the dampness in her hair as it tumbled onto her shoulders, just inches from his fingertips.

He swallowed, tearing his gaze from Callie. "Meet the newest member of the Fallen."

"Those are the people who used to be faeries, right? Hazel explained it some," Callie said. "I don't really get it."

Rowan searched for a way to explain it that she'd understand. "What's the one thing you want more than anything in the world?" he asked.

Callie hesitated.

"It's okay. You can tell me."

"Family," she said.

A sharp ache lanced through Rowan's chest. He ignored it. "So imagined you had a family. Parents, siblings, the perfect suburban life wrapped up and tied with a bow. Then, all of a sudden, you're not worthy of that family anymore, so they kick you to the street, refuse to speak to you, refuse to acknowledge you exist. *That's* what it's like to become Fallen."

Callie looked uncertain. "Hazel made them sound evil."

"I don't know. I guess it all depends how far you're willing to go to have everything you've ever wanted." He pushed to his feet and held out a hand to help Callie up. "You've got to get back. Sapphire will worry."

ℬ Six ℭ

CALLIE WOKE THE following morning to an empty cottage. In the past five days, she'd grown used to Sapphire, head bent over the vegetables in her garden, humming the morning away. The silence reminded her too much of being alone. Callie dressed quickly and headed outside.

Dark clouds stretched across the sky, lumbering against the horizon as if they were just waiting to strike. At least it'd stopped raining. The day before still worried at the back of Callie's mind. She'd really hurt Rowan with her powers. She had to learn how to control them, and fast, especially if they were to continue growing. If she ever did get to go home, she'd hate to see what kind of havoc she'd cause a human who didn't have the ability to heal.

The path to the city seemed strangely empty.

She'd expected Ash to be at her door demanding she practice, but Callie was grateful for the solitude and time to collect her thoughts. She sat on the porch, letting the sounds of *Eirensae* wash over her. Birds whistled in the trees that surrounded the city. The stream gurgled cheerfully. She inhaled, smelling the morning and the faint, acrid scent of lightning from the night before.

If she was still enough, quiet enough, she swore she could hear the grass growing, and more faintly, the soft sound of petals unfolding into blooms.

Then, footsteps.

Callie's eyes flew open.

Elm stood before her, furious. "You shouldn't be here," he said.

Rage rose within her, battling for dominance over her fear. She could still feel his fingers around her throat. "You're lucky to be here," she countered, pushing to her feet.

Elm ran a hand through his hair. When it dropped to his side, it curled into a fist. "You think I'm afraid of you? A child? I fought in the original battle, back before the fae split into cities. You're nothing more than a minor disturbance. Easily squashed."

Callie tasted metal on the back of her tongue. "I don't know why you hate me. I haven't done anything to you."

"Perhaps not," he said, moving closer. The muscles in his arms bunched. Callie pressed herself against Sapphire's door. "I know Hazel is planning something. I know you're working with her. Maybe I can't challenge her, but I can certainly take you out."

A few cottages away, a door opened.

"I'm not working with anyone," Callie argued. She felt power tingling beneath her fingertips, skimming along her scalp. "You better get away from me," she gasped. She bit her lip, fighting the sensation.

"Hey, Callie," Ash was there, his feet squeaking against the wet grass. He glanced at Elm. "Hey."

Elm ignored Ash.

"Back up, Ash. I don't want to hurt you," Callie said, voice desperate. Her skin vibrated, a numb, incessant feeling.

Elm pressed his face close to hers. He smelled rancid, as though hate spewed from every pore. "I want you gone."

Ash's fist came out of nowhere. The sound of bones on bone crackled through the air. Elm's head snapped backward.

"You leave her alone," Ash said, fist ready to strike again. Elm was nearly a full head taller than Ash, but Ash had his chest right against the bigger man's.

"Ash," Callie said, horrified, certain that Elm was going to crush him.

Elm took a deep breath.

"Go on," Callie said. "Go away."

"Yeah," Ash said, shoving Elm's chest. "I heard what she did to you last time. You want her to finish the job?"

Elm turned his angry gaze on Callie. Veins in his forehead pulsed. Callie fought the shiver that inched up her spine. "I'm a patient man, Calla Lily. Remember that."

As Elm retreated, Callie sagged against the door. Ash cradled his hand. "Shit," he whispered, turning to Callie. "That hurt." He reached behind her and opened the door, shuffling her inside.

Callie went to the pitcher on the counter and poured herself a glass of water, drinking it slowly.

"What is his problem?" Ash exploded. He waved his arms. Winced. "Just wait until I tell Hazel about this."

Callie shook her head. "No. You can't. I've already caused enough trouble. I really just want to fly under the radar, you know?" She'd had her fill of attention.

Ash lifted an eyebrow. "Radar, yeah. I understand."

Callie smiled. "Let me see your hand."

He had two split knuckles and a bright red mark spreading across the back of his hand. She wet a towel with the cool water in the pitcher and held it over the wound. "You shouldn't have hit him. Are you insane?"

"Maybe a little," he admitted. "But this is nice." He held up their joined hands, covering the back of Callie's hand with his palm.

Uneasiness wormed into her gut. "Ash—"

He smiled, green eyes luminous. "Yeah?"

Callie sighed, fighting the urge to pull her hands away. She remembered the other day, when they'd held the blooming flower. The petals falling around them like a perfect, magical moment. She extracted herself from his grasp. "Where is everyone, anyway?"

His grin widened. "It's initiation day. How can you not know?" He tossed the bloodied towel onto the counter. "We're naming a new prophetess. Sapphire is going to be great."

Callie's throat closed. "Sapphire?"

"She didn't tell you?"

"Guess not," Callie said. She pushed away from the counter. "Maybe she just forgot, with everything else going on." Through the window, she saw Rowan stalking up the path to the city. Did he always look so high-strung? Maybe having your brain exploded did that to you. She turned back to Ash. "You can teach me how to control my power, right? I don't want to hurt people."

Ash nodded. "You'll have it in no time. I mean, I hardly ever set accidental fires anymore."

Ash caught Callie's horrified expression. "Hey," he said, touching her shoulder, "you'll be fine. You have nothing to worry about. You're exactly perfect."

"Um," she said.

He cradled her cheek. Callie recognized this look. It was the one he'd had when he almost kissed her in the caves. She ducked away. "I can't do this, Ash."

"Do what?"

"Whatever it is you think is happening." She opened the cottage door. "I'll see you at the initiation, then?" she said, hoping she hadn't thoroughly smashed his heart.

"Okay," he said, moving toward the door.

Callie breathed a sigh of relief when he was gone.

She had to find some way to control her anger. And it'd be really nice if Ash got a clue. She wasn't interested in a relationship.

℘◆℘

Rowan strode through Ash's door, not bothering to knock. The sunset shone through the windows, turning everything burnt orange. Ash sat on the couch, hands folded in his lap, eyes far away.

Rowan slammed the door, making the other boy jump. "Are you meditating?"

Ash's neck reddened. "No."

"Then get up and get dressed or we'll be late for the initiation. I figured you'd be with Callie..." Rowan left the question unsaid though his insides churned with worry.

"I was this morning. I haven't seen her since." Ash stood and stretched, flexed his fingers.

Rowan crossed to Ash, inspecting his knuckles. They were bruised and split. "I'd avoid you too, if you hit me."

Ash rolled his eyes. "I didn't hit *her*. I hit Elm. The asshole."

Rowan grunted in agreement and went to the kitchen, pillaging for something to eat while Ash changed. Rowan was already dressed for the evening, in a dark blue tunic and loose pants. To the fae, it would just be another celebration, another night to drink and party and ignore responsibility.

Rowan found a crusty loaf of bread, a block of cheese, and two withered apples. Sighing, he shut the cupboard door. What he really wanted was to go to Sapphire's. He was certain Callie was avoiding him after last night, because in truth, he was avoiding her. Rowan could still feel her energy, thick and intoxicating, soaking into his skin. If he saw her, he'd want to touch her—and if he touched her, he'd never want to stop. If this continued, he'd have to up his training schedule just to distract himself.

Ash emerged from the bedroom wearing the same thing as Rowan in forest green. "Let's go," Ash said, dragging a hand through his hair.

Last night, after Rowan had walked Callie back to Sapphire's, he'd slid into the night, body humming with electricity. He felt as though he could run for miles and miles and miles and never tire. He'd gone back to his cottage and lay staring at the ceiling, dissecting what he'd found in Callie's mind.

What if she opened up to him? What if her past knitted them closer together? What if he couldn't leave her when his time was up?

Rowan gave up on sleep when sunlight streamed through his window this morning. He'd spent three hours training, and ran the perimeter of the city twice, though he wouldn't admit the second time he was solely looking for Callie.

He and Ash made the short walk to the palace, which lit up the growing dusk. Laughter, the melodic thrum of a harp, and the clink of champagne glasses spilled from the open doors and windows. The fae greeted Ash when they reached the ballroom, resting their forearms against his as they said, "Blessed evening," and, "Blessed night." They ignored Rowan, eyes skipping over him as though he was as transparent as a ghost and just as negligible. Resentment smoldered, a simmering coal in his belly. He healed them when they were sick or injured, he studied their history, he knew more about the fae of *Eirensae* than they knew of themselves. Yet they treated him like a pariah, the bastard black sheep they'd sell first to slaughter.

The Elders lined the stage, dressed in their finest gowns and tunics, the women's faces glamoured to reflect the twinkling orb light. There was no reference to the recently deceased prophetess. The murder was nothing more than a memory. Rowan knew they'd have a funeral in two days' time. The prophetess would be dressed in layers of silk and shimmer, her skin glamoured to youth and perfection. Then they would burn her body and scatter the ashes in the river.

For now, they partied as though a faerie hadn't died for a new prophetess to be initiated.

Rowan was disappointed that Callie hadn't arrived yet, and resorted to following Ash around like a trained dog. A few fae spoke to him— Cypress, Sapphire, and Chicory, greeted him from atop the stage. Gardenia, the oldest faerie in the city, said a polite hello. Even Hazel spared him a brief scowl, and Rowan wondered if he was moving up in the world. When they reached the end of the raised platform, Rowan noticed Ash glaring at Elm. Despite Ash's ravaged knuckles, Elm's face was unmarked. Rowan hoped Ash would hit him again, just to make the evening more interesting. He'd love to get into a fight in defense of his friend. Hell, he'd love to get in a fight for *any* reason.

Rowan knew the second Callie stepped into the ballroom. The air in his lungs vanished. She wore a simple white lace dress, belted at the waist with a silk sash. Her face was free of glamour makeup, blonde curls hung loose over her shoulders. Even from across the room, he could see fatigue lining her eyes and mouth. Beside her, Willow talked a mile a minute, probably describing the initiation. Callie didn't look like she was listening. She scrutinized the crowd, eyebrows sliding lower and lower, until finally, their eyes met. She looked away and said something to Willow, who launched into another breathless spiel.

Rowan pushed through the crowd, ignoring protests from the other fae as they struggled not to spill their drinks. Ash was right behind him.

The ceremony started before they reached the girls, Hazel's voice expanding to fill the room as she spoke in Gaelic. Rowan translated without even thinking about it.

Welcome, Sapphire, woman of the fae, servant of Eirensae. Do you accept your place as prophetess and with it, vow to devote yourself to the service of the city, forsaking previous ties and commitments? Will you speak the oath and pledge yourself to the fae and to the city?

Hazel's pronunciation wasn't perfect, but it was close, and Rowan knew that eventually the language would die with the Elders. They no longer taught the returning children to speak as their ancestors had, and the words were only used as part of the ceremonies. His knowledge of the language was mostly self-taught, aided by Cypress. Rowan's desire to learn came when he'd read every book in the library, save the ones in Gaelic. He'd devoured the nuances of the language with insatiable hunger, and then later, the books. The fae had a long, sordid history, and he suspected that the majority of them living today had no clue, either because they were too lazy or too uninterested to learn.

Ash and Rowan reached the wall and had to backtrack through the crowd to come up behind Callie and Willow. The Elders were placing long strands of flowers over Sapphire's head and kissing her pink cheeks. Callie's head was up, gaze focused on Sapphire as she accepted her new position as prophetess. Rowan moved into the space behind her.

"I heard you explode brains for fun," he whispered.

Callie whirled, smacking Rowan in the face with her hair. "That's not funny," she hissed.

"Maybe you should light me on fire again?" He lifted one shoulder, ready to tease her further, but Callie's expression made him say, "What's wrong?" instead.

She looked over her shoulder toward the stage. "Sapphire," she said, just loud enough for Rowan to hear.

Ash appeared beside them, finally pushing his way through the bodies. "Are you okay?" he asked, touching her arm. Rowan followed Callie's movement as she folded her arms and slid away from Ash.

"I was worried after..." Ash said, trailing off when Callie gave him her back. Ash glanced at Rowan and shrugged.

Rowan couldn't help feeling a little smug over Callie's dismissal of Ash. No wonder his friend was so pouty. Callie had turned him down. Rowan inched closer to Callie, pleased when she didn't step away. "She'll make a great prophetess," Rowan said, leaning in close enough that loose strands of her hair tickled his face.

"Why didn't she tell me?" Callie asked

A frown tugged at Rowan's mouth as he remembered what it was like to be new to the city, oblivious to the traditions and rules. "It's her place, determined by the previous prophetess." And it would put Sapphire directly under Hazel's thumb.

He tracked Callie's gaze to the stage where Sapphire accepted the final string of flowers from Hazel. Sapphire grinned, happiness radiating from her despite what she'd told Rowan. She may know terrible things, but this was what she was born to do. Knowing your place had to feel like coming home.

Hazel and Sapphire held the pile of blue, violet, orange, and yellow blooms, mouths moving in a silent chant, the words too ancient for Rowan to understand. As they watched, the flowers shivered and started to coil Sapphire's arms like vines creeping up a tree trunk. Sapphire's eyes fluttered shut. With a hiss, the flowers melted into Sapphire's skin, staining her arms with a colorful new imprint that marked her as prophetess.

While it was meant to be an uplifting ceremony, Rowan felt dread pool at the base of his spine, remembering Sapphire's words about King Arol and *Fraeburdh*. He glanced at Callie. Sapphire had to be wrong. There's no way Callie, who was terrified of hurting people with her powers, would join the City of War.

Then again, Rowan had never anticipated joining the Fallen, either, but that would soon happen.

He shook off the thoughts and gestured to the stage. "You want to get closer?"

ℝ♦℞

"Congratulations?" Callie said, lifting the end of the word into a question.

Sapphire laughed and they embraced. The new prophetess's skin tingled against Callie's as though the imprints were charged with electricity. "Thank you," Sapphire said. She released Callie and moved to greet Willow, Ash, and Rowan, kissing their cheeks. "I'm so nervous," she admitted.

Callie thought her sister looked beautiful, happiness rolling off her skin and infecting the gathered crowd. "Why didn't you tell me?"

Sapphire caught Callie's hands and squeezed. "I would've, but you were out so late last night, I didn't want to wake you."

Callie's guilty gaze slid to the side then up to Rowan before returning to Sapphire. "You knew?"

Sapphire winked. "I know *everything.*"

A dark skinned man approached, carrying two glasses of bubbling liquid. Something about him tickled the back of Callie's mind but she couldn't quite place why he looked familiar.

"Ladies," he said, bowing. He handed a glass to Willow and Callie, a smile splitting his face. He presented his arm to Sapphire. "My prophetess." They touched arms and he lifted Sapphire's fingers to his mouth. "You look ravishing, as usual." Sapphire's cheeks pinked further and she was pulled away by the crowd.

He turned to Callie. "Gorgeous, Calla Lily." He took her hand and bowed gracefully. "It's a pleasure to formally meet you. I am Bonsai, but you may call me Sai. May I introduce Hawthorne and Jack," he said, gesturing to the two fae accompanying him.

The first boy, Jack, had wide blue eyes framed by pale blond lashes that matched his mop of curling, sunshine hair. Callie liked him immediately, even before he ignored her offered arm and pulled her into a hug. He broke into a smile, still holding her hand, leaking gentle energy into her skin. "Callie, that's a beautiful name."

"Thanks," she said, an answering smile on her lips.

Hawthorne stepped forward next. Where Jack was light, Hawthorne was dark, with brown hair and eyes. When they touched forearms, his energy tore into Callie like an insatiable beast. They jumped away from each other, Callie with a small sound of surprise.

"Nice to meet you," Hawthorne said, recovering first, his voice much deeper than Callie anticipated, tinged with a slight accent she couldn't place.

"You, too," she said, relieved when Sai launched into a story and the attention was diverted from her.

Callie tried to listen to the boys; Jack kept interrupting Sai as they reiterated their search for a missing fae child that should've returned to the city by now. Her eyes kept going to the crowd, searching for Elm. He'd stepped off the stage and she'd lost sight of him. She wasn't afraid that he'd approach her again, more that he'd ruin Sapphire's initiation. He was the kind of person that wouldn't shrink away from retribution, justified or otherwise.

Distracted by the search, Callie lifted the glass to her lips, realizing what she'd done only after the taste of flowers and berries burst on her tongue. "Damn it," she said after it'd slid down her throat. It was the reason she couldn't remember what had happened to prophetess, why her entire welcome ceremony was a giant black spot in her mind.

She hadn't meant to drink it.

The faerie wine worked its way into Callie's veins, leaving her limbs loose and tingling. The music swirled around them, sneaking between the bodies, turning the air ethereal. Callie took another sip.

"Would you like to dance?" Jack asked, holding out a hand. He wiggled his eyebrows.

"Uh—" she looked around, trying to stall, afraid that she'd lose her mind again to the drink.

Ash looked irritated and Rowan looked like he couldn't care one way or another. He'd found a glass of bright green wine, it dangled at his side from two fingers. His eyes were focused on a spot beyond

Callie's head. Sai captured Willow and spun her onto the dance floor. Hawthorne snagged a drink and headed off into the crowd.

"Come on. I don't bite," Jack said with a wink. *"Much."*

Callie finished her drink and handed the glass to Rowan.

"You've done this before," she said as Jack twirled her into the churning mass of bodies. She had a vague, fuzzy memory of Rowan doing the same thing at the welcome ceremony.

Jack nodded. *"Eirensae* is known for their parties. I just like to look the part." They passed Willow, who struggled to keep up with Sai as he flung her around. "I apologize for missing your welcome ceremony. I hear it was grand, even if it ended so tragically. But, we must not speak of the sad things today."

He spun Callie under his arm. When she regained her footing, he flicked his hand at the band and the music sped up. They spun faster and faster until Callie was too dizzy to keep herself upright. Finally, Jack led Callie to the edge of the floor and she collapsed into a chair, relieved. The faerie drink twisted in her brain, making all the colors appear brighter. Sai returned with more drinks and a panting Willow who fell into a puddle beside Callie and wiped sweat off her forehead.

"We should," Willow said, taking another breath, "go back to your place." She gestured to the guys. "Have our own party."

Sai's teeth gleamed white when he smiled. "That's an *excellent* idea."

Jack clapped and whooped, "Private party!"

"I'm in," Rowan said, downing the rest of his drink and handing it to a passing waiter. "This party is dull anyway."

Callie would've argued with him just for the sake of arguing and defending Sapphire, but the drink made her thoughts and voice disconnect. So when Ash pulled her to her feet and the group left the room, she followed.

❦ Seven ❧

BRIGHT AFTERNOON LIGHT streamed through the window. Callie's body ached as she forced her eyelids open. Cracking her neck, she sat up and gasped, trying to make sense of the scene before her. She was sprawled on the floor, legs underneath the spindles of a wooden coffee table, and looking around, she wasn't sure whose house it was.

The space was in shambles.

Decorative plants lay torn from their stone pots, roots exposed like veins ripped from skin, dripping dirt crumbles. Champagne glasses littered the floor, some shattered, others half-full of multicolored liquid. The couch behind her was turned on its side, pillows spilled across the floor. She sat up further, groaning. A few feet away, Willow and Sai were entangled on the couch, his dark skin stark against the paleness of hers. If not for their different skin tones, Callie wouldn't have been able to determine where one ended and the other began. Willow's hair was a riot of red, exploding across Sai's chest.

She swallowed the dry foulness in her mouth. At the kitchen counter, Ash slept, head pillowed in his hands. Underneath the table, Jack laid prostrate, arms and legs akimbo, snoring softly. Callie stood, bare feet crunching the remains of something. She braced herself against the table, dizzy.

Callie took stock. She was still fully dressed, but couldn't remember a thing from the night before, just a giddy blur of colors and flashes.

One side of the dress she'd borrowed from Willow was covered in blue goo. She rubbed the sleep from her eyes and picked her way to the door, careful not to disturb the others.

She trudged toward Sapphire's, every moment in the sun a reminder of the wine's harsh side effects. The light slid into her eyes like knives.

Fae hurried through the city, in pairs or groups. Callie left the shelter of the tall buildings and emerged into the afternoon sun. In the distance, a structure was beginning to take shape. Several men, chests bare and imprinted, were working together, hauling branch-stripped logs as thick as legs. The steady thunk of wood against wood reached her ears.

Callie wasn't sure what they were building. The base was bigger than the top, which was flat as a table. As she reached the height of the path, she saw rows and rows of green covered chairs. Curiosity warred with her desire to shower as she turned away from the men, toward the cottages.

Rowan stood in the emerald grass, barefoot, the sun glinting off sweat on his chest. Callie's steps faltered as he lifted a staff, the wood smooth and wrapped with thick leather on each end. He swung, the staff arcing in a great circle over his head that ended with a sharp jab.

She watched, transfixed, as he retrieved the weapon and stretched his neck. Callie's gaze followed the gentle curve where it met his shoulder, and lower, where muscles rippled beneath his skin. Rowan had the body of a dancer, long, lean. *And flexible,* she thought as his feet flew over his head and he landed in a defensive pose. He pushed his staff in front of him on a horizontal, sliding one foot behind the other for balance. His body was fluid, mercury allowed to slide across a tabletop as he repeated the motion. Rowan was breathing hard when he settled the length of the weapon on his shoulder and flicked hair out of his eyes.

Here is beauty and grace, she thought. There was passion behind the movement, restrained desire. Where had he learned to fight like that, and worse, had he ever needed to use that knowledge?

Rowan cleared his throat.

Heat filled Callie's face. "What are you doing?" she asked, gathering the length of her hair over one shoulder, realizing how terrible she must look, dirty and hung over. Whereas Rowan, dripping sweat, looked beautiful and all sorts of indecent.

He scratched an exposed hipbone, drawing Callie's eye to the flat expanse of his stomach, the ridges of muscle there. As she watched, dry-mouthed, a bead of sweat dripped from his chest to the waistband of his loose pants and disappeared. Callie couldn't drag her eyes away; they kept going to the little V created by bone and muscle. She wanted to touch him there, see if his skin was as smooth and perfect as it looked. She dug her nails into her palms.

"Callie?"

She startled, blush burning hotter. "What are you doing?" she repeated, finally forcing her gaze to his face.

The skin around his eyes crinkled and he lifted one eyebrow. "I said, *I'm training.*"

"With that stick," Callie said, knowing the moment the words left her mouth that they were horribly inaccurate. It wasn't a *stick,* it was a flowing extension of Rowan's body that he handled with intimate knowledge, as one might know a lover. She waited for the acid of his tongue, and it came, right on cue.

"That *stick* is a quarterstaff," he muttered, gaze sweeping over her like a touch.

Callie pressed her arms over her stomach, recoiling as the blue goo smeared, cold and sticky, across her skin.

"You look awful," he said.

"Thanks," she said. She suddenly felt okay and was certain it had something to do with the adrenaline rush of watching Rowan train. She imagined learning to move like that, with lightness and confidence. She pointed to the men in the distance, desperate to change the subject. "What's that?"

"Funeral pyre for the prophetess." He came closer, so that Callie could smell the sunshine and sweat on his tan skin, sense the shiver of energy. "After they burn, we scatter the ashes in the river."

Horror clogged Callie's throat as visions of burning bodies filled her mind. It seemed inhumane, barbaric, even. She ripped her eyes from the pyre, turning so it was behind her. "That's kind of awful."

"It's the way of our people." He tapped the end of his staff against the ground, distractedly.

"So this stick…"

"Quarterstaff."

"Quarterstaff," she corrected. "You fight with it?" Callie poked at the stretched leather, intrigued. "Why a staff?"

"For shits and giggles, mostly. Occasionally, I use it to intimidate Ash and unsuspecting humans." His expression sobered. "If you haven't noticed, someone breached our wards and killed the prophetess. We could all use a little more training around here. *Eirensae* is complacent, has been for a while. The people are weak, but don't listen to me. I'm just the illegitimate, unimprinted idiot. I wouldn't know anything about fighting or strategy. It's not like I've read all the history books in the library." His lips twisted.

Callie digested that. Rowan had read *all* the history books. She hadn't counted, but there had to be thousands of thick bound volumes in *Eirensae's* library.

"Will you teach me?" Callie asked, looking up at him. Rowan stood half a foot taller than her, making Callie feel tiny.

"Will I what?" he snapped.

"I want to learn how to fight." Her thoughts went to Elm, to the energy pulsing beneath her skin. Maybe it would help her learn to control it. "If the people that killed the prophetess are after me, at least teach me to protect myself."

Rowan's glare turned wary, and then interested. He sucked his lips inward, deciding, and then blew out a breath. "Fine."

Callie hadn't expected him to agree. "Fine?"

"Fine." He held up a finger. "One condition." She waited, expectant. "Go shower. No way am I touching Willow's puke."

8O ✦ Q8

Rowan followed Callie's approach with a mixture of dread and anticipation roiling in his gut. Freshly showered and changed, she'd plaited her hair into a heavy, dripping braid. He'd used her absence to practice more, going over the familiar routine time and again until his muscles shook.

It hadn't been enough.

She wore a green tank top that exposed the gentle curve of her throat and collarbone. Rowan swallowed. He should've pushed himself harder—he should've been too tired to think. He reminded himself that Callie was nothing more than a student, the same as the young people he'd taught before he'd come to *Eirensae,* but his gaze found her calves, summer bronzed under matching green leggings. Her feet were bare, her toes unpolished. Was it weird to find toes erotic?

Callie stopped, squinting against the sunlight. She had to feel awful. A headache throbbed behind Rowan's eyes, but that was no reason not to train. Whoever had killed the prophetess wouldn't make exceptions for hangovers. He hefted the extra quarterstaff he'd gone to get for Callie. "Ready?"

She nodded, staring at the staff, uncertainty clouding her expression. Suddenly, Callie's situation became real. There wasn't much time left for Rowan, eventually they'd cast him out. She had to learn to protect herself, because he couldn't trust the city to do it when he was gone, not with Hazel lurking over Callie's shoulder.

"The first thing you have to learn is how to fall." He tossed the staff. It landed in the grass with a muted thunk. He used Callie's distraction to attack. She fell easily beneath him, the air that rushed from her lungs smelled like flowers with a light tang of fermentation underneath. Her eyes widened. She was soft and solid at the same time and he didn't let himself linger, though he did imagine a hundred different variations of the same scene.

Rowan fought a smile as he stood and offered a hand. "That was the wrong way to fall."

Callie ignored his hand and dragged herself to her feet, elbows already stained green and brown. A little furrow appeared between her eyebrows.

Rowan planted his feet for stability. "Push me."

She frowned and shoved his shoulder. There was no weight behind it and Rowan hardly moved. He sighed. "Like you mean it."

This time she used both hands, holding her palms together as if she intended to give him CPR. Aside from the thrill of her hands on his bare skin, there wasn't enough force to throw him off balance.

"This may be more difficult than I imagined. Even though I'm toned to perfection and that makes you believe I'm thin—I'm actually quite substantial." He leaned in closer, enjoying the wariness that crossed her face. "Push *harder.*"

Callie's shoulder rammed into his chest and he got a face full of her sunshine and lilac scented hair.

"Are you hugging me? We could skip the training if you just want to mess around." He was smiling, the expression hidden where she couldn't see.

"I thought I was supposed to be falling," she grunted against Rowan, struggling to knock him down.

He bit back a laugh. "As you wish." Rowan countered Callie's weight and she collapsed. He heard the snap of teeth as her head connected with the ground.

To Rowan's delight, she climbed to feet seconds later, livid, the muscles in her jaw tense.

"The first rule of falling is to let your body go slack," he said, reverting to teacher mode, deciding it wasn't fair if he enjoyed *every* second of training Callie. "Why do you think drunks always survive car accidents that would kill a sober person? They're ragdolls, they just…" He mimicked flopping with his hand. "You can't tense up. Try to relax." Rowan didn't give her time to prepare, just went in low, tossing her to the ground.

She glared up at him. Rowan offered a hand, and this time Callie allowed him to pull her upright.

"Am I going to do a lot of falling?" she asked, brushing the dirt from her arms and backside.

"Oh yes," he said, lips stretching into a smile, "a *lot* of falling."

Callie hurt everywhere. Her elbows were dark with grass and the dirt. She knew her backside was bruised, and she could hardly turn her head to the right—but she'd survived. Rowan came toward her again and Callie tensed, anticipating another fall. She'd lost count of how many times she'd met the ground, at least fifty, maybe more. Instead of knocking her down, Rowan pressed his palm to her belly. "You've got to relax from here. Contrary to popular belief, your core controls everything."

Though the touch was light, Callie felt Rowan's hand like a punch to the stomach. She flinched and stepped away.

Confusion flitted over Rowan's expression and then he smiled. "I think you've had enough for today."

She went weak. She wasn't sure she could handle even one more fall. Rowan, as if sensing this, made one last attempt to knock her off balance. Callie let her body go fluid. She hit the grass and rolled away from him in the same motion, the collision less jarring than the others.

Rowan sprawled next to her, sweating. "That was good," he said.

Callie rolled over onto her stomach, feeling all the tendons in her back pop. She couldn't remember the last time she was so tired.

The sun had dipped in the sky, dusk wasn't far off. Callie turned, settled her arms over her stomach, and watched the clouds. She picked out shapes, a tree, a fish, the creepy smile of a jack-o-lantern. Rowan breathed steady beside her. He smelled of sweat and the raw earth and grass stains. Heat poured off his skin. His closeness made Callie's throat tickle.

Rowan propped himself up on one elbow and gazed down at her, eyes troubled. "You'll be sore tomorrow."

"Mm," she said.

"If you want me to heal you..." He let the proposition hover between them.

"I'm okay," she said. And she was. Though battered, bruised, and weary, Callie was exhilarated. For once she felt stronger, one step closer to being able to defend herself. She hoped next time they started with the quarterstaffs. Knowing how to fall wouldn't get her far in a fight. Besides, letting Rowan heal her would be admitting weakness.

She closed her eyes and tried to access the burning energy she felt whenever she was angry. It seemed far away. Unreachable. She had to do this every day, she decided.

Next to her, Rowan tensed.

"Can I ask you something?"

There was a long pause, Callie couldn't open her eyes. She didn't want to see his face, didn't want to know his thoughts. She felt one finger trail softly over her bare stomach. She flinched and rolled away, jerking her shirt down. She sat up, finally looking at him, breathing hard. A scream built in her chest.

Rowan's lips parted. "Callie—I…"

"Don't," she said, the word just audible behind clenched teeth.

He sat up slowly, coming to his knees.

Callie dug her fingers into the dirt, nails bending backwards. If Rowan wasn't there, she might've just kept digging. Clawing out clumps of dirt until the hole was big enough for her to hide.

"I'm sorry. I didn't—"

"Forget it," she snapped. The power was back, pulsing beneath her fingers, needing to escape. She scooted away from him, terrified of what might happen.

Rowan blinked once, swallowed. "Did someone hurt you?"

She pressed her lips together so hard that her teeth slid into the flesh. Rowan hurried to explain. "I mean—you just…"

"I, what?" She tasted metal, remembered the blood.

"If someone hurt you—just tell me, and I'll—"

"You'll what?" Callie stood, dizzy with memories, drunk with energy. "Thank you for the lesson, Rowan," she said, backing away. When she was far enough that she wouldn't feel like an idiot, Callie turned and ran to Sapphire's cottage, slamming the door behind her. The mirror on the wall fell to the ground and shattered. Callie pounded her dirty fists against the door, wishing the wood planks were enough to hold back the past.

As her heart rate returned to normal, Callie realized how empty the cottage was. Her lonely mattress lay in the corner, Willow's puke-stained dress a crumpled pile at the foot. The pegs that held Sapphire's scarves poked from the wall, bare. Callie slid to the bed, the pressure of the past few days collapsing like a pile of stones.

Sapphire was prophetess—and though Callie didn't know what her duties entailed, it meant Sapphire wouldn't be there when she woke in the morning.

Tears collected in her eyes and she pressed her face into the pillow, smothering a sob.

Three soft knocks drifted through the cottage and she pulled herself upright. If Rowan thought she wanted to see him, he was wrong. She could still feel the soft brush of his fingertips on her skin. The weight of his body had pressed the air from her lungs while they'd trained, but that was okay, as long as she didn't think too hard about it. Callie stood and swiped the wetness from her face. She flattened her hands on the door when she reached it.

"What?"

"Callie? It's Ash."

Sighing, she pulled the door open. Ash stood on the other side, clean and looking much improved from the passed out boy he'd been earlier. He must've taken some miracle hangover drink, because his eyes were bright and focused.

His face fell as he looked Callie over. "What's wrong?"

"I'm tired," Callie said, moving to let Ash into the cottage. "Rowan's training me." She caught a brief change in Ash's expression. "With the quarterstaff."

"I thought you might want to practice. I didn't realize you were working with Rowan, too." He sat on the edge of the table and frowned. "It's weird without Sapphire's stuff in here."

She nodded, another sharp lance of loneliness stabbed her heart.

Ash waited outside while Callie scrubbed the stains off her elbows and changed into fresh clothes.

"Mind control," Ash said with a grin, "the stuff of dreams." He tapped his temple. "I want you to get inside my head." He folded himself in the center of the training room and motioned for Callie to do the same. "Not many fae can do it, and it's especially rare for one to have more than one power," he paused, lifted his brows, "but since we already know you have *three*, why not *four?*"

Three, Callie thought. She already had three powers. *Fire, water, and the brain explosion thing.* She didn't want anymore—she didn't want what she had. Had Rowan told anyone what she'd done to him?

The more she learned of her powers, the more freaked out she became. She felt venomous, not to be trusted. Maybe they were right to bind her to the city, cage her in like an animal at the zoo; at least she wouldn't hurt anyone.

The ground was cold under Callie's legs, her backside tender from falling. Ash took her hands and pressed them to his face. For a second, Callie was back with Rowan, healing him. Ash didn't feel anything like Rowan, though. The energy he emitted was softer, gentler, and his skin smoother. Callie felt his smile beneath her fingers. "Close your eyes and focus on my energy."

She did as he instructed, finding the green smoke of Ash's power. It undulated, a lazy slide of mist from a waterfall inside him. It caressed Callie as though tasting her, deciding if they should mingle.

"Got it?"

She nodded, not opening her eyes, hoping it was supposed to come this easy. It was nothing for Callie to trace the energy up his arms and into his heart. It was as though they shared the same body, their heart rates steadied into rhythm. Her breathing slowed, matching Ash's, and she was inside him.

Ash's mind unfolded like the petals of a flower, exposing a vast, swirling space filled with thoughts, emotions, and memory. It was pure, safe, all the edges brightly lit. No shadowy twists lurked in the corners, no demons draped his memories with sticky fear. She glimpsed his childhood, a day at the park, his foster mother bandaging his knee. The uncertainty of his first day in *Eirensae,* the joy of finding his amulet. She saw herself as he did, silky blonde hair to run his fingers through, soft skin to trail his lips across, a tender soul to protect.

And desire, pulsating white hot, at the center.

Callie gasped and fell away from him, severing the connection. Couldn't she just have *friends*, for once? No pressure, no commitment?

Moments later, she was on her feet, while Ash still sat, legs crossed, confused. "Did it work?"

She faltered, backing away, unable to find air in the stifling cave.

Ash stood now, moved toward her. "What is it?"

"I—" She kept feeling Rowan's fingers on her stomach. "I'm tired." *I can't do this.* She turned on her heel and hurried away from him, unable to look him in the face. These boys, they meant well. They weren't the one who hurt her, but rationality didn't have a place alongside the terror and every touch turned her into a mess of uncertainty. The cave walls moved passed her, as though she stood still and the world spun on.

Ash caught up in the great room, dropping a hand on her shoulder. "Callie, stop."

"I'm sorry," she muttered, the response on autopilot. She couldn't remember how many times she's said those words to Nate. *I'm sorry I can't. I'm sorry, I have to go. I'm sorry. I'm sorry. I'm sorry.* She was trapped here, unable to escape, bound to the city. All she wanted to do was run.

Ash caught her chin, lifted it until she met his gaze. Face to face, they were the same height. Freckles bridged his nose. "What do you have to be sorry for?"

She didn't have a good answer, though she had plenty of awful things to be sorry about. Ash touched her cheek, tentative. Callie swallowed.

"You shouldn't touch me. You don't know what I'll do. I can't—"

Ash ignored her. "I don't know what you're afraid of," he said, slipping the hand around her neck. It was warm and electric and soothing at the same time. Callie felt the gaping hole inside of her grow wider, threaten to suck her into its depth.

"You can talk to me," he went on, "about anything. I don't know if it's about Elm—but not everyone here is like him. I only want to help."

His fingertips were heavy on her flesh, driving his point. "I'd never hurt you. Not ever. Come on," he said, sliding his hand down to hers.

The image of herself through Ash's eyes flowed through Callie's mind. Taking a breath, she pushed down the insistent flash of power in her fingers. Then, she followed him through the rock wall.

༨ Eight ༩

ROWAN STOOD AT Sapphire's dresser, eyeing the assortment of sparkling clips, blooms, ribbons, and bands.

"Hand me that flower," Sapphire said from in front of the mirror.

"Which one?" he asked, trying to keep the irritation out of his voice. He hadn't come to help Sapphire dress for the funeral, he'd come for information on Callie. Being here at all was forbidden, no one was allowed in the prophetess's house unless invited by Hazel. Rowan had never been much for rules, especially ones that restricted access to information.

"The violet," she said, twisting her hair into a bun. Their fingers brushed when Rowan handed her the flower. Sapphire's hands were freezing. She pinned the petals into her hair and smiled at her reflection, gaze going to the new imprints on her arms.

Rowan looked too, never having seen the previous prophetess this closely. Her imprints were magical, alive and ever changing, as though he viewed them through rippled glass. Sapphire shivered. In less than an hour, she would light fire to the body of the previous prophetess, turning her to ash so she could rejoin the earth. If the idea bothered Sapphire, she didn't show it.

"I know why you're here," she said, turning away from the reflection.

Rowan felt a scrape of unease in the back of his throat. He couldn't say that he was close with Sapphire, but she was someone he trusted.

Sapphire touched the flowers on her arms. "Everything is changing, and not just in the city. I know you care for Callie—I know you want to fix everything—I know the things you've seen in her, and I know what you hide in yourself."

She smiled now, sadly, and Rowan was terrified of the knowledge behind her eyes. Sapphire was prophetess, and if he asked, she might tell him his future. He couldn't decide whether it was worse to be oblivious or have your life laid out like a map before you.

Sapphire took his hands, leeching a bit of warmth from him, though he wasn't certain she realized it was happening. "I would give it to you, you know, that power to change everything," she paused, searching his face, "if I could." Sapphire dropped his fingers and went back to the mirror. Instead of looking at herself, she met his eyes in the glass. "I'm bound to service of *Eirensae* and its leader." Her face stilled with the importance of what she was trying to impart, gaze boring into his. "I can't betray that. This city wasn't meant for you."

Rowan's heart sank. He'd known all along that he didn't belong in *Eirensae*. Hearing it aloud made it real. He wanted to ask *where* he belonged then. The thought made him sick.

The Fallen. Perhaps he'd always belonged to them.

"We'll go to war," Sapphire said. "We'll stand on opposite sides."

Rowan stilled, his unease turning into horror.

"I know you don't understand, but you will soon. I can't stop this path we're on…the one you'll follow with Callie. Just promise me," her voice shook, "promise that you'll stand beside her. That you'll never stop fighting. Promise that no matter how far or how deep you two go, that you'll always pull her back. Eventually, you'll have to bring her home."

"I promise," he heard himself say, his words tinny as though they came from the end of a tunnel.

"I want her to stay, but I don't see how."

"I can try—" he broke off. He could try what? Forcing Callie to stay within the city walls? Hadn't Hazel already bound her? "I'll find a way to make her stay here," he said.

"The future is ever changing. Maybe I'm wrong." She didn't sound like she believed him. "You'll find your place, too, you know. Maybe it won't be what you expected, but that's not always a bad thing. Just protect Callie. No matter what happens." She returned to the mirror, shoulders curled inward, as if the weight was too much to hold.

Rowan turned to leave, but Sapphire's voice stopped him at the door, hand on the knob. He couldn't make himself face her again, not knowing that *Eirensae* would never be his home. It shouldn't have hit him so hard. He'd known it, but he'd always hoped it wasn't true.

"And Rowan? Just because it's dark doesn't mean it's impossible. Hope is always greater than fear. Your lives intertwine like the branches of two trees trying to survive in the same space. There will be sacrifice, but also beauty. The fate of *Eirensae* is in her hands, and her fate? That's in your hands. Protect my sister."

ℰ✦ℛ

Callie collected shards of the broken mirror, careful to avoid the sharp edges. She palmed the biggest piece, a triangle the same size as her hand, and peered into it. Several stubborn strands of hair had escaped her braid and hung limp. Her hand lingered at her neck, trembling, remembering Elm's hand there. A sob caught in her throat. There, just below her ear, she fitted her fingers against the faint scars, almost invisible now. She traced their downward descent and shuddered.

The memory was like air. It crawled beneath Callie's clothes and made her retch. She cried out, the sound a strangled cough. Suddenly she wasn't in Sapphire's cottage surrounded by broken glass, but underwater, hurting and screaming and drowning.

Dying.

"Such spirit. Such spirit."

Pink bubbles. They stung her nose, made her gag. The smooth edge of porcelain was freezing against the backs of her thighs.

"Such spirit."

A piercing dart of pain ripped Callie back to the present. Blood dripped between her fingers where she clutched the mirror. She

104

dropped the glass. It broke in half, both sides smeared with red. Her hands flew to her mouth to stifle the cries.

"No, no, no," she repeated over and over, each one more desperate than the last. Callie forced her eyes wide, made herself see the shiny pieces of broken mirror, the worn-smooth wood of Sapphire's kitchen table.

The shards exploded into tiny, glittering slivers. The scarlet of her blood turned brilliant, electric blue.

She was here.

Not back in that tiny, cracked bathroom, small and helpless. She was here, where she had power beneath her skin and strangers who actually cared what happened to her. She was here, where the past couldn't reach beyond the wards to find her.

Callie's fingers curled inward, scraped down her cheeks. She bit the tip of her index finger, tasting metal and salt. Bit, until the pain centered her thoughts. The crying cut off and she took a deep breath of here, letting it fill her lungs, expand her stomach and shoulders, until nothing else fit beside *here*.

"I am here," she said.

Another breath.

She gagged. It was then that Jack strode through her door, dressed for the funeral, blond hair combed neatly to one side. Callie looked up at him from her knees. She couldn't remember when she'd wrapped her arms around her middle, but they brought no comfort. Gagging again, she felt the hot tears on her cheeks and was grateful it was Jack, and not Rowan or Ash.

Jack shut the door with practiced calm. In two steps, he fell beside her, oblivious to the glass that cut through his pants and slashed at his knees. He pulled the bloody, sodden mess of Callie into his arms, held her against his chest like a small child. He didn't speak, but she felt his energy everywhere, pale blue, warm, safe. The airy magic expanded in her veins and after a while, Callie's breathing slowed.

She could think again. The cottage took shape, her mattress, the chairs, the kitchen, Willow's ruined dress. A knock on the door had her flinching against Jack.

"Is she in there or not?"

"Hawthorne," Jack mumbled into her hair. "Just Hawthorne. I'm going to send him away." He eased himself from her and was back in seconds, resuming his position.

She swallowed hard, breathed in his scent, citrus and sunlight, and closed her eyes, relieved when the memory did not resurface. She felt Jack's fingers at her throat, gentle as he slid damp hair from her neck. He stiffened, and she knew he'd noticed the scars.

Jack swore.

"I can't control it," Callie said. "It's inside of me and it always wants out. I can't do this. I'm sorry. I'm sorry."

"Hey," Jack said, trailing a hand over her hair.

"I'm going to hurt someone."

Jack leaned away and caught Callie's injured hand. He carefully dug out a lingering piece of glass while Callie sniffled. He tied her palm with a scarf from his pocket. "There is nothing you can't overcome. You're not broken."

Callie looked away, unable to take the sorrow in his eyes.

He caught her face, bringing her back. "You're not broken."

"I don't know how stop being afraid. They did this to me, you know? If I was just human…if I wasn't *this*," the glass rained around them, a shimmering storm, "it never would've happened. I might've had a family…parents. I wouldn't have been…weak."

"You're not weak," Jack argued.

"It was two years of my life, Jack. Two years of hell that I'll always have inside of me. I'll always have *him* inside of me. You know why it stopped? Because he died, not because I was strong enough to fight him off or the state finally realized what was happening. No. He had a heart attack and died in his sleep. He didn't even suffer. And *they* did this to me. Everyone keeps talking about me being happy, about having a home here. They have expectations that I can't fulfill for them. The fae can't lie, but I feel it all around me. I didn't ask for this."

Callie closed her eyes as Jack's arms came around her.

"Please don't tell anyone," Callie said, curling her injured hand into a fist. "Ash thinks he wants to date me…and Rowan—oh god, I don't even know. I don't even know who I am."

Jack sighed. "You are Calla Lily, the strongest faerie in *Eirensae*. If you have nothing else, you will always have that."

Callie spoke, so softly it barely reached her ears, "But what if it's not enough?"

℘✦℘

Rowan arrived at the funeral just before Sapphire. Fae gathered in chairs left out for them, Elders surrounded the pyre and the small body of the prophetess. Dressed in gold, her body lined with flowers that spilled over the dais, she was beautiful. She'd lived 347 years, but her face was unlined and peaceful, and Rowan knew behind her closed lids, her eyes were the luminescent green of a holly leaf. He wished he'd had the opportunity to know her better.

Torches lit the path between the chairs and the pyre, bright spots against a dusky sky. Rowan searched out Callie, finding her next to Jack in the third row. She had a scarf wrapped around one hand. Was that another present from Hazel? Something else to prevent Callie from leaving the city? He hoped so. She needed to stay where Sapphire could protect her.

Ash, Willow, Hawthorne, and Sai took up the seats behind Callie and Jack. He made his way toward the empty seat next to her. Callie spared him a brief glance before turning back to Jack. She looked pale, the skin around her mouth pulled tight, eyes puffy.

After the way their training session had ended earlier, Rowan did not expect a warm welcome. He felt useless, unable to offer comfort or kind words. He wanted to fill the darkness in Callie with light. He didn't know *how*, and worse, he couldn't fight a source he couldn't see. He had to find a way to keep her inside the city walls. If Callie's safe future depended on remaining in *Eirensae,* then he would make that happen.

No matter what it cost.

The gentle cadence of the Elder's voices mixed with the smoke and flower scented air.

"The Elders are asking for her safe return to the earth," Jack whispered to Callie. "When they're done, Hazel will talk and then Sapphire will light the pyre and wish the prophetess farewell."

Callie's face paled further. The flame of the torches danced in her eyes. "Sapphire?"

Her voice was ragged and made Rowan's throat ache. Had he done that to her with his questions? With his touch? Had Hazel said something to her?

"It's her duty to guide the prophetess over the divide." Jack patted Callie's leg and Rowan was envious of the other boy. "It's beautiful, really."

Sapphire was on the path now, dress glistening in the fading light. Her imprints seemed to glow as she slipped between the other fae, chin held high, gaze only on the lost prophetess.

"I fail to see how lighting someone on fire is beautiful," Callie said.

"*Domhan go talamh, luaithreach a luaithreach, deannaigh a deannaigh.*" Rowan said, catching Callie's eye as she returned her gaze to the front.

She turned her back to Rowan and asked Jack, "What does that mean?"

"Earth to earth, ashes to ashes, dust to dust," Jack supplied.

"Is that from a poem?" Her eyes were wide now, the flames brighter.

"It's from the Bible," Rowan said.

Sapphire and Cypress embraced, holding each other for a long moment. Cypress's shoulders shook and they spoke in words too low to hear. Finally, Sapphire stepped away and waited for Hazel to join her.

"Blessed evening," Hazel said, words splitting the night. Behind her, the sun cast a final slant of light before sinking below the horizon.

"Blessed evening," the fae murmured in response.

"We celebrate the life of our prophetess. Though short, her life was full. She devoted herself to her people, and served them well. We must not mourn, but celebrate the journey we took together." Hazel placed her hands on the dead woman's face. *"Codladh maith mo pháiste, go dtí go gcasfar le chéile sinn arís."* She kissed her forehead, lingering, as though sharing a telepathic message.

By the time Hazel stepped down from the pyre, Sapphire had a torch. Rowan saw Callie's face go green. He lifted his hand, intending to comfort her, but she tossed him a glance that made him curl his fingers and let them fall.

Sapphire kissed the prophetess's cheeks, the flame held over them like a beacon. *"Slán, mo dheirfiúr,"* she said quietly before touching the fire to the dry tinder. The pyre lit with a whoosh, the fire consuming the flowers, higher and higher, igniting the prophetess's dress. Soon, she was wreathed in flames.

Next to Rowan, Callie wiped away tears and finally, buried her face in Jack's shoulder.

୫୦ ✦ ୯୧

Callie returned to the cottage alone, feeling like a scraped out shell, tears still drying on her cheeks. She was sore from training with Rowan, the cuts on her hand stung, and the ache in her chest was no less painful. The funeral wasn't as awful as she'd imagined, though it wasn't pleasant to watch a body burn. Callie found some saturnine beauty in the fact that the prophetess would return to the earth as ashes. It had to be better than decomposing.

She'd wanted to say something to Rowan, apologize for acting so childish earlier, but she'd left the gathering before she could gather her nerve. Maybe it was better if she said nothing.

Stars shrouded the moonless evening in ethereal light. Sapphire's cottage, though it looked identical to the day Callie had arrived, seemed lonely, nestled against the trees. Candles burned in the windows of the surrounding buildings and her eyes went to Rowan's cottage. It was dark and just as desolate.

Stepping inside Sapphire's—now Callie's—cottage, she rubbed the night from her arms. A low fire burned, hardly more than embers. Callie added another log and tried not to remember the flames devouring the woman's body. It made her feel like an out of control car, spinning and spinning, the world a kaleidoscope around her.

It had hit her all at once and she wished she could take it back. It was too much—the past, her new powers, Sapphire, all of it. She wanted to be strong, she wanted to smile and go on as though nothing was wrong, it was what was expected, after all.

She went to the kitchen, stomach rumbling, trying to remember the last time she'd eaten, amazed that she had an appetite at all. Without Sapphire to force fruit and vegetables into her hand, Callie had a hard time remembering to eat. Snagging an apple from the fruit bowl, she bit into it, the first taste making her mouth water and her stomach gurgle.

She should go to Rowan's, apologize for acting so stupid. At this rate, she'd be lucky if she kept any friends. Half the people thought she was a liability and the other half, who actually *wanted* to get to know her, she drove away with her insecurity.

Callie felt equally enamored with and terrified of Rowan. He was intense, and she couldn't read him. Ash, on the other hand, she read all too well. Jack, she trusted. She had to, especially after he'd bandaged her cuts and helped her to the funeral.

Callie's stomach growled, an angry sound that reverberated. She set the apple on the counter and pressed her hands there, certain she was going to be sick. Hot pain lanced up her throat. The apple rolled and thumped on the floor, gathering a thin layer of dirt. Callie curled around the ache, bending in half and sliding down beside the apple.

Agony was a barbed wire snake in her gut. It slithered into her chest and filled her mouth with rancid foam. She coughed, spattering the front of her dress with red.

She couldn't breathe.

Such spirit! The words were on autopilot. She heard his voice over and over, tasted imaginary soap.

Panicking, Callie shoved her fingers in her mouth, trying to scoop out the suffocating substance, but there was more and more, pouring over her hands like a faucet. Her lungs burned. Fireworks exploded across her vision.

She had a single, irrational thought that warred with her desire to lie down and give in. She needed to get outside, lie in the grass of *Eirensae*, and see the perfect velvet of night sky one last time. With that thought came the unwavering certainty that she wanted to belong to *Eirensae*, grow old there, be with her sister, finally have *friends*.

Her face was damp when she crawled to the door, trailing red, every inch more brutal than the last. The pain came in vicious waves. Her fingers slid across the handle, slick with blood and sweat. She shook, arms, legs, hands. Shuddering, airless sobs crashed through her chest. She fought to open the door, wanting to see her home and burn the image on the inside of her eyelids so she'd remember that she died in faerie and not flailing in a half-full bathtub in Pennsylvania.

Using one last spark of energy, Callie released the door hatch. She slid down the two tiny steps into the crisp grass. The sky swung above her, a blanket of black and *stars*.

I am here, she thought.

Everything grew heavy and the night settled across Callie.

She relaxed.

€♦C&#x3;

Rowan said goodbye over the smoldering remains of the pyre. Ash, and the others with fire magic, had sped the process. The prophetess had burned in a glorious rainbow of flame. In the morning, they'd collect the ashes and Sapphire would spread them in the river. The chairs were put away, the dying fire the only reminder of what had transpired.

The grass was cool beneath his toes as he strayed from the group. The imprinted headed for their homes in the city. A few stragglers went his direction and disappeared into cottages. The night was warm and dry, but away from the heat of the fire, Rowan shivered. It was nights like this when he thought of his foster home, the modest house on the modest street. For the longest time he'd had a normal life, even though he'd never belonged in it. He'd worn the human world like an ill-fitting suit to a high school dance. No matter how hard he'd tried, it'd never worked.

Much like everything, that life was a mistake.

Callie's cottage came into view, her windows glowing with firelight. He debated stopping to apologize. Part of him wanted to keep his distance, but Sapphire's words haunted him. Their lives were intertwined, what was the point of staying away? As he thought this, her door flew open and something fell out.

At first, he thought she'd thrown something outside, a pile of clothing, a blanket, but as he drew closer, she took shape, arms and legs becoming a full body.

He started to run.

"Callie?"

She was frozen that way, chin tilted to her chest; legs sprawled on the stairs. Blood smeared her face and the front of her dress, a thin stream of crimson drizzled from the corner of her mouth. He dropped to his knees. Her skin was clammy when he touched her cheeks.

"No. Wake up." Energy slid into Rowan's fingertips and he felt it drain into Callie. "You're going to be fine," he ordered fiercely. "Come on." He willed his power to work faster, harder, anything that would make her okay.

Through the gift of healing, Rowan saw Callie's insides, torn to shreds. He saw an apple, laced with poison. Heat radiated from his palms and warmed Callie's face. He felt her stir. "Callie?"

Her eyelids fluttered. She took a deep, rattling breath, spat blood. Rowan's insides twisted as he lifted her carefully.

"The apple," she murmured, voice ravaged.

Callie was a rag doll. The back of her neck was damp and feverish against his arm. He held his muscles tight around her, making a cage, but she cried out every time his feet struck the ground. He had to get her to Hazel. Of all the things he knew, natural healing was the least of it. He could mend any injury, but he couldn't stop poison. It would continue to eat away at Callie, ripping through her insides, until it left her system or they found a remedy for it.

The city hunched in the night, so far away. Callie groaned and a stream of bubbling red erupted from her mouth. Rowan paused, lowering her to the dirt path, protecting her head from the fall. He summoned his energy again, healing the ruins inside Callie. She cried now, thin rivers of tears that washed through the streaks of red and dripped cool onto Rowan's hands. She quivered, her face tensed, and finally smoothed. He caught her up and continued to run.

After what seemed like hours, they reached the city. Rowan collided with Ash around the first corner. "Hey," he said, before his eyes dropped to the limp body in Rowan's arms. "Callie?" Ash's expression dissolved into horror. "What happened? Is she…is she—"

"It's poison," Rowan said already moving.

Ash followed, jogging to keep up. "Why aren't you healing her?"

"I did. It starts all over again as soon as I'm done." Rowan's breath came in sharp pants. He had a stitch in his side. Callie's graying face kept him going.

Callie coughed, splattered Rowan's shoulder red.

"The blood," Ash breathed.

"I know." Rowan stopped again, dropping to his knees. Callie's head lolled to the side. She moaned. He touched her cheeks, felt the pulse in her throat, sprinting fast as hummingbird wings. The energy at his core lagged as he tried to send it to Callie, the edges of his vision went dark and stayed that way, even after her face relaxed. Callie's wounds were too much for him, and if they didn't get help soon, he'd lose consciousness. "Get Hazel," he ordered, lifting her into his arms once more. He didn't wait to see if Ash obeyed.

Callie's mouth opened and she gulped greedy mouthfuls of air. *"Rowan,"* she gasped, a world of pain in that one word.

"You'll be fine," he said, relieved to see the palace rise before him.

Her eyes met his for a moment before rolling backwards. She convulsed. Gagged.

Went still.

"Damn it." He stopped to heal her, feeling every second as an eternity. Rowan had tunnel vision and even the parts he could see were blurry. His hands shook as he pulled Callie against his chest. Rowan gritted his teeth and stumbled forward. This time, he'd only taken a few steps when Callie started writhing again. His healings were growing less and less effective.

"Rowan," she gurgled, curling in on herself.

"Stay with me." His voice reached his ears as though coming from a great distance. "Hazel will fix this. You'll be fine."

Callie's eyes closed. Each breath rattled. Rowan knew that sound— the calling card of death.

"Callie? *Callie!*" He careened up the palace steps, fumbling the last one and sprawling against the limp mass of Callie's body. Energy stuttered into his fingertips. Rowan shut his eyes, finding her cooling cheeks beneath his fingers. He'd been here before, unable to heal someone he cared for.

He searched deep, for any reserve that hid in the abyss of his core. The flicker of energy was faint. Rowan forced it into his arms, relieved when it heated Callie's face and her breathing evened out. He brushed stiff strands of hair from her forehead. Rowan saw her through a gray screen. "You'll be okay."

Hazel appeared beside him. Her hands were pale against the bloodstained skin of Callie's face, her face a measured mask of concern. "Ash, go the library and get the old herb book." She looked up and Rowan noticed the smudged moon faces of the small crowd that had gathered. "Jack, find Cypress and Sapphire and bring them to the hospital quarters. Hawthorne, check the wards and confer with the guards. I need to know if there's been a breach. Everyone else, follow me." Her eyes moved to Rowan. "Can you lift her?"

Defeat rose within him, bitter and debilitating. He knew he should say no, let someone less weary take over. His mouth refused. Instead, he nodded, and pulled the small weight of Callie into the shelter of his arms. If this was the only thing he could give, then he would give it completely, until there was nothing left. She sagged against him and he tightened his grip.

They drifted through the palace doors in the slow motion of a dream. His feet were lead, every step, agony. Between breaths, he could feel Callie's pulse hammering against his. It kept Rowan moving forward. They found the stairs.

"Set up the infirmary," Hazel barked, her voice disjointed from the ephemeral scene around him. "We need blankets and a mortar."

114

He slogged upward, feeling the steps would never end. Maybe they'd already given up, given in, and this was the road to heaven—a never-ending staircase.

Callie's withered voice broke through the fog. "Needs an elevator."

Rowan felt his mouth curve. He would do this for her.

৪০◆ଔ

She lay on a cot, bowed against the pain. Rowan was there, across from her, bruises shadowing his eyes. He'd aged decades. Lines radiated from his eyes and mouth, his skin was waxy, the color of stone. Blood stained his shirt and hands. Callie knew she should worry, but all she saw was Rowan. He reached out a hand, and their fingers connected. The usual snap of energy never came. He closed his eyes, his lashes two dark marks resting on the sharp angle of his cheekbone.

The angry monster inside Callie reared again, rending her flesh, trying to rip itself free. She cried out, not as loudly as before, but enough to rouse Rowan. His hands crept up her body, a wounded animal seeking shelter, and found her face.

She tried to push him away. "No more."

Rowan captured her weak fingers, drew them away. "Let me fix it."

"It's killing you." She choked on blood.

The world swung over and around them. Hazel called out orders, someone brought blankets. Sapphire arrived, Callie felt her hands in her hair, smelled the scent of flowers as she wiped ichor away.

Rowan's healing energy caressed her skin, what once was a powerful force, now just a feeble flutter. Still, coolness washed her, and she relaxed.

When Callie opened her eyes, Rowan was silent.

Still.

"Rowan?" She grabbed his hands, still resting on her face. They were slack. Dark strands of sweaty hair covered his closed eyes. His chest was eerily motionless.

Ash skidded through the door and slammed a heavy, bound leather book onto the counter. Hazel was there in an instant, flipping pages.

115

"Rowan?" Callie shook his hands. "Help him," she croaked, eyes going to the gathered fae. *Why weren't they doing anything?* "Help him."

"Jack," Sapphire called, her eyes never leaving Callie. A serene calm surrounded Sapphire, but Callie saw the panic in her eyes, felt it in the static of her power.

Jack's face appeared above Callie, his eyebrows furrowed with concern. He bit his lip, tears in his eyes.

"Give Rowan your energy," Sapphire said.

"No," Rowan said. His lips barely formed the word.

Cypress blew through the door then.

"Cypress is here, Row. She'll take over." Urgency layered Jack's voice.

"No," Rowan mumbled again. He opened his eyes, caught her gaze, and Callie's stomach turned over.

Cypress took over for Rowan, chasing away the pain, clearing Callie's mind. She felt Cypress, her hands loaded with cool, healing energy, and Rowan, his body a bottomless pit of loss. With unconscious decision, Callie directed the energy into Rowan's body.

Mere seconds passed and he tore out of her grasp, expression hard. "Get me away from her," he said, rolling backwards and nearly off the cot. Callie watched as Jack and Ash helped him to the corner. They talked in whispers, and the whole time, Callie felt Rowan's gaze on her.

"I found it," Hazel declared a while later. She rambled a litany of herb names Callie didn't recognize, giving orders where to find each item.

Rowan was sitting now, Jack's hands in both of his. Rowan's face was a picture of displeasure, as though he found the entire process repulsive. Some of the color had returned to his cheeks, and still, he watched her. Jack shook all over, and at first, she thought giving Rowan his energy was painful, but then she realized Jack was crying, his shoulders shuddering every time he looked in Callie's direction.

One by one, the others trickled back, carrying flowers, pieces of bark, long leaves. Soon, a glass of thick green liquid was tipped to Callie's lips. She bit back a gag as the bitter slime slid into her mouth.

Everyone huddled around her, even Rowan pushed through the crowd to stand at her head, though he had to grip the cot to remain upright.

"Well?" he said, impatient.

"Give it a minute," Hazel said.

Gentle coolness spread from her center outward, eradicating all the crevices of pain. Callie coughed, splattering her hand with fresh blood.

"I'm healing her again," Rowan said. Nobody moved to stop him.

The rawness in her throat eased, the burning monster disappeared. His hands lingered, wiped hair and sweat from her brow. "Better?"

They held their breath, waited.

Callie swallowed, relieved when the motion felt normal, and nodded. Their faces eased and Jack clapped, letting out a whoop.

"Hazel?" The voice came from the doorway. The fae parted, showing an older man standing just outside.

Hazel's words were clipped. "What is it?"

"I need to speak with you." He shifted his weight.

Rowan seemed oblivious of the newcomer. He'd intertwined his fingers with Callie's, which was enough to sidetrack Callie from what was going on. His hand was warm, not quite as electric as usual. He stroked the pad of his thumb across the back of her knuckles. On the other side, Ash had her opposite hand tucked into his.

"I'm busy," Hazel snapped.

Rowan's thumb paused.

"It's important," the man said.

"Fine." Hazel motioned to the rest of the group to follow her.

Rowan's thumb started the soothing circles again.

Ash patted Callie's hand, returning it to the destroyed sheets. "We'll be back." He looked to Rowan, who hadn't let go. "Come on, Row. She'll be okay."

Rowan didn't look up. An unnamed emotion flickered on Ash's face.

"Go ahead." Rowan climbed onto the cot next to Callie and adjusted the pillow under his head, their hands still joined. "I'm tired."

For a moment Callie didn't think Ash would leave. He looked between Rowan and Callie, expression shuttered. Eventually he turned on his heel and followed the rest outside, closing the door quietly behind him.

ℰℭ Nine ℭℛ

"ARE YOU AWAKE?" Callie whispered into the darkness. She wasn't sure how long she'd lain there, staring at the pale gold ceiling. It felt like hours—days, even—and still, she couldn't find sleep. They'd been fussed over, fed, and ordered to rest. Before leaving the last time, Ash had offered some of his energy to Rowan, who'd refused, of course. Then everyone was gone and the night closed over the two of them, the sounds of the palace growing fainter and fainter until all Callie could hear was the gentle cadence of Rowan's breath. She'd squeezed her eyes shut and willed herself to sleep. Every time she came close, Rowan's breathing broke through the veil and reminded her that he was just inches away.

"Yes," he said, close enough that it fluttered strands of her hair.

Callie tensed.

When Hazel said goodbye and flipped off the lights, Callie had turned her back to Rowan. They were both exhausted. Besides, Callie didn't know how to thank him for what he'd done. She'd agonized over the perfect words. Everything sounded stupid and insincere. The lack of conversation had swelled between them, larger and larger, until Callie couldn't stand it any longer.

She rolled over. Rowan's face was a pale moon against the sheets, close enough she could reach out and touch his cheek. His eyes were surprisingly bright, vivid blue even in the dim light. He looked healthier, his skin smooth, his color returned.

"You look better," she said.

Rowan didn't answer.

She grew uncomfortable under his gaze. "What is it?"

"I thought it'd be harder to get you into bed."

"And you're *feeling* better." Callie's face heated.

"Relax, I'm kidding." He flopped onto his back and pillowed his hands behind his head. "The million dollar question is: how are you feeling?"

"Okay." She sat up and tugged the blankets tight around her shoulders. She could smell him, the sweet scent of soap and something earthy. "Thank you."

"For what?"

"You know—"

"Did you really think I'd let you die? Chivalry is not dead. Besides, saving you was about the only thing I've been allowed to do around here."

"Well, thank you."

"Now, let's talk about how you're going to return the favor."

"I—*what?*"

"Kidding." He chuckled. "You are so gullible."

Callie stared at him, the wheels shifting slowly in her mind. Who was this and what had they done with the pensive, sullen boy that usually wore his skin? Maybe some of Jack's positive attitude had slipped in along with the energy. She looked at him for so long that he finally glanced her way and wiggled his eyebrows.

"Did you tell Ash about—you know, when I tried to blow up your brain?" Her face grew hotter. *Why* was it so hard to talk to him?

"No."

"Why not?"

"I never play all my cards." The bed shifted as he sat up. Their knees knocked together and Callie jumped. "For the love, Callie," he breathed, rubbing his knee.

Shirtless, Rowan was beautiful, hard lines and angles. Callie's hand lifted before she realized what she was doing. It hovered in the air between them, awkward, derailed from its destination. She let it drop into her lap.

Rowan smirked.

He looked so *approachable*, with his hair tousled and the rumpled sheets cocooned around his waist. She never would've thought it possible for Rowan to look soft. It was as if she could actually reach him, and not just the arrogant boy he wore on his sleeve.

It unnerved her.

"Why didn't you tell him? He's your best friend."

"He's the closest thing, anyway," Rowan agreed.

"You didn't answer my question."

"That's the plan. Keep them guessing."

Callie blinked. "You know, everything that comes out of your mouth is a riddle."

Rowan shrugged and brushed loose strands of hair off her face. The gesture was so intimate that for a moment, she could only stare as silence welled between them. He'd lowered his hands to his lap, but the touch lingered for a long while.

"They won't let you become Fallen…will they? Hazel wouldn't want to give up one of her own. Right?" After how hard they'd worked to heal her, she couldn't imagine that they'd just let Rowan wander off into the human world without a fight. He was smart, a trained warrior. They needed more fae like him.

"They will. My amulet's not here. I already told you." He ran a hand over his face and into his hair, mussing it further. "Six others have returned since me. Every one of them, apart from you, has found their amulet. It's not *hard*, Callie. It's instinct. They went right to it— like a gut reaction. They just *knew*." Quieter now, "It's never been like that for me. *Eirensae* has never felt like home."

"If it's not here, then where is it?"

Rowan hesitated, speaking carefully. "I don't know."

The cot squeaked when Callie pushed to her knees. "I'll help you find it. We can look together. If it's so easy, then it won't be a problem. Two sets of eyes are better than one, right?" She was excited, talking fast. This was how she could repay him for saving her life.

Rowan's careful expression remained. "That's—" He sighed and rubbed his forehead. "How about we search together for yours. If we find mine—"

"Oh, we'll find it," she said, no doubt in her mind. She wasn't going to let Rowan become Fallen. She needed him to keep training her to fight.

He smiled as though he wanted to believe her, but knew better.

What if he's right?

Callie shoved the thought away. She'd learned about the wards. Only the fae of *Eirensae* were allowed through. If Rowan was in the city, then he belonged here, just as she did.

The wards. Someone had broken through them, or worse, it was someone on the inside. Hazel had kept everything quiet, but she knew something about the attack. Someone wanted Callie dead—and they knew how to make it happen. Callie felt removed from the information, as though she'd watched it and not experienced it firsthand. She'd gotten lucky this time.

"What are you thinking about?" Rowan asked.

"Dying."

Silence.

"I always knew you were weird."

Callie fidgeted, crumpling the edge of the blanket in her fist and smoothing it again. Hurried footsteps passed the door. She wished that Rowan would say something to break the tension. They were too close, with the night pressing in around them. She found herself staring at Rowan's bare feet, scrubbed clean. His second toe was longer than the first. She remembered learning something about that in anatomy, but the fact escaped her.

Rowan let out a breath. "This is stupid. We should be in our own beds."

"Mm," she agreed. Her nails made an awful sound against the blanket.

"We could go back."

"Someone tried to kill me. I'm not going out there."

"I wouldn't leave you," Rowan said, suddenly serious. "I'd stay. I'm not going to let anything happen to you."

Callie's mouth went dry at the thought of Rowan in her cottage.

"I think we should stay here."

Rowan sprawled on the cot as if that's what he expected her to say all along. His long body almost too big, his feet hung off the end.

"So when did you decide that you wanted to stay in *Eirensae*?"

Swallowing, Callie pulled the blankets tighter and lay down. "I didn't, really. It's like you said before, I can't really go back to the human world with this demon beneath my skin. I'd be shot down by the police or something."

Rowan smiled. "I don't think the police would get anywhere near you."

"I don't want to be like this. I wish that I had your power, not this awful one. I don't want to be a monster."

"Please," Rowan said, still smiling, "you're far too beautiful to be a monster."

"Yeah. Remember that next time I explode your brain."

His smile stretched. "At least I'll die happy. Night," he mumbled, closing his eyes.

Callie stared at him for a long moment, drinking in the curve of his bicep, the hard angle of his hipbone, gaze lingering on the soft ridge of his lips. He'd called her beautiful. It shouldn't matter. She wasn't some silly superficial girl who needed a man to make her feel justified. Still, it was nice to hear.

She could reach out and bridge the space between them if only she had the courage.

With a sigh, she buried her face in her pillow. "Night," she whispered.

୫୦ ♦ ୧୪

Rowan slid off the cot, flinching as it creaked. He'd watched daylight travel across the wooden floor as the sun rose. Callie was asleep, blankets tangled around her waist, with one hand pillowing her face and the other balled under her chin. She looked better, with a sleep-induced rosy hue riding on her cheekbones.

Last night, Rowan had been terrified, certain she would die, worried that he would. He couldn't understand this raging desire to protect Callie. Now that he had confirmation from Sapphire that they were essentially connected, at least he didn't have to fight it so hard. But Rowan was still himself, and he knew he wasn't like the other fae in *Eirensae,* which meant he was bad for Callie. Maybe she couldn't see that now, but it was only a matter of time. His clock ticked down with every passing day.

Rowan pushed open the hospital door, surprised when it met resistance. Ash groaned and stumbled to his feet, eyes bleary. Rowan's brows lifted. "You slept on the floor?" He leaned against the now closed door. "Were you afraid I'd steal her virtue?"

Ash made a rude noise and smoothed rumples from his shirt. He looked like hell, with puffy eyes and hair sticking up in all directions. "I was afraid someone would try to kill her again."

"I think I'm offended."

"Get over yourself." Ash glanced over Rowan's shoulder, as though he could somehow see Callie through the door. "I know you don't care—or you *pretend* to not care, but the wards weren't breached last night. This was an inside job."

"Elm?"

"I don't know." Ash lifted a shoulder. "What about the prophetess? Would Elm have killed her?"

Hawthorne came around the corner before Rowan could answer. He greeted them formally. "How is she?"

"Asleep," Rowan said, sizing up the other boy. He'd never gotten along with Hawthorne. Not that he got along with most people, but he found Hawthorne repulsive in a way he couldn't explain. "Why are you here?" Rowan didn't bother hiding his displeasure.

"Guard duty," he answered. "Hazel's orders."

"Is there any news about who poisoned Callie?" Ash asked.

For a moment, Rowan pitied his friend. Ash was a teacher. It was destiny given to him by the prophetess, yet he'd always longed for more. Rowan could understand his interest, not only because he cared for Callie, but also because it was a chance to do something other than teach.

Hawthorne frowned. "Nothing solid."

"And the wards?" Rowan prompted.

"Intact." Hawthorne gave him a strange look.

"Hm," was Rowan's response.

"Do you think it someone inside the city? A traitor?" Ash asked, leaning in closer.

It took Hawthorne a long time to answer, so long that Rowan didn't trust his careful response. "I think that Callie is special and that someone knows more than they're saying." He glanced at Rowan. "Whatever this is—it's not the end." Then he propped open the door and surveyed the room.

"See you later," Rowan said, striding off.

"Bye?" Ash said, confused.

Rowan muttered an excuse about training. He lingered around the corner, just out of their sight, listening. A large part of him wanted to remain stationed at Callie's bedside until she woke, and possibly after that as well. If her poisoning was an inside job, then he couldn't trust anybody. But, if Hazel wanted Callie as badly as Sapphire thought, then Hazel would protect Callie with everything she had.

"Guard duty, huh?" Ash said, voice filtering down the hall. "Nothing like tracking."

Hawthorne made a rude sound. "It's boring. Besides, I can't figure out why everyone is so taken with her. She's just a child."

Ash made a noncommittal sound and Rowan almost laughed.

"Hazel has us guarding her twenty-four seven now, and she's restricting her to the palace. Personally, I think it's a waste of time," Hawthorne said.

Rowan listened for a few more minutes, but the boys had grown silent. He moved farther down the corridor, intent on seeking out Hazel. He didn't have to go far before he heard her voice seeping beneath a closed door. Rowan pressed himself to the wall to hear better.

"I should kill you for this," Hazel hissed.

A laugh. "Kill me? You couldn't. The girl wasn't part of the plan."

Rowan recognized the voice. Elm. Anger burned the back of his throat.

"Forget the plan," Hazel said. "She's going to take me farther than anything you came up with."

Elm laughed again. "Arol will only use her against you."

"I'm not afraid of Arol."

There was a long pause before Elm spoke again. "I won't let you have her. It's supposed to be me at your side. She's supposed to die."

"That's not really your choice anymore," Hazel said.

"Have you forgotten what I know?" Elm whispered. "I killed Orchid so you could have Sapphire. Callie is the perfect fall for that. You can't cast me out now. I know all your dirty secrets. I'll tell them what you did."

"I'm not afraid of you, either," Hazel said.

A loud thump shuddered through the floor. Rowan pushed away from the door, making it to the stairs just as the door swung open. He flattened against the wall, just out of sight. Hazel emerged. She looked both directions and smoothed her skirt before shutting the door and locking it from the outside.

৪১✦ଔ

"You can't keep showing up here. Someone is bound to notice," Sapphire chided. She stood at her kitchen table, which was piled high with stacks of books from the library.

Rowan lifted a shoulder and pretended to be interested in a volume about horticulture. "Elm poisoned Callie." Even though Sapphire was the nicest person in *Eirensae,* he always felt small when he stood beside her. Her chin came to his shoulders. Her presence made up the difference.

Sapphire sighed and pushed hair from her face. "I know."

Rowan told himself he wouldn't yell at the prophetess, that he wouldn't get angry. The hard edge of his restraint softened. "Why didn't you stop it?"

She sighed again and closed her eyes. "Don't you think I wanted to? It's not that easy. I can't just impede fate, Rowan, no matter what I know."

He broke his promise not to yell. *"She nearly died."*

Sapphire's shoulders shuddered and she pressed both hands to her mouth, stifling a sob. Quieter now, "I know."

"You could've gone to Hazel. You could've come to *me*. I would've protected her."

"No." She shook her head. "No."

"What aren't you telling me?" he yelled.

Sapphire jumped and the tears she fought spilled down her cheeks.

Rowan backtracked. "I'm sorry—"

She slid into a chair at the table, shoulders curved as though she hefted a heavy burden. "When the prophetess died—"

"Was murdered."

"Was murdered," she amended, "I didn't expect it to happen so soon. Time is long for us and somehow it was over before…before I even had a chance to comprehend what was happening. I've had the visions *forever,"* she glanced at Rowan with watery eyes, "but I never really understood what they meant. But now…Callie will bring the next war, Rowan. Her powers are too great for any one fae. Whatever city has her will rule. I've seen her next to Hazel, I've seen her with Arol. It's as though her path changes every day."

Rowan felt the blood drain from his face. "What do we do?"

"Train her to fight—and to use her powers." Sapphire bit her lip as thought debating how much to tell. "She's strong, but not invincible." She reached out, covered his hand, her touch cold. "Hazel wants Callie's power. And she'll do anything to have it. She'll ruin the entire city."

"We have to keep Callie away from Hazel. She had Elm kill Orchid. She could come after you."

Sapphire swallowed and nodded. "We're in great danger, Rowan, all of us. I'll find a way to remove the binding spell from Callie. But you have to know, out there in the human world she's a target. The Fallen will hunt her and so will Hazel. She's not safe anywhere."

℘ ✦ ℚ

Rowan looked up when Ash strode into the library sometime later. "I thought you were with Callie," he said.

"I was. She just went back to the palace for the night."

Rowan shut the book and made to stand.

"Jack is with her. She's fine, Row."

He sat back down. "Last night—" Rowan broke off at the emotion in his throat.

"I know," Ash said. "She scared me, too. But she's safe now, because Elm admitted to poisoning Callie and Hazel banished him."

Rowan's insides went cold. "Who told you that?"

"Jack. Said they sent him out of the northern gate a couple of hours ago." Ash flopped into the chair across from Rowan. "I always knew he was an asshole, but to poison one of your own? I'm surprised, even from him."

Rowan made a noncommittal sound, deciding to keep what he'd overheard to himself. Elm was either dead or banished, and Callie was safer with him gone.

ജ Ten ❦

ROWAN TOSSED THE quarterstaff. It landed next to Callie in the grass, where she lay face-up, gasping for air. She pushed up on her elbows and squinted through the sweat dripping in her eyes. Rowan stood, arms crossed, waiting for her to stand. Though they'd spent nearly two hours training, he looked as he had when they started, calm, cool, and remarkably sweat free.

"Get up," he ordered.

Callie sighed and climbed to her knees. Two weeks had passed since the poisoning and things had returned to normal, if one considered being locked in the palace normal. Callie lived for training with Rowan, though it left her exhausted, bruised, and sore. She rubbed her arm where a fresh welt rose from the bite of Rowan's staff. It'd join the rest of her mottled skin, which ranged in tones from purplish-blue to jaundice-yellow. She'd never admit it to Rowan, but she took a scalding shower every night to work out the kinks in her muscles. Sometimes she hurt so badly that it was torture just to drag herself into bed.

She never complained, no matter how hard it got, no matter how many times she fell. If she wasn't out here in the sunlight with Rowan, then she was stuck in her room at the palace, studying and staring at the four walls. Mornings and evenings, she worked with Ash, and afternoons, when the sun was the brightest and warmest, she spent with Rowan. Occasionally, she was allowed to search for her amulet, never with Rowan like she wanted to, and always with a guard.

She'd thought the night in the hospital would change her friendship with Rowan, that he'd become less reserved, but she was wrong. Even though they spent hours together every day, Rowan retreated further inside himself. He didn't speak to Callie, unless it was to correct her form, and anytime she mentioned searching for his amulet, his eyes grew dark and he went on as though she'd never brought it up.

Sometimes, she wondered if he regretted saving her life, or thought training her was too much of a burden. She devoted herself to being the best possible student, but Rowan's mood never improved.

To add to her list of displeasures, Callie had two guards with her at all times. They flanked her as she crossed the grounds to train, searched every room she entered, tasted her food before she ate it. She found the entire process mortifying. Today her guards, Jack and Hawthorne, watched her train from the edge of the grass. Jack lifted his arms, mimicking a hit with the staff, and pointed to Callie. Hawthorne chuckled and both their gazes turned toward her again.

She'd like to see them fight Rowan. She caught up the quarterstaff and stood, anticipating the next blow. Rowan feinted right and struck low. Callie swung her staff to parry his hit. He recovered in less than a heartbeat and used the other end to knock her feet from beneath her. Callie slammed into the ground. Her teeth snapped together and she tasted blood. Sparkles danced behind her eyes and she was grateful to be lying down. Rowan shoved a hand in her face, and she let him help her up.

"Again," he said before the pain had time to recede.

Callie took a slow breath, clearing her head. She searched for repetition in Rowan's movements, some precursor to his intentions, but found none. It was as though he moved by impulse, never by thought. This time, she struck first with a weak hit to Rowan's ribs. When he moved to counter, Callie jammed her staff into the ground, used it as leverage to get her feet in the air, and slammed Rowan in the chest. His counter move as he fell back thunked uselessly against her staff and his eyes widened.

The motion threw her off balance, and she tumbled to the ground after him. Callie rolled away and on to her feet, expecting another attack. Rowan, for once, was on his back, staring up at the sky, his staff discarded at his side.

He didn't move.

She gloated for a moment in victory, insides dancing with glee. It was the first time she'd taken him down.

Fear skittered into her stomach when Rowan remained still. Across the field, Jack and Hawthorne stood.

"Rowan?" She crossed the short distance. His mouth was twisted into a grimace, eyes squeezed shut. "Are you okay?" Her gaze traveled over his face, down his arms, across his legs, searching for broken bones. She hadn't hit him *that* hard.

Suddenly his hands were on her ankle. He twisted and she flew off balance, crashing into him, limbs flailing. Rowan slammed his arm across her chest, rolled, and pinned her underneath his body faster than Callie could cry out in surprise. When the world stopped swinging around her, she glared at him, pissed that he'd taken her glory.

"You couldn't let me have that one, could you?"

A rare smile twitched on his mouth. He eased off her and offered a hand. "That was a good attack, I think we're done for today." When she stood, he kept hold of her arm, frowning at the bruises. "I'm being too hard on you."

Callie pulled her arms away and hid them behind her back. "It's okay. I'm learning."

Rowan continued to stare at her until she swallowed, uneasy.

"I mean it," she insisted.

He shrugged. "Whatever you say." He hefted the staffs and started toward the palace.

She hurried after him, biting her lip against the pain in her legs. "Can you teach me hand-to-hand combat?" she asked when she caught up. Rowan's last move had taken her by surprise. She didn't want it to happen again.

Rowan slowed and tucked the staffs under his arm, catching her hand. For a second she thought he was going to hold it and before she could decide her feelings on that, he lifted it to his eye level, examining the bruises and scrapes. "You should let me heal those." Another smile. "I feel bad—only a little—but still bad."

She tugged her fingers away. "Hand-to-hand?" she prompted.

Rowan sighed. "Tell you what. You let me heal you and we'll talk."

"You promise?"

"I guess," he said, lifting a shoulder.

"That's not a promise."

They'd reached the inside of the city where the buildings blocked the sun. Jack and Hawthorne trailed behind, still talking about her training session.

"Do you want me to swear it with my true name?" Rowan asked.

If you knew a fae's true name, you had absolute control over them. Of course, he was being ridiculous, but Callie wondered *what* Rowan's true name was. She had a hard time picturing him as Jonathon or Matthew or Keith. Rowan just fit.

"No. I just want you to do it," she said.

"Fine. Tomorrow." They stopped at the porch of the palace. "Do you want me to come up?" He didn't look at Callie as he asked, and like usual, she got the impression that he expected her to say no.

One battle at a time, she reminded herself. He'd agreed to hand-to-hand, maybe tomorrow she'd work on their friendship. "I have homework," she said, leaving it at that.

He walked away.

She waited for Jack and Hawthorne to catch up before entering the palace, watching Rowan until he disappeared between the buildings.

"Tired?" Hawthorne asked with a smirk as they climbed the stairs.

Callie groaned, making her feet move. Every step jammed into her sore muscles like a knife. "Shut up."

Jack chuckled and held up his hand. "You are badass! You took him *out!*"

She laughed and slapped her palm halfheartedly into his. "Thanks, but I think he won that round."

Jack mimicked Callie's attack. "You were like *bam!* Take that!" He shoved Hawthorne, who lifted his eyebrows.

They climbed the mountain of stairs to the second floor, Callie lagging behind. She still thought the palace needed an elevator. Hawthorne went inside to scour the room while Jack stayed in the hallway with Callie. It seemed unnecessary for them to search the rooms when the palace was locked down like a fortress. Guards stood at every entrance. Very few were allowed inside.

Willow was on the shortlist, and sprawled across Callie's bed when she finally entered the room. Callie shut the door, leaving Jack and Hawthorne outside. If she couldn't see them, they didn't exist.

"I have news from the human world," Willow said, tossing Callie the fashion magazine she was reading. Whenever the trackers went into the human world, Willow bribed them. She always had books, magazines, and music brought back for her.

The glossy pages hit the floor and Callie debated leaving it there. She groaned the entire way down to pick it up. She took it to the bed, a four poster swathed in white linens and gold trim, and collapsed next to Willow.

"I'm *tired.*"

Willow frowned and propped her chin on her hands. "I don't know why you bother with all that. For one, women aren't supposed to be warriors, and two, we don't have anyone to *fight.*" She blew strands of unruly hair from her forehead. "In case you haven't noticed, the people of *Eirensae* are pretty mellow. We're not like *Fraeburdh.*"

Callie had studied the other cities, *Fraeburdh,* the City of War, possessed the sword, *Macántacht,* the City of Honor, had the spear, and the fallen city of *Cloch,* had once possessed the stone of truth, but it was lost during the last war, along with the city. And *Eirensae,* the City of Fertility, had the cauldron. Long ago, the four cities were one magnificent city, *Aontaithe,* where the fae lived in peace. Over time, discord grew between them. The fae books taught that every faerie has the ability for good or evil inside of them. As time passed, *Fraeburdh* became known for its cruelty, *Eirensae* for its indolence, and *Macántacht* for its inability to choose a side. Rarely did the fae of the cities mingle, and as far as anyone would tell her, no one had seen someone from *Fraeburdh* or *Macántacht* in many decades—since the last war.

"Elm wasn't mellow," Callie said. Her mouth tasted bitter every time she thought of him. Though she knew he was gone, banished to the Fallen, Callie couldn't help looking over her shoulder. No matter how far she went, the shadows always remained.

Willow made a noncommittal sound and went back to the magazine. Now that Callie lived in the palace, Willow visited every day. Callie suspected Willow liked it better than her apartment. Callie had a walk-in closet filled with more clothes than she could hope to wear. Her bathroom featured a giant claw foot bathtub and double sinks—like she really needed two. The fireplace across from her bed was large enough to walk in when it wasn't occupied with flames.

And everything was trimmed with gold.

The unfamiliarity made Callie's skin itch. She understood now why Sapphire had stayed in the cottage when she could've moved into the city. It was ostentatious, and far more than Callie needed to survive. She would've gladly traded Willow places, if Hazel allowed it.

Plus, she missed Sapphire. She'd only seen her sister in passing over the past two weeks. Callie was always busy, but what she really wanted was an evening of doing nothing with Sapphire.

It'd never happen, of course.

Willow flipped a few pages. "I saw you practicing with Rowan today."

"Spying on me again?"

"Hardly. More like spying on Rowan. He is *hot.*" She speared Callie in her green-eyed gaze. "Tell the truth. You're into him."

Callie rubbed a knot in her calf. "He's alright."

"You're into Ash, too," she said, smug. She took Callie's silence as her answer. "I knew it. You slut!" She clutched the magazine to her chest and made stupid girly noises. "So which one are you going to choose?" She said it like it was the most important decision ever.

"Neither." Callie slid off the bed, not in the mood for conversation with Willow. She only had an hour before Ash would show up with more homework.

Willow scowled. "If you're not interested, I'll gladly take him off your hands."

Callie froze, mid-stretch. "What would Sai think about that?"

"Sai?" A pause. "I have no idea what you mean." Her face flushed pink.

The knot in Callie's calf refused to relent, so she gave up and worked the stiffness out of her arms. "He's interested."

"Well, yes, but—" she sputtered.

Callie laughed. "Not being able to lie sucks, huh?" She went to the bathroom and shut the door, but not before catching Willow's look of frustration.

She turned the water hot as she could stand and undressed in front of the mirror. Her arms and legs looked the worst, covered with all shades of blue, purple, and green. A long, linear bruise spread across her ribs and even the gentlest touch sent fire across her skin. Beneath the battle wounds, Callie saw the beginnings of muscle swelling in her arms and shoulders. She'd thrown everything into training for the past two weeks, and it was finally paying off.

Callie pulled the band from her hair and reached for her brush, dropping it when a spider scuttled from underneath. Black fur covered the tiny body, interspersed with yellow spots.

She screamed.

The spider froze, mid-scuttle. Its hairy legs twitched, and then the entire thing exploded in a firework of guts that left a gooey smear across the counter.

Callie screamed again.

Willow threw open the bathroom door. "What is it? What's wrong?" She looked Callie over, eyes lingering on the bruises. "Holy shit! Rowan beat the crap out of you."

Callie waved an arm. "No."

"No? Look in the mirror. Clearly that says, *I've been beaten.*"

From the depths of her room she heard Hawthorne and Jack approach. "Callie?" Jack yelled. Their stomps carried into the bathroom.

She took a breath to calm her racing heart. She'd exploded the spider. Blown it up like a grenade. "There was a spider," she called to her guards before they came charging into the bathroom.

"You screamed like that for a spider?" Willow said, incredulous. She shut the door in the boys' faces. "She's naked you perverts." She searched the floor and ceiling. "Well, where is it?"

"I—uh...I killed it..." *with my mind.* Callie swallowed the bile in her throat, horrified at what she'd done without even *trying.* "It's definitely dead."

Willow scrunched up her face. "Gross."

☙◆❧

"Wait outside," Callie said to her guards as she knocked on the doorframe of Hazel's study.

Eirensae's leader sat behind a sprawling raw wood desk, parchment spread before her. She gathered up the papers and shoved them into a drawer as Callie entered. "What can I do for you?" she asked with a smile.

Hazel gestured to the couch that sat facing her desk and Callie perched on the edge of a cushion. Hazel folded her hands, watching Callie with bright, violet eyes.

Callie hesitated.

"Go on, child," Hazel encouraged.

"I've been training with Ash for a while now," Callie said, trying to organize her words into something that wouldn't sound whiny.

"I hear your progress is phenomenal."

"Yeah. About that. I need to know how to control it. Every time I think I have it, I end up exploding something," she stopped there, hoping Hazel wouldn't question her further.

"Exploding something?" Hazel lifted an eyebrow.

"It's not just people," Callie said. "It's things, too. A mirror, a spider. I never know when it's going to happen."

Hazel leaned forward. "Can you demonstrate for me?"

Callie waved her hands helplessly. "I've never done it on purpose. Besides, I don't want to hurt you. Can't you bind my powers like you bound me to *Eirensae?*"

"Hm," Hazel said. She sat back in her chair and folded her arms. "I think your powers are something that need to be cultivated, not oppressed."

"So you want me to keep breaking things?"

"Of course not. What I want is for us to understand the scope of your power, Callie. With Elm, it seemed to be attached to your fear. Is that a safe assumption?"

Callie thought about the spider, the mirror, and the time she'd attacked Rowan. "Fear," she murmured. It fit.

"It's not your magic that needs controlling, child, it's your fear." Hazel stood and came around the desk to sit next to Callie. She draped a gentle arm around Callie's shoulders, pulling her close. "Embrace your life here, Callie, and let go of your fears. Elm is gone, you're safe now. All that's left is finding your amulet."

"How am I supposed to find it when I'm always stuck inside the palace?" Callie grumbled.

"Jack," Hazel called and the boy appeared in the doorway as though he'd been waiting to be summoned.

"Yes, Hazel?" His cheeks were red as if he was guilty of eavesdropping.

"Take Callie to search for her amulet."

℘✦℘

"I'll just *know* where it is?" Callie said, hand resting in the crook of Jack's arm. The river gurgled next to them, the sound of a million voices in a high ceilinged room.

"It's hard to explain," he said.

Her feet sunk into the soft bank, toes squelching. Though she knew the fae couldn't lie, she trusted Jack above the others. His pale face was honest, his eyes clear. It was easy for Callie to avoid being sucked into his mind as she had been with Ash. Besides, she decided, she didn't want to know what went on inside others. Dealing with her own emotions was enough.

Speaking with Hazel hadn't helped Callie know how to stop hurting people, but at least it'd gotten her outside.

"Does it hurt—the imprint?" she asked.

Jack shook his head. "Not exactly. It's warm and tingly. The marks aren't a tattoo. It's not a scar; it's more of a birthmark."

Callie slowed now. The forest rose in front of them. She knew if they continued on this path, they'd reach the northern gate to the city. *Eirensae* had two entrances, the one she'd come through beneath the reflection pond, and one to the north that exited in Ireland. Part of her was deeply curious to step through the portal into the countryside—not that the binding spell would allow that. She imagined rolling hills and clear blue skies. Pretty much, she envisioned *Eirensae,* but *bigger.* The faerie city existed somewhere in Europe, the exact location a mystery hidden by magic. So technically, she could already be in Ireland—though she'd never stepped foot on an airplane.

They stopped, toes nearly in the edge of the river. From what she understood, imprints were deeply personal to the individual. Curiosity won out over common courtesy. "Show me."

"Bossy much?"

Jack's face pinked and Callie felt stupid for asking. He lifted the hem of his tunic until his chest showed, revealing a light dusting of blond chest hair and a flat stomach. Green lines twisted there, shaped a naked, elegant tree.

Callie curled her fingers into a fist so she wouldn't touch. "How do you know what it means?" All the imprints were beautiful, flowers, trees, plants, delicate lines, but none of them made sense, pretty pictures, not some roadmap to the future.

Jack tugged his tunic down and smoothed the front. "The prophetess tells us." He held out his arm again and Callie tucked her hand there, comforted by his light, cheerful energy. "Sapphire is a great prophetess, you know."

Her lips dipped into a frown. "Actually, I don't know. What exactly does a prophetess *do?*" They stepped into the cover of trees. The air cooled and filled with the green scent of leaves and damp earth.

"She focuses mostly on bringing the fae home. When a child comes of age, trackers are sent to retrieve them. Or in your case, you klutz-fall into the pond." He flashed a smile. "She's involved in the births, divining the futures, spelling the amulets…" he trailed off with a little shrug. "She watches for threats to the city, not that there's been much to see. Until you, of course."

Callie sighed. "I didn't ask for this."

"People are jealous. I wouldn't worry overmuch. Between the guards, the increased ward strength, and Rowan as your personal protector—"

She arched an eyebrow, not liking the part about Rowan. "He's not—"

"Have you ever heard the saying about jumping in front of a speeding bullet?"

"It's not like that," she argued.

"It is."

Quiet settled around them, heavy as a blanket, as if forest held its breath, waiting for Callie's response. She chewed her lip, irritated that everyone noticed what she didn't. First Willow, now Jack. "And why does it matter to you?" she asked eventually.

"Gossip, darling, was created by the fae. Along with vengeance, greed, envy, gluttony, a million other things that involve glamour and magnificence. Though I only consider myself envious, well, that and magnificent. I've been here years and nary has a head turned in my direction. Honestly, what's a boy to do?"

She smiled and rested her cheek on his shoulder. "I'll turn my head your way."

"Ah," he patted her face with a cool palm, "a pity turn. Lucky me."

It was the most relaxed Callie felt in weeks. Maybe it was because she knew Jack wasn't interested in her, or being away from the palace, but she found herself talking. "I was running from a guy when I fell through the pond."

"A hot guy?"

She shook her head. "Not your type. Football sort, you know, *my muscles are bigger than my brain.*"

"Too bad, kind of ruins the mental picture—continue."

"We'd dated for months—but I couldn't," she swallowed the monster in her throat, hating its claws, "I could never…"

"Seal the deal?" Jack supplied.

"Yes. That."

"I imagine it was his loss, not yours. *Men,*" he made a disgusted sound, *"pigs.* I'm assuming he's not the one who…" Jack let the question hang between them, and she knew he was thinking of the day he'd found her in Sapphire's cabin surrounded by broken glass.

Callie was silent for a long time.

"There's more to this story, isn't there?" he asked.

They'd reached the northern gate. Four guards stood watch; though Callie wasn't sure how effective they'd be with their hands empty, unless they thought their surly expressions would maim any fae that attacked. She wondered if they had offensive powers like hers, a monster hidden beneath their skin.

Jack nodded at the guards and they turned around, headed back for the city.

"I don't have to tell you about the *more,* do I?" She could still feel the cold porcelain against her thighs. The impossible, never-ending pain.

"Of course not."

They didn't speak until they emerged into the sunlight. Her skin warmed and she turned her face upward. "What kind of power do you have?" She wanted to ask every fae she saw, hardly restraining herself. Ash had said that most fae have one power, not a handful as she did.

"I sense things. I guess you'd consider me an empath. I can read emotions."

"Oh."

"Yeah. Not very cool."

"No—it's not that."

He laughed. "Don't worry, I'm not offended. In the grand scheme of my life, it makes sense. It works both ways, though. Because I already know what you're feeling, it puts you at ease. People will tell me anything I want to know."

"So that's why I told you all that stuff about Nate!" she said.

"The meathead has a name," he crowed. "I shall hunt him and pluck his nose hairs individually, with blunt tweezers."

It was Callie's turn to laugh. The sound died on her lips as the cottages came into view along with harsh male grunting. They reached the final bend just in time to see Rowan slam Ash to the ground. Ash's head bounced off the grass and his teeth snapped together with a crack.

"Rowan," Callie yelled, letting go of Jack and running to them. "What are you doing?"

Rowan squinted and pushed a damp tangle of hair off his forehead. "Teaching."

Callie gaped at him. "What?" She dropped to her knees and lifted Ash's head. Dirt smudged the side of his face and a bruise highlighted his jaw. He moaned.

"Ash?"

He moved his head slowly, first one side, then the other. His neck popped and he sighed. "I'm fine."

"See?" Rowan said, smug.

"He's not fine," she argued, glaring at Rowan. "Heal him."

"No."

"What is your problem? Heal him."

"I don't need healing," Ash grumbled.

"Besides, he asked for this," Rowan said.

Callie stilled, fingers in the middle of brushing dirt from Ash's cheek. "Asked? He *asked* for you to be a dick?" Anger gathered in her veins, hot as molten lava. Jack took a few steps away and rolled back on his heels, clearly sensing her emotions. Callie stood and shoved Rowan's shoulder, hating the firm resistance. He took a tiny step to regain his balance. "You want to fight?" she yelled. Several fae turned in their direction, pausing on the path between the cottages and the city.

"Callie," Ash said from the ground, "I asked him to teach me how to fight."

"You *what?*" She held out a hand and pulled Ash to his feet. He wavered, unsteady, and Jack came to the rescue, keeping Ash upright. "This isn't funny." She pushed Rowan again. "You could've really hurt him."

"I'm fine," Ash repeated, forcing a smile. His teeth were bloody. "Really."

"He's *fine,"* Rowan mocked.

Ash stepped away from Jack and Callie and straightened his shoulders, wincing. He blew a breath through his teeth. "Let's go again."

Rowan gestured for Ash to make the first move.

Callie stepped between them. "You're not doing this. You'll kill him," she said.

Ash rolled his eyes. "Rowan is teaching *you* to fight. I'm pretty sure I can handle it."

"How about two-on-one?" Rowan suggested.

"You're on," Ash said, limping forward.

Callie stopped him with a hand on his chest. "Stop it. What is the matter with you two?"

"You don't see me fighting anyone. I'm more of a lover than a fighter," Jack interjected.

Rowan smirked. "Me, too. Let me prove it."

"No. No one is proving anything. Go *away* Rowan. I need to train with Ash." *Before you kill him.*

Rowan looked disappointed. "Tomorrow, then?"

"Yeah," Ash said, nodding. "Tomorrow."

৪১♦৫৪

"Why would you possibly think this is a good idea?" Callie demanded, opening Ash's door and waiting for Jack to go inside and search the place.

Ash sulked. He leaned against the wall and refused to meet her gaze. "I don't know why you have to make a big deal out of it. No one said anything when you wanted to learn to fight."

"That's different," she said, though she didn't have a good reason why. She wanted to fight to protect herself, maybe that's what Ash wanted too.

She didn't believe it.

Looking back, she'd probably overreacted. Rowan was volatile. She might've made it worse for Ash. A midnight blue bruise covered the top of his foot and the sleeve of his tunic was torn from the seam. "What did he do to you?" she muttered.

"All clear," Jack said, returning from the depths of the apartment. "I'll just wait out here." His expression said, *no way am I getting in the middle of this.*

She dragged Ash inside and left him on the couch, nursing his wounds. Callie scrounged up a towel and used a sweating pitcher on the counter to wet it. When she touched them to Ash's jaw, he flinched.

"Ow." His eyes flew open.

"Rowan's good," she said.

"I'm realizing that." He covered Callie's hand, pressing it harder to his face.

"Why do you need to fight, Ash? You're a teacher."

"Not a warrior, thanks for reminding me." He sighed. "I like you taking care of me."

Callie stilled. She wished Jack had come inside with them. Suddenly Ash's apartment felt cramped and close. She wanted to be back outside, in the sunlight. "You could've just asked me over. You didn't have to get beat up."

"I know it's stupid. I just—I see the way you look at him. I fought Rowan to get to you."

Callie's eyes widened. "You did?"

"God, I'm a moron," he muttered. "I don't even want to admit it."

Ash was beautiful, not in the dark and dangerous way that Rowan was beautiful, or in the innocent and carefree way of Jack. Ash's skin had a gentle glow from the sun, not quite golden, but pink. Freckles peppered his nose and tiny blue veins snaked the skin on his eyelids. She slid her hand from beneath his, touched the darkening bruise.

"The night he saved you, I wished…I wished it were me. That I could do something like that," Ash said softly. "I thought maybe I could learn to be more like him. Stronger…better, somehow."

There was a long pause before Callie said, "You're *jealous?*"

His lips curved. "I have a concussion. I'm not liable for anything I say."

Ash's cheek was prickly beneath her hand. "I don't know what to say. I'm not—" she mumbled.

"So don't say anything." He sat up now, catching her fingers. "What are you so afraid of?" He pressed a finger to her mouth when she tried to answer. "It's a rhetorical question. I have zero expectations here. If you want to run away," his hand slid from her lips to cup her cheek and finally to the back of her neck, "run away." He searched her face.

Callie thought of Hazel's advice. *Face your fears.*

She took a deep breath. She could see the gold rings in the center of Ash's irises as he leaned in closer. His eyelashes were darker than his hair and cast shadows on his cheek when his eyes closed. Her heart thudded.

There was indecision and panic. She felt hot and cold all at once.

Then their lips met.

His mouth was warm, soft, and despite his fight with Rowan, he smelled sweet. He didn't drag her into him or deepen the kiss, just waited until she either accepted or denied him. Callie surprised herself by returning the gentle pressure. She didn't know what she felt for Ash, yet this felt okay. She waited for the instinctive reaction to push him away or Ash's cry of pain when she accidentally exploded him, but they never came.

Ash pulled away first and rested his forehead against hers. Callie's heart pounded beneath her ribs, she felt lightheaded. Ash's hand still claimed the back of her neck. He kissed her again, quickly.

⁊⋄ભ

It was very late into the night when the quiet knock filtered through Callie's dreams. She came instantly awake, heart pounding a frantic tempo. The sound came again. Callie kicked free of the sheets tangled around her legs and climbed from the bed. She found Rowan waiting on the other side of the door.

"What's wrong?" she demanded, looking over his shoulder at the dim, empty hall, expecting someone to be with him. "Where's Jack?"

Rowan lifted a shoulder. "Around."

"What did you do to him?" Callie opened the door wider. "Did you decide to teach him how to fight, too?" She was still furious with Rowan for how he'd treated Ash.

Rowan eased himself into the gap, forcing Callie back into her bedroom. "He's fine. I need to talk to you." He closed the door without a sound.

"About what, Rowan? It's the middle of the night." She sat on the bed and folded her arms across her chest, glaring at him.

Rowan stood backlit by the fireplace. The flames gave him a rust-colored halo. He looked as though he hadn't yet been to bed. He ran a hand through his hair. "I've been to see Sapphire."

Callie's gaze found his. "Hazel told me that's forbidden. I've asked to see her dozens of times. How is it that she allows you—"

"I wasn't allowed. It doesn't matter. She's had visions of your future, of *Eirensae's* future. There is war coming to the city and Hazel plans to use your powers to defeat our enemies. She has you exactly where she wants you. She had Orchid killed to set this plan into motion. She has Sapphire under her control, and by default, she has you."

Callie absorbed his words like a blast of ice water to the face. "The prophetess was killed because of me?"

"You are what she's been waiting for, a power strong enough to defeat King Arol and *Fraeburdh*. But she's overconfident, because Sapphire sees you with King Arol." Rowan moved closer to the bed. "She can't win against him, his city is too powerful. They have training that we don't. He will pluck you from her hands as though you are nothing more than an infant. He will use you to destroy *Eirensae*."

"How can you know this? Hazel wants nothing more than to protect me. I saw her this evening, she was nice to me. She wants me to be at home here."

"She wants to use you. Can't you see it? She bound you to the city. She has your sister as good as captive. You are right where she wants you, and you're falling further and further into her hands every day. *Fraeburdh* will attack *Eirensae*. It's only a matter of time."

Callie pushed to her feet and went to the window, gazing out over the city. A few candles still burned in the windows of the apartments where Ash lived. Much farther out, she could see the dark roofs of the cottages. "I can't believe this," she said, voice hitching. She was supposed to be safe, here in her new home beneath the reflection pond. She finally had a family. She was supposed to belong.

Rowan came to stand beside her. "It was her plan all along, Callie, something she plotted with Elm, and when she went against his wishes, he tried to kill you. He knew you could give Hazel everything she wants."

She shook her head. "That makes no sense. Why wouldn't Elm want the same things as Hazel?"

"He was her right hand, but when you showed up, you threatened his position. He knew you were more powerful than him. He knew that Hazel would lose interest in what he could give her. He tried to control Hazel, and she banished him for it. Elm is greedy, Callie, but so is Hazel. The difference is, she already had the status, where Elm had nothing."

Callie frowned and rubbed her forehead. "I want to see Sapphire."

"You can't. Hazel is watching her."

"I need to ask her what to do. I need proof. If this is true—" she broke off, turning to face him.

He touched her shoulder. "It is true. You have to decide what to do. If you stay here, *Fraeburdh* will attack. If you leave, the Fallen will find you."

"So I'm dead either way?"

Rowan's face softened. The moonlight turned his skin pale and deepened the blue of his eyes. "I promised Sapphire that I wouldn't let anything happen to you. I'm going to keep that promise." He looked away and dropped his hand. "There's something else you should know."

Callie's insides froze. More bad news? She could hardly comprehend what he'd already told her.

"I don't belong in *Eirensae*. Because of the magic used to make her prophetess, Sapphire can't speak freely to me, so I only know that I don't belong here. She couldn't tell me anything else."

Realization spread through Callie's gut, as caustic as a tidal wave, destroying everything in its path. "Where?" she whispered, though she already knew.

"*Fraeburdh*. I'm not certain—"

"But how would you end up here? The wards wouldn't admit you."

Rowan shrugged. "Stranger things have happened. You're here, after all."

"Maybe if I speak with Hazel," Callie said, waving her arm. "Maybe we could figure this out. It could just be a misunderstanding. Sapphire told me she's wrong sometimes. The future can change. It's not set in stone."

His hands were hot on her face, forcing her to look at him. "Listen to me. You need to stay away from Hazel and tell no one about this. We'll find a way to get you to Sapphire, but Callie, you have to be careful. You don't know who is loyal to her."

Tears formed behind Callie's eyes. She swallowed hard.

"You can trust me," Rowan said.

"And if you belong to *Fraeburdh*, what then? You'll find your amulet and join them?"

Rowan closed his eyes and drew a deep breath. When he opened them again, they were hard as flint, determined. "I will do whatever will keep you safe. I swear it. You'll never be alone in this."

She moved out of his grasp, stomach churning. She wished he'd never come to her door, that she was still lost in oblivious dreams. "I need to think," she said, going to the door and holding it open. Jack waited outside.

Rowan nodded once.

"How much time?" Callie whispered as he slipped into the hall.

"Until I have to leave," he said. "You can come with me. It won't be easy, but I promise—"

Callie closed the door, shutting out the boys, and returned to her bed. She pulled the covers up to her chin and shut her eyes. Sleep took a long time to come, and when it did, she dreamt of death.

ℰ Eleven ℭ

IN THE MORNING, Callie found Hawthorne standing outside her door. He nodded in greeting. His eyes swept over her, making her stomach turn cold. Callie didn't like the dark-haired boy. He seemed out of place in the city, too distant and cool to belong.

It kind of reminded her of Rowan.

"Where's Jack?" she asked, smoothing the skirt of her dress. She wanted to talk to him about what Rowan had told her. She needed another opinion, and she was limited on people she could trust.

"Sleeping, I'm sure," Hawthorne said. "Just me until this afternoon. We're short until the trackers return."

Callie squashed her moment of excitement over a newcomer. She'd heard that there was another child scheduled to return home. The city wasn't safe for her. She should be planning, not worrying over some fae child she'd likely never know.

Not that she'd made any kind of decision. Rowan's warning rattled around inside of her brain like the ominous breaths that preceded death.

She had options, of course, but none of them were very comforting.

"Shall I escort you somewhere?" Hawthorne asked, offering an arm.

Callie frowned at it before shaking her head. "No, thank you. I'll just wait here until Ash comes for me." She moved to shut the door, but changed her mind. "Actually, I'd like to get a head start on my studies. Would you mind taking me to the library?"

"As you wish," Hawthorne said.

Callie made her way out of the palace with Hawthorne on her heels. She could feel his gaze on the back of her neck the entire way, much colder than the cheery yellow sun above her. She couldn't wait for Jack to come back. Perhaps she would request a different guard.

Except, that would mean talking to Hazel.

She drew a deep breath, frustrated. The palm of her hand tingled where Hazel had bound her to *Eirensae*. Rowan's words made sense. They fit like the final pieces of a puzzle snapping into place.

Still, Hazel had been nice to Callie. Accommodating. She'd stood up to the Elders when they'd questioned Callie's sudden appearance. She'd made Callie feel safe.

Was it all part of Hazel's master plan?

Callie stepped through the portal into the caves. Hawthorne appeared beside her. For the briefest second, his gaze moved to the tunnel that led to the cauldron.

"What do you know about the wards?" Callie asked, turning toward the library.

"Trying to break Hazel's binding spell?" Hawthorne asked.

Callie went still. She hadn't thought of that. "Of course not. It's not a secret that Rowan can't locate his amulet," she said. "There has to be some sort of explanation why he's here."

Hawthorne's breath lifted the strands of hair at Callie's neck when he spoke. "My guess is that the prophetess saw him bringing destruction to the city. Sometimes their amulets are destroyed and the faeries are banished to the Fallen."

"But Rowan has done nothing wrong," Callie argued. "And the future can change, anyway. Nothing is certain."

He shrugged. "I'd say that only death is certain, but not for a long, long time. As for your boyfriend, there are likely many things we don't know."

"He's not my boyfriend."

Hawthorne's face split into a bone-chilling smile. "My mistake. You two seem rather fond of each other."

Callie opened her mouth and then shut it again. She didn't have to explain herself to Hawthorne, or anyone for that matter. They reached the library a few seconds later.

"Wait out here," she ordered Hawthorne.

His smile widened. "I must first check for your safety, Calla Lily, then I will stand guard."

She waited, fingers tapping against her leg, while Hawthorne did a sweep of the library. He nodded when he returned. "It's empty. Enjoy your studies. I'm right here if you have any more questions."

Callie went to the stacks, running her fingers over the bindings. So much knowledge in one room. Of all the places in *Eirensae,* she liked this one the best.

She found a book with *Fraeburdh* written along the spine and pulled it from its slot. Rowan thought he belonged to the City of War. Callie refused to believe it. She flipped through the pages with shaking hands.

Weapons, blood, devastation, death. Each page was more horrific than the last. Their history was black as the infinite depths of the ocean, scattered with torture and an insatiable hunger for power.

She slammed the book shut and shoved it back on the shelf, fingers finding a book about the City of Honor.

A fine filigree of gold lettering caught Callie's attention and her hands moved of their own volition to remove the book from its home. The rich, dark leather warmed her skin as she squinted to make sense of the looping calligraphy which rose from the branches of a tree. Instead of a trunk, the golden leaves crowned a woman's head. She held her arms outstretched and four objects spanned the top edge of the cover. A cauldron, a sword, a spear, and a stone.

Callie's insides began to buzz.

The Four Treasures and the Divergence of the Fae.

The cover sent electricity through her hands, as though it carried faerie energy within its pages. Callie's heart thudded in her chest, pounding out her anxiety. She touched the edge, hesitant, and finally opened the cover.

There, nestled just inside, was a brilliant blue stone about the size of Callie's palm. It was the sky over *Eirensae,* the color of the night roses that lined the river, the exact shade of Callie's energy. A fine latticework of iridescent white shot through the stone and undulated, so that the surface looked different from every angle. Knotted through a hole in the top, was a simple leather cord.

Callie exhaled. *Her amulet.*

From the entranceway, Hawthorne began to whistle and Callie jumped. The amulet slid against the thin parchment of the pages, almost touching her skin.

"Ash is coming," Hawthorne called.

Callie eased the cover shut, trapping her amulet inside, and slid it back onto the shelf. She should tell Rowan. Everything inside of her screamed to tell him, to tell Sapphire, to tell *everyone.* She swallowed, feeling the non-truth lodge itself in her throat.

Up until last night, this had been everything she wanted. Now, she wasn't sure. If Hazel found out that she knew where her amulet was, she'd force Callie to put it on. If that happened, Callie would have no choice but to accept Hazel's rule. To be her weapon.

She didn't want that, but she didn't want to run from the city, either. What was she supposed to choose when all the choices were bad?

Callie made sure her hands were steady as she stepped out of the stacks to greet Ash.

"There's my student," Ash said, his grin darkened by the bruise from Rowan's attack.

She forced a smile, anxiety eating away at her gut. "What are we learning today?" she asked, accepting the kiss that Ash planted on her cheek even though it made her nauseous.

"I thought we could get into faerie history, when the fae diverged, the qualities of each city."

"How about we work on mind control?" Callie blurted. He'd see her amulet and then he'd have to tell Hazel. Ash was good, through and through, Callie knew, but he was also loyal.

Rowan had told her to trust no one. Did that include Ash?

Ash's face brightened at her suggestion. "I knew you'd grow to accept your powers." He gestured to the passageway where Hawthorne waited. "Let's go to the training room." He reached for her hand, intertwining his fingers with hers.

Yesterday, she had let him kiss her.

Today, everything was a jumbled mess, including her feelings for Ash. She kept telling him no, but she knew somewhere inside of her there was a part that wanted to say yes, and it lived right next to the part that wanted Rowan.

It wasn't fair to either one of them.

Before she could slide her hand from Ash's, Rowan appeared through the portal. He froze, his eyes going from Ash to Callie, to Ash, and finally coming to rest on Callie. His nostrils flared. "There's been another murder."

"What?" Callie said. Her thoughts went to Sapphire. "It wasn't…"

Rowan must've read her mind because he said, "A child." He frowned and shook his head as though clearing it. "There's a meeting at the palace and Hazel wants Callie where she can keep an eye on her." He met Callie's gaze, a warning, before turning on his heel and retreating back into *Eirensae,* with Callie and Ash right behind him.

⬡✦⬡

The fae of *Eirensae* pressed together in the grand entranceway of the palace. Their voices rose over each other and bounced off the ceiling, turning the palace into utter chaos. Hawthorne disappeared as soon as they entered. *Some guard,* Rowan thought bitterly.

Rowan and Ash kept close to Callie, one at each elbow as they pushed into the fray. The crowd was so riled they hardly noticed.

They found Willow near the center of the room, eyes bright with excitement. "I've never seen them so angry," she yelled. On cue, a litany of curses lit the room, followed by an answering string of profanity.

"They're not angry," Rowan said, scanning the room. "They're scared." Part of him thought this was a good thing. They'd spent far too long hiding in their city, content in their safety. How long had it been since they'd interacted with the other cities or even acknowledged they existed?

Sai's dark head bobbed toward them, expression wary as he made his way through the horde. "Willow," he said with a small smile, touching her shoulder. Her face pinked.

"What's happening?" Rowan asked.

"One of the children," Sai said, face grave. "We found her drained of blood. All the markings of the ceremony were there."

Rowan's face paled. "An Immortal." It was as awful as he'd imagined when he'd heard the news. Not only would they face attack from *Fraeburdh,* now there was an Immortal to contend with.

"The Elders are calling for mutiny. Blood for blood against the Fallen," Sai said. He moved closer to Willow, sliding an arm around her waist. She leaned into him.

"We can't fight an Immortal," Rowan said, incredulous. He found himself stepping toward Callie, wishing he could pull her into his side as Sai had done to Willow.

"We don't fight," Willow said. "Ever." All their eyes went to her. "I mean," she backtracked, face growing redder, "we haven't in a long time."

"Blessed afternoon," Hazel started. There were few who responded in kind. Her gaze roamed the crowd and Rowan wondered whom she was searching for, but of course, her face relaxed when she found Callie.

Now Rowan did move closer to Callie. She gave him a wide-eyed stare. She looked terrified. He hadn't wanted to go to her with what he knew, but what choice did he have? She deserved to have some say in her future. If anything, he should've told her sooner.

"One of our own, a child, has been slaughtered," Hazel said. The group shuddered and exploded into furious shouts. Hazel waited them out. "At this time, we do not know the culprit, though there are few suspects to consider. The Fallen, of course, the fae of *Fraeburdh,* and less so, those of *Macántacht.* I've sent scouts to search for clues, but we may find none. We have increased protection in the city. I don't think there's any reason to panic. I will dispatch warriors to bring her home, and they will conduct an investigation."

The air around Rowan sizzled with restrained energy. This was a child, an innocent fae robbed of her life before it'd even begun. Her parents were in the crowd, and though familial ties were secret, Rowan knew they would feel the loss.

A small worry nudged the back of his mind, then grew and grew until he acknowledged it. *Elm.* He was Fallen now.

He could be an Immortal. He could come after Callie and they'd be too weak to stop him.

"We must continue life as usual. Anything else would be giving in. Loss happens," Hazel said, and her eyes met Rowan's for a brief moment, "but we must persevere. We send our children into the human world to protect them, yet we know there is always risk. Our hearts are heavy for the sister we lost."

Her words were meant to comfort, still the gathering grew more and more unstable the longer Hazel spoke.

"You'll never be Joshua!" someone yelled, their face hidden in the crowd. The fae murmured and churned as they either accepted or denied his words.

Hazel's magic buzzed through the room, fogging Rowan's mind. He hated her power, which muddled the brain and left the victim grasping to find reality. The fae surrounding him groaned. Ash rubbed his forehead and Callie winced. Rowan fought it.

He'd longed for the day that the city questioned Hazel's rule. Joshua was Hazel's husband and the previous leader of *Eirensae*. He'd led them through the war, only to fall at the hand of the king of *Fraeburdh*. Hazel had taken her place as leader following his death. No one spoke his name, not unless they wanted to face Hazel's wrath. Hazel lifted her hands and a stronger wave of energy coursed through the room. Several fae doubled over and held their heads.

"You *dare* bring up Joshua," she said, moving closer to the man, hands still raised. "You *dare* question my authority. Are you challenging me?" she screamed. Her hair had come loose from her bun. It whipped around her face in the wind created by her power. "Say the words."

Rowan stepped in front of Callie, panic eating his gut. They had to get her out of here before things got ugly. What better way for Hazel to stake her claim on Callie than to have her fight in a challenge? They would all have to choose a side to support, and Callie would pick whatever side Sapphire chose. The prophetess was required to support the leader.

"We've got to go," he said, yelling over the crackling static of welling energy.

Around them, fae gathered their powers. The room lit in all colors of energy, citrus yellow, vibrant orange, midnight blue. Most of their faces were turned to the oncoming fight, but a few were looking at Callie. Word had spread of Callie's power, her ability to explode a mind with her thoughts. Perhaps it was no longer a secret that she would become Hazel's greatest weapon.

Rowan tucked Callie behind him and turned so that his body blocked her from view. She fit perfectly in the circle of his arms. This close he could see flecks of green in her eyes, which widened.

Rowan's arms tightened. He could protect her in a physical fight, but not a magical one. Callie was better suited to that. She hadn't had enough training, a fact that had Rowan ignoring her protests.

"I challenge you!" The voice crashed through the room, rattling the walls and shaking the floor. It wouldn't take long for the entranceway to become a war zone.

The palace shuddered now and a deep rumble sounded through the hall.

"Go," Rowan said, pushing Callie backwards as Ash struggled to shove people out of their way. Rowan lost sight of Willow and Sai, but he couldn't worry about them. He had to get Callie out. He had to keep his promise to Sapphire.

They'd moved only a few feet when he chanced a look over his shoulder. Sapphire and Cypress had moved behind Hazel.

"Sapphire," Callie gasped.

"No," Rowan said as she tried to pry his arms off. "She'll be fine." He willed the words to be true. Uncertainty didn't count as a lie in faerie edict, but he knew Callie would never forgive him if he were wrong. "This is exactly what Hazel wants," he hissed in her ear.

"I have to help Sapphire." She fought Rowan harder, trying some of the things he'd taught her during hand-to-hand training. Callie was tough, but Rowan was stronger. "Please," she said, her voice filled with determination.

Their progress slowed as sconces shook loose from the walls and crashed to the floor. Rowan shoved Callie into Ash, using their combined weight to barrel through people. Callie stumbled, body pressed against his tight enough that he could feel the ridges of her ribs when she breathed. He kept his arms iron tight around her, lifting her to keep her from falling. They crept toward the door at turtle speed. The fae were choosing sides.

An eerie silence moved through the room, prickling the back of Rowan's neck. The lights dimmed from the energy surge and went out.

Then the screaming started.

Tremors rocked the room. He kept hold of Callie as he struggled to remain upright in the darkness. Bright colors flashed, illuminating faces with bursts of color, pale green, iridescent violet. Chunks of stone rained down from the ceiling. Glass shattered. People lay prone and he tripped over them.

Callie no longer fought his grip but held on, both arms locked around his chest. Energy sizzled, disorienting Rowan. How far away was the door? Ten feet? A hundred? He couldn't remember. He wasn't even sure if Ash was still in front of him. They stumbled forward, blind. Rowan hoped it was the right direction.

A bright, white light exploded above them. It hung suspended, like a frozen moment in a camera's flash, showing the destruction of the palace. Dust and debris hung in the air, halted in the process of falling. The fae were crushing each other. Arms and legs tangled, glamours were lost. He saw leaves and fur and bark and glowing eyes.

From across the room, he saw Hazel looking right at them.

Rowan swore. The doors were just ahead, hanging open, one of the hinges broken.

Rowan shoved Callie forward just as he felt Hazel's power probe at his mind. The edges of his vision went blurry and gray. Then he and Callie exploded through the entrance and off of the porch.

His mind cleared but the urgency didn't leave him. He had to get Callie far away from Hazel until the fight was over.

Maybe Hazel would lose and suddenly *Eirensae* would become a safe place for Callie. Maybe this was a blessing in disguise.

A mottled purple sky hung above them, roiling with thunderheads. The fight had called a storm. Wind blew Callie's hair into Rowan's eyes and he realized he hadn't let her go. He released her and she lurched away from him. They'd lost Ash.

Her eyes were furious. Lightning turned her skin pale as paper and her hair lifted from her scalp, combed by invisible fingers. "What is going on?" She took deep breaths as though trying to calm herself.

Rowan smelled ozone and the oily scent of burnt flesh. The palace rumbled behind him.

"I'm going back," she said.

"Like hell you are. We're getting as far away as we can. Didn't you feel Hazel trying to control you?" He caught her bicep.

Callie's expression turned murderous. The energy from her skin under his palm nearly scalded his fingers. "Sapphire is in there. She needs me."

"Sapphire is a marked fae. She can handle herself." He pulled, but she dug her heels into the grass.

"Let me go," she hissed, wrenching her arm, still breathing deep.

His fingers turned white. "No."

The wind blew harder now, sneaking under their clothes and snapping at the fabric. It'd started to rain, but the drops sizzled before reaching the ground, turning to steam. Cries tumbled from the open palace doors.

"It's my choice," she argued.

Rowan ignored her.

In the end, he dragged Callie back to Ash's apartment. He wanted to take her to his place, but it was too far away and the weather had turned nasty. Lightning streaked the sky every few seconds and giant bolts of electricity arced for the forest. The storm howled as it descended on the city, its giant maw ready to consume everything in its path.

Then they were inside Ash's and Rowan jammed a chair beneath the door handle. Callie stood in the center of the room, shivering. Her blonde hair tangled at her shoulders and her cheeks were red with anger. She wrapped both arms around her middle and glared at him.

Rowan had never wanted to kiss her more. Instead, he ran both hands through his hair and over his face. Everything had gone to hell—Hazel, the child, Elm, all of it. But Callie was with him and she was safe...for now. If they had to run, he'd find a way to break the damn binding spell himself.

ଚ Twelve ଓ

CALLIE SAT ON one end of the couch, legs pulled underneath her. She wasn't sure how much time had passed. The storm continued to pound the windows like a determined, unwelcome visitor. Rowan paced near the door, blade in hand. He slid it absently between his fingers, and she wondered how he didn't cut himself.

Her anger faded, little by little, replaced with bone-chilling dread. Aside from Rowan, everyone she cared about was inside the palace. Sapphire, Ash, Willow, Jack. The ache to go back overwhelmed her insides and grew until she couldn't swallow around it. She knew Rowan would never let her go. Maybe his intentions were purely for her protection, but it didn't matter. She felt insignificant and useless trapped in Ash's apartment.

She dozed for a while, dreaming of things she'd never seen. Dark places where faeries tormented humans and tricked their lives away. She saw Hazel, limbs torn from their sockets, bleeding on the palace floor. She saw Elm with hollow, soulless eyes, lapping at Hazel's blood with greedy, red stained lips curled from teeth sharpened to daggers.

When she woke, Rowan sat across from her, elbows balanced on his knees. A great rumble shook the apartment and Rowan went still. Callie sat up and stretched her legs. Their eyes met. Rowan's expression was dark and unreadable. They'd never lit any candles, but the storm illuminated his face as he looked away.

He stood and went to the window, silhouetted there, shoulders taut.

"What is it?" she said, panic unfurling in her chest.

"I don't like waiting."

Callie joined him at the window. It was impossible to see through the rain pelting the glass. Rowan continued to stand there, staring outside. Humidity made the hair as the base of his neck curl. In the dim light, his eyes were black. She imagined them as steel doors, keeping all his secrets inside. She knew he had many things that shaped him into the sarcastic, distant boy he was now. She'd felt close to him that night in the hospital, as if she could actually touch him. Now, he seemed far away, despite the promise to protect her.

Suddenly Rowan was in front of her, hands on her face. For a second she thought he would kiss her, and she couldn't decide if she was terrified or thrilled. His thumb stroked her cheekbone. She worried he could hear her heart beating.

"I promised that I wouldn't let anything happen to you. I'm trying so hard to keep that promise. Maybe I'm not what you want, but I keep my word, Callie."

Her hands were on top of his, holding them to her face, even though she hadn't told them to do that. And she thought maybe she would kiss him, instead. He exhaled; sweet breath across her face, it smelled green and she wanted to know if it would taste the same. He leaned in, she leaned in.

She waited.

Then she was inside of him, settling into his mind as she'd done with Ash. Their energy collided, sparks flying as they tried to consume each other.

His mind was shadowed, much darker than Ash's. She felt small there, as though she could never produce enough light to brighten the space.

"What are you doing?" Rowan said and the sound came from inside her head—*his* head.

She didn't have an answer.

Everything was unfamiliar, like tasting the wrong flavor in something you'd eaten many times before. His thoughts cowered in darkness, surrounded by black energy that battered against Callie's. All the channels to thought and memory were heavily guarded. Numb, creeping coldness stole through her.

"I can feel you," he whispered.

Callie came back to herself, slipping from Rowan like fog burned off by the sun. She rubbed her forehead where a headache pounded between her eyes. When she looked up, Rowan was staring at her.

"What?" she said, annoyed. She couldn't decide if it bothered her more that it'd happened or that Rowan hadn't stopped her. She wasn't a malicious mind snatcher, and she hated that she even had the capability.

Rowan licked his lips and a sudden clap of thunder brought them closer together. "You felt…warm."

"I'm sorry," she said, heat spreading across her cheeks. "I didn't mean—"

"Want to try again?" he asked, eager.

"No!" The word leapt from her mouth much too fast. "I mean, it was an accident." She kept talking, some horrible, projectile word vomit. "I don't want to hurt you. We don't know what I'm capable of and I almost exploded your brain and I'd never forgive myself—"

"I'm not afraid," Rowan said, interrupting her monologue.

Callie stilled. "I know." She pressed her thumbs into her eyes, surprised to find them wet. She caught the tears with her palms and hoped Rowan didn't notice. When his hands settled over hers, she couldn't hold it back anymore. Her shoulders quaked with a sob. It all came pouring out of her eyes, her grief for Sapphire, the confusion over her newfound powers, what she felt for Ash and Rowan, anger at her own powerlessness. The emotion spilled from her hands only to fall into Rowan's. "This isn't me," she said when he pulled her against him. Callie buried her face in his tunic, inhaling the scent that was purely his. Rowan's arms went around her and he whispered things that mixed with the thunder and rain, words she couldn't hear.

She stayed there for a long time, much longer than she thought possible. Callie wasn't scared of Rowan's body against hers; his hands on her back didn't make her run, even his lips close to her ear made her shiver instead of shudder.

"I wish you'd try again," he said. They were still pressed together and his breath fluttered strands of her hair and tickled her neck. "No matter what you decide, I need you to be able to protect yourself."

Callie swallowed and removed herself from his arms.

"I'm just—I know I'm going to leave…become Fallen," he said. "And if you choose to stay here, then you have to be strong. You have to understand what you can and can't do."

A lump rose in Callie's throat. Though her powers frightened her, she said, "I'll try again." If Rowan knew he'd become Fallen and he still found the courage to go on, she could at least master her gifts. She hesitated for a moment before bringing her palms to his. He smiled and laced their fingers.

Callie closed her eyes and tamped down on the anxiety in her chest. She exhaled. *Rowan.* She swept away all thoughts except for his name.

Sliding into Rowan felt like stepping into icy water. Inky blackness swirled around her, pulsating against her energy, threatening to devour it. It pressed against Callie, and finding no resistance, mingled like oil and water, together, but separate. The second they mixed, she was transported into his memory.

An angry man stood over her, so tall that she had to crane her neck to see him. Greasy blond hair fell across his face and his lips twisted into a snarl. Spittle flew from his mouth as he screamed. She doubled over, covering her ears. Her stomach ached empty. Ached and ached and ached.

The scene shifted and she stood on the edge of a small stream with a net in her tiny, pudgy hand. Then she was in the stream, soaking wet and freezing as the net drifted away. Two boys stood on the riverbank, howling with laughter.

Another jump and she held her bleeding knees to her chest, sobbing. In the distance, someone yelled at her to get up.

She was older now, in a gym with a red padded mat worn thin with use. A large boy stalked a circle around her, quarterstaff held ready. When he swung, he knocked the wind from her lungs and her feet from underneath her. She hit the mat with stars spinning behind her eyes.

She stared into a mirror, disgusted by the reflection with its bleeding lip and swollen eye. She pulled her fist back and slammed it into the mirror. The glass exploded around her like shrapnel.

She lay bleeding, her skin shredded to ribbons. A woman filled Callie's vision, her skin gray with death, her eyes wide.

Then, she was standing outside a cottage, the entrance nearly hidden by vines and flowers. The door opened and Sapphire stood smiling on the other side.

Callie flew from Rowan's mind as one might jump from a sinking ship. Her vision blurred with fresh tears and she buried her face in her hands to avoid his gaze. He touched her back, gently at first and then firmer when she didn't pull away. She could still feel the glass slicing her fist.

Someone banged on the door and they both jumped. The knob rattled. "Open up," Ash called. "It's over."

Rowan removed the chair and let Ash in. He stood just inside the apartment, gasping. His clothes created a puddle on the wood floor and his hair plastered his forehead. "Hazel," he said between breaths, "she won."

Callie caught the look of dread that passed over Rowan's features. Then his face hardened. "And the others?" he asked.

Ash's lips flattened. "The palace is in ruins. We need all the healers."

"Sapphire?" Callie breathed, feeling her throat close.

"She's okay," Ash said.

♦

Smoke slithered from holes in the palace walls. The porch sunk into itself as though it'd taken on one too many burdens. The jeweled doors lay thirty feet away, broken in half. Callie couldn't reconcile the scene before her. She blinked, willing the destruction to disappear. Once a grand, four-story structure, the palace was reduced to crumbling rubble.

Injured fae lay strewn in the grass, too weak to maintain glamours. For the first time, Callie saw scars and imperfection, a missing finger, a jagged, scarred cheek.

She searched for Sapphire, but found Cypress instead. The older woman crouched next to a man, healing the nasty gash on his forehead. She stood and wiped her face, smearing grime and blood. The dampness of her clothes chilled Callie's skin when they embraced. She smelled of smoke and sweat and despair.

"I was so worried."

"Sapphire?" Callie said.

"She's fine. She fought beautifully. You should've seen it."

"But she's okay?"

Cypress nodded. "This isn't anything we can't handle."

Callie went weak with relief. "Can I see her?"

Cypress glanced at Rowan and they shared a significant look. Cypress *knew* about her situation, Callie realized.

"I'm sorry, Callie. Hazel won't allow it," she said. Cypress hugged Ash and then Rowan, keeping a hand on Rowan's arm. "Walk with me a moment," she said, leading him away with an apologetic smile.

Callie assumed he was needed to heal the others. Their moans rose over the fading thunder and the random rumbles from the building settling into its new form. Her gaze went to the place that had been her prison for the past few weeks. When had she started to think of it as home? She'd miss the echoing emptiness of the corridors, the opulence she didn't deserve. She'd even miss Willow's intrusions and knowing Jack stood guard outside her door.

Then a worse thought—*where would she go?* Back to Sapphire's cottage, where the absence of her sister felt too full to withstand? To the apartments where Willow lived?

Ash's arm slid around her waist. "It's awful," he said, words laced with regret. Callie leaned into him. Though it'd stopped raining, the storm left the air damp and cold. Ash's clothes were wet, but heat from his body seeped through, warming her. "Hazel wants to see you."

Callie found herself searching for Rowan. He'd disappeared with Cypress into the chaos. Nausea filled her stomach. "Shouldn't we wait?"

She caught the darkness that traveled across Ash's face. "He can take care of himself," Ash said, misinterpreting her meaning. He used his arm to steer her away.

Callie hesitated.

"Or we can wait, but Hazel had a hard fight, we shouldn't—"

"Let's go then," she interrupted. She thought of sliding into Rowan's mind, how easy it was to see his memories. Maybe she could do the same to Hazel, actually see the truth for herself.

A hard little ball of fear lodged itself in her chest as they neared the portal to the caves. Callie felt responsible for the discord in *Eirensae*. Everything seemed so peaceful when she arrived, and despite her attempts to remain under the radar, every move she made seemed magnified—blown up until it affected every fae in the city.

What if Hazel knew Callie had found her amulet? What if she was waiting with it right now?

Callie almost asked Ash to turn back.

She bit her lip. She could be strong. She was more powerful than Hazel, wasn't that what everyone was telling her?

They stepped through the stone and Callie inhaled the heavy scent, comforted. She glanced at the library where she'd spent so much time with Rowan and Ash, longing for the familiarity and indifference of the books. Of all the beautiful things she'd seen here, the library was her favorite. She turned away with a sigh.

The blue orbs brightened when they entered the passageway to Hazel's pond. Hazel sprawled on her dais, eyes closed, head laid back. The coppery length of her hair was singed and hung in ragged chunks from her scalp. Her once gold gown was torn and bloody, showing pale, mangled skin through the rips. She opened her eyes, slowly, and gestured Callie closer.

"Leave us," she ordered Ash, her voice hoarse.

He dipped his head and backed through the mouth of the room, giving Callie an imploring look before he disappeared. She knew he wanted to stay, and if she were honest, she wished he could.

The older woman patted the cushion next to her, scooting to make room for Callie. She climbed up, noticing the blood that smeared the pillows. Hazel didn't seem to care. The suspended perch swayed in a slow, undulating pattern over the water.

"Hazel," Callie started when she didn't speak, "shouldn't someone heal you?" Thin lines of crimson spilled from gashes on her neck. A dark bruise, blue as an angry ocean spanned her forehead and blackened one of her eyes.

Hazel sighed and rubbed a dirty hand over her face. "Accepting a healer now would be admitting weakness. I will mend the old-fashioned way, though I assure you, I'm far from death's door. As a race, we are resilient. It'd take far more than one disgruntled faerie to take me down. When no one could find you after the challenge," Hazel drew a deep breath, winced, and continued, "I was worried. Sapphire had a vision of your future."

Callie's stomach leapt. "She did?"

"It's not much, just muddled flashes, but she's certain you'll leave us."

Callie swallowed, tasting the smoke that clung to Hazel's ruined dress. She remembered the human world she'd escaped; her foster family, the boy she'd never loved, the despair, heartache. Callie didn't want to go back. Then, even more awful, she imagined the Fallen, a faceless enemy that grew in her mind until they all resembled Elm.

Except one.

Rowan.

"What do you mean by leave?" she asked finally, keeping her tone neutral. She could evade the truth if she had to.

"She saw you surrounded by darkness. The vision is hazy, changing, but she thinks as the events draw closer, the images will clear. I've ordered daily reports, but I thought you should be aware." Hazel caught Callie's gaze and lifted her eyebrows. "You do realize how detrimental your departure would be for the city, especially after all the," she waved a hand, *"indecision* surrounding your arrival and the chaos I've moderated."

"I don't want to leave," Callie insisted. It wasn't a lie. Even though Rowan had given her that option, she didn't want to leave Sapphire, not if she didn't have to.

"Perhaps it'll be by force."

She froze. "Force?"

Hazel slid lower into the cushions, closing her eyes. Her words were soft. "It is your destiny to stand beside me. I won't accept anything less. Everything I've done is to keep you safe. I need to know where you stand."

The hairs on the back of Callie's neck stood. "Where else would I go?" Callie asked, thinking of the binding spell.

"There is no other safe place, child. I hope you know that. Find your amulet, bind yourself to me—to the city. Let me protect you." Her eyes opened to slits. "You do realize the danger we're in, under attack from all sides. You may be the only one who can defend the city, Callie. I need all of you. Sapphire needs all of you."

"But the wards," Callie said, thinking of the protection everyone seemed to take for granted.

"You're not listening." Hazel sat up and caught both of Callie's hands. "You *will* bind yourself."

And just like with Rowan and Ash, Callie slid inside of Hazel's mind.

She saw greed. It tasted bitter and black. She saw a man she didn't know. And she saw herself, wedged between Hazel and the man, her eyes vacant as a blank sheet of paper. A sea of unglamoured faeries stood before them, and as the man spoke, the faeries fell to their knees. A sharp, victorious smile spread across Hazel's mouth. Rowan was among them, an inky imprint spreading across his chest. He kept his gaze on Callie, even as his body bowed under the weight of her power.

Callie tugged her hands from Hazel's grasp and herself from the woman's mind, ignoring Hazel's sound of protest.

"I—uh," Callie said, backing off of the dais, dread filling her throat. "I gotta check on Sapphire."

"Sapphire's fine," Hazel called after her. "I saw her myself and you're not allowed…"

Hazel's voice faded away as Callie ran for the tunnels that led back to the city. Was this the future Sapphire had seen for Callie? She shuddered. She wouldn't be used. She felt stupid for trusting Hazel. Callie had played right into Hazel's hands.

Even now, with Sapphire under Hazel's control, Callie questioned herself.

She didn't know what to do.

ଔ✦ଈ

Rowan looked out over the wreckage, feeling his insides tighten. This was only the beginning of a long path of destruction. Beside him, Cypress wiped her hands and stood. He'd lost count of how many injured he'd healed. His head felt full of sandpaper, his ears rang.

"Not many more," she said with a smile. "The city is lucky to have you."

Rowan snorted and regretted it. "Doesn't seem that way."

"I know otherwise." Cypress hesitated and then led him out of earshot of the others who were working to clear the area of debris. "I've spoken with Sapphire. She's told me of your involvement with Callie."

He lifted his eyebrows, impressed with the risks Sapphire was willing to take for Callie. How did it feel to be so central to someone's existence? Most days, Rowan was an island. Uninhabited. *Lonely*. Yet, any other possibility terrified him. Love and caring were a two-way street. If he gave part of himself away, he became responsible to that person, his decisions would affect them.

It was better to remain alone.

"I know it hasn't been easy for you here." Cypress continued, laying a gentle hand on his arm. So few people touched him that the contact surprised Rowan, and he fought to keep his expression blank. "Sometimes I think you're stronger than any of us…more vital. I'm not Sapphire, and she's limited on what information she can give me." She

169

squeezed his arm and some of her healing energy cooled his skin. "She said you promised to protect Callie, and I wanted to thank you. We've lived this way for so long, I think we lost sight of what change feels like. I'm guilty of it just as much as anyone else."

Rowan swallowed and felt some unnamed emotion catch in his throat. He imagined it was something like love. Cypress and Sapphire, they'd always believed in him when no one else did, listened, when all other ears would rather tune him out. She made him wish he could stay.

"I don't know details, it's safer that way." She smiled now, and it transformed her face. Rowan thought he saw the same curve that turned Callie's mouth upwards. "Loud, disorderly revolutions never change the future. It's the quiet, determined movements that shape our paths and bring about change." She touched his face and then pulled him into an embrace. "I hope, one day, when we've put all this behind us and peace instead of war appears above our horizon, that we will sit and you will tell me the story in full." She hugged him tighter. "Just in case I don't get to say goodbye."

As Rowan moved on, stooping to heal a broken arm, he made his decision, or maybe he'd made it long ago. He'd stay two more weeks; spend as much time with Callie as he could, train her to defend herself, and then hope she made the right choice when the time came.

A little over a month remained of his two-year time limit to find his amulet. Sapphire had admitted that he wasn't from *Eirensae*. If he didn't leave on his own accord, his powers would be stripped, his longevity removed. Once outside, he'd have two weeks to figure out where he belonged and locate his amulet. If not, he'd have to accept life as a human.

There were worse things.

Still, the possibility of leaving Callie behind in *Eirensae* made him ache. He'd have to respect her decision, whatever it was.

♋ Thirteen ♋

"GOOD, YOU'RE BACK," Rowan said, striding toward Ash and Callie and catching Callie's elbow. "You're staying with me tonight." Before he said the words, he hadn't realized that was his intention. Jack, Callie's usual guard, had left along with Hawthorne and a few others to bring home the body of the child. He didn't want her out of his sight. Rowan let a chill fall over him. He'd keep her close, but not too close. It wasn't fair if he tried to muscle her out of *Eirensae*.

Next to Callie, Ash stiffened. "He'll protect you. You can worry about all this and everyone else in the morning. You need to sleep and you'll be safest with him, away from the city." Ash turned his back to Rowan, blocking Callie from Rowan's view though he still held her arm. "Please?"

Rowan felt rather than saw Callie's distracted frown. He tugged her arm. "Come on. You heard the man."

A few minutes later, Rowan held his cottage door open. The walk had been long and silent and Callie was shivering as she stepped around him and inside. Rowan shut the door and slid the wooden plank he used as a deadbolt into metal hooks.

"I thought nobody had locks here," she said, rubbing her arms. She was backlit by the dying fire. It turned her hair and skin golden.

"I do." He went to the fireplace and added a log, waiting until he could feel the flames.

Callie prowled his space, wearing her restlessness like armor. The cottage was neat. A single mattress took up the corner, covered with a green blanket. A cup was drying next to the sink. Apples and oranges filled a bowl in the center of the scarred table. His collection of weapons resided in the corner, the quarterstaff resting atop a sword, bow, and an overabundance of knives. She paused at his bureau.

"Are you tired?" he asked.

Callie startled and turned, wide-eyed. She lifted a shoulder. Her gaze traveled to the bed.

Rowan's stomach clenched. "It's the middle of the night. You should try to sleep."

She looked at him, face full of terror. He wished she would tell him who had hurt her so badly. He wanted to go to her as he had earlier, take her into his arms. He could still feel her there, soft weight against him as she cried. Needing his hands to be busy, he went to the counter and lit the two taper candles. When the tiny flames danced before him, he sat at the table and folded his hands, resting his chin. He wished she were tired. Rowan felt exhaustion in every inch of his body, but knew he wouldn't sleep, not with Callie this close.

Her voice broke the stillness. "I think you should apologize to Ash."

"For what?"

"You know what." She crossed her arms. He felt the ice of her stare from across the room.

"I'm sure Ash wouldn't appreciate you questioning his decision. It's safer for all of us to know how to fight. I'm sure he wouldn't like that you're a better fighter than him, either." He punctuated it with a grin, just to goad her further.

"Have you seen the bruises? That was more than training, Rowan, and you know it."

"It's nothing a little glamour won't fix. He can pretty up his face and while he's at it, maybe doctor up his body to be more to your liking."

Callie grew quiet, her gaze turning inward. He'd expected her to have a sharp comeback. She spent so long thinking that Rowan felt sweat bead in his hairline.

"You were right," she breathed. "I saw it inside Hazel's head."

"You saw Hazel?" Rowan said, pushing from his seat. "I told you to stay away from her." He went to stand next to Callie, as though too much distance between them put her in some kind of danger. "God, Callie. I meant what I said."

"I know," she exploded, waving her arms. "It was terrifying. I had this blank look, like my eyes were empty. All these fae were bowed before me. And Hazel was with some man." She met his gaze then. "You were there."

"So you'll leave, then?" he asked, quietly, afraid of her response.

Callie shook her head. "I can't. Not until I talk to Sapphire. I can't abandon her. Not without knowing what Hazel would do to her."

"It's too dangerous. Hazel will know."

"If it's so dangerous, how come you've done it? I saw it in your memory. I know where she lives."

Rowan flinched. "Sometimes you're too powerful for your own good."

"I need time to think. Elm already tried to kill me. If he's banished to the outside, what's to stop him from attacking me as soon as I leave? Plus there's the binding spell. It's not just going to disappear." She swallowed hard. "This isn't a choice I can make arbitrarily."

"I know." He wanted to touch her again. His insides ached with want of her. Silence swelled between them. Rowan took in the curve of her jaw, the way the scent of smoke clung to her clothes and skin. Callie was fragile and beautiful as glass. If he held her too tightly, she would shatter beneath him. He curled his fingers inwards to keep them at his sides.

"I want you to teach me about glamour," she said finally.

"What?" Rowan said, derailed from his fantasies.

"The night of the welcome ceremony, you said you'd show me what you look like sometime." She kept her gaze trained on the wall behind his head.

"No, I said *maybe* I'd show you sometime."

"Rowan…" Callie sighed, long and heavy. "Please. I need—" she broke off. "I need the distraction."

He could tell it cost her to ask. Rowan dragged a hand through his hair, catching tangles. He gestured to the seat across from him. She took it and mirrored his pose, resting both arms on the table.

"What do I need to do?"

Rowan thought of what hid beneath his glamour and offered her a grim smile. "Glamour is nothing more than a mask. Once you realize that, the edges of it become visible. It's like searching for a layer that's always been there. It's easier to ignore it than seek it out so our mind automatically skips over it." He touched his jaw. "Here's a good place to start. Focus right here until the lines of my face blur."

He watched, amused, as she went cross-eyed staring at his jaw.

"I don't see anything."

"Focus," he encouraged. When her eyes started to twitch, Rowan laughed. "Stop," he said between chuckles, "before you hurt yourself." He leaned back, enjoying her irritation. "My face isn't glamoured."

Callie glowered. "If you're going to make fun of me, I don't want to do this."

"I'm not making fun of you," he said, though the grin refused to leave his face. "I just wanted to see…" he trailed off. "Never mind." Standing, he slid out of his shirt. He knew what she saw, tanned, smooth skin over muscle. Hard lines and angles. She saw exactly what he'd put there.

"What are you doing?" Her cheeks turned pink.

"This," Rowan said, gesturing to himself, "is a glamour."

Confusion washed her face and she glanced up, searching him. "Are you trying to tell me you're actually fat?"

His lips quirked. "No." He touched the edge of his ribs. Callie's eyes followed his fingers and her gaze felt warm as a touch. "Start here."

෪◆ଓ

Callie inhaled slowly, held it, and let it go. If she didn't know that glamour existed, she'd feel like an idiot. Rowan's skin was perfect, spanning a flat stomach, layered over muscle and the sharp curve of bones. His waist tapered inward where his pants hung from his hips. His expression, stretched tight as though he wished to be anywhere else but ensconced in the dark with her, made Callie's stomach tingle with nerves.

"Concentrate," Rowan said, voice tense.

He was edgy, and that didn't make her feel any better. She fixed her gaze where his fingers rested against his ribs, glad that the exercise called for staring. There was something about the boys of *Eirensae,* something that made them unbelievably attractive. Maybe it was a faerie thing.

This time, instead of only seeing skin and bone, Callie found a shimmering edge, a layer that didn't belong. "I see it," she said, excited.

"Good." His words sounded off. "I want you to peel it away like the dead skin of a sunburn."

Callie ignored her disgust. She imagined the thin, almost invisible layer curling, stretching, and pulling away from Rowan's golden skin. She watched, fascinated, as the glamour obeyed, inch by inch. What lay underneath was littered with raised scars. They crisscrossed over the bone, angry pale marks that distorted his torso. She managed only a thin strip before the glamour fell back into place. Without thinking, she pressed a hand to his side. It was warm and firm under her palm, electric, smooth.

She glanced up. "What happened to you?"

Rowan remained frozen, so still she wasn't sure he was breathing.

"So you did it then. Good." He stepped away and moved to the fireplace, adding another log. The sound of fire devouring wood crackled through the room.

She stared at his back, now finding the edge of the glamour easily. It peeled away just above his shoulder blade, revealing more scarred skin. Nausea turned her stomach and she swallowed it down.

"Rowan?" She remembered being inside of his mind, seeing his flesh torn to shreds. It was true, then.

He tensed. Balled his hands into fists. Callie's steps scraped across the dirt floor. Rowan didn't turn. The heat from the fire and Rowan's scent hit her at the same time. She lifted trembling hands. They hung in the air between them, indecisive. She couldn't breathe.

"Go ahead," he said, hoarse. He lowered his head and hair fell across his face, hiding his expression.

Callie wished she knew what he was thinking.

She touched him gently, as though the scars still caused him physical pain. The glamour dissolved, and Rowan—the *real* Rowan—stood before her. Scars covered his torso and arms, some long and straight, others jagged as though someone had torn through his flesh with a serrated blade. She traced a thick, hard ridge in the center of his back and he tensed further. This scar had an equally ugly twin on the opposite side, just as wide and rough.

A deep desire to seek justice boiled inside Callie, bitter and burning, taking her by surprise. Her throat ached and she bit her lip, fighting emotion. Rowan's memories swept her mind. His foster homes were not safe places to live.

Someone had hurt Rowan, and hurt him badly.

She moved closer, sliding her hands from his back, over the ridges of his ribs, until they stilled on his chest. The fire warmed his skin and their energy mingled with the contact. She flattened her palms, feeling the slight down of chest hair, the stilted rise and fall of his breaths, and underneath, the steady drumming of his heart.

Callie pressed her cheek to Rowan's ruined back. She wished she could take it away.

Seconds passed, and then minutes. Rowan didn't move.

Wetness pooled beneath Callie's cheek, silent tears that slid from her eyes and trailed Rowan's skin. The fire continued to crackle, the cheerful sound at odds with the emotions tumbling inside her.

His scars tore at her insides as though she'd experienced them herself. No wonder Rowan had walls to keep everyone out. She knew exactly what that was like. If you let your guard down, even for a moment, you risked everything tumbling out.

And he'd trusted her with this. Fresh tears filled her eyes.

It was a long while before Rowan turned from her touch. She let him go, dropping her arms. They faced each other. Rowan's expression was guarded and distant. Callie felt like she'd just leapt from a hundred-story building. Her stomach was in her throat when their eyes met. The glamour was back, she realized, his chest and arms now smooth.

Rowan brushed tears from her cheeks with his thumbs. "Please don't cry." His voice belied the calm of his expression, too heavy and thick. "It was a long time ago. Don't cry for me."

"I'm sorry," she whispered.

Rowan rested his forehead against hers. One of his hands traveled to the back of her neck. His palm was damp with her tears. He pulled away too soon, leaving her lips parted and expecting.

She ached all over, her skin stretched taut as though it wasn't quite strong enough to hold everything inside. She'd felt powerless before, so inconsequential that she'd wished she would disappear. This was different. No amount of grief or words would heal the damage. She wished she were like Rowan. She wished she could touch him and heal it all.

She flashed back to when she was inside his mind, when he lay broken and bleeding. She wanted to ask why. The words scraped against the end of her tongue, but refused to fall.

How could she look at Rowan the same? She'd always know what he carried underneath, what haunted him. Part of her wished she could push the rewind button and unlearn.

"Don't you want to see yourself unglamoured?" Rowan asked.

Callie wiped her eyes, feeling foolish. He hadn't shown her his scars as some attempt to win her over, or seek her consolation; he'd shown her as a teaching tool. She sniffed and swallowed the thickness in her throat.

Rowan led her to the tiny mirror above the sink. The glass was cracked in one corner and mottled her reflection. Her eyes were red and swollen, her cheeks pale. Rowan's face filled the space next to hers.

"This glamour is harder to peel away," Rowan said, businesslike. "The one I wear is something I did myself, not as strong as the glamour given to us when we're born and sent into the human world.

It's thick and durable, drawing from the collective energy of *Eirensae*, and involves much more magic than simply hiding a few scars. It doesn't waver like mine would if I was injured or weak."

Callie frowned and met his gaze in the glass. "So those scars—they aren't what you really look like?"

"Yes and no." He put his hand on her shoulder. "The scars are real, but there's more. We'll get there in time. Right now let's focus on you." He slid his fingers to the sensitive skin of her forearm. "Let's start here. Your faerie form involves your entire body."

"It does?" Callie said, remembering the alligator lady with green scales from head to toe. She hoped she wasn't green. Or scaly.

Rowan chuckled, obviously sensing her distress. "Don't be scared. It's not bad. I promise." He lifted her arm, gently encircling her wrist with his fingers. "Find the edge of the glamour just like you did before. You'll need more concentration to remove this one and it won't work if you get frustrated."

Callie's arm looked the same as it always had. A small trio of freckles gathered on her wrist, and further up, she had a mole shaped like a heart. Her arm hair was sparse and bleached from the sun. But there, just at the edge, she caught the flicker of glamour. "Found it," she breathed. Rowan remained silent as she tried to peel it away. The glamour was such a tiny difference that she had a hard time keeping hold of it. Every time she pulled it away with her mind, it snapped back into place.

She sighed.

Rowan dropped her arm. "You can't get upset. Think about something else for a minute."

"Like what?" she grumbled, feeling the first pains of a headache between her brows.

He narrowed his eyes. "Ash?"

"Seriously?"

Holding up both hands, Rowan said, "It'll work. Trust me."

She stared at him. Was he being obnoxious on purpose? "Fine," she said. Closing her eyes, she pictured Ash, the endless green of his eyes, the way his copper hair curled at his hairline. She thought of the freckles that bridged his nose and the webbing between his fingers when he was unglamoured.

Her heart squeezed.

She was in over her head with all of it.

At least here, with Rowan beside her, she was safe.

Callie rolled her shoulders, ready to try again. She let her thoughts dissipate like smoke in a breeze. When she lifted her arm, she was pleased to see that it was easier to locate the line of glamour. She exhaled, finding the energy that curled inside her. She willed the glamour away, as she'd done with Rowan. Millimeter by millimeter, the glamour lifted. Brilliant blue light escaped through the tiny crack, nearly blinding her in the darkness.

She gasped, and the glamour slid back into place.

ꕥ♦ꕥ

"I'm blue," Callie said.

Rowan grinned. He focused on her until he saw what she did. Callie's skin glowed gentle blue, her energy swirled just beneath the surface, wispy as clouds at sunset. She was pure power, so strong that her skin couldn't contain it.

"You're beautiful," he said, willing his glamour away. The light from her skin turned his scars purple.

"Why?" she asked, relief evident in her expression. "Why am I blue?"

"We just *are*. There's not any one reason for our abilities."

She turned her arm over. The skin was thinner there, and darker blue veins snaked under the surface. Her blood glowed, too, pulsating just beneath fragile skin.

"This is crazy," she said.

Rowan hesitated, hand still resting on her arm. He couldn't believe what he was about to do.

"What is it?" she asked.

"Do you want to see me?" He wished he could take back the offer. But the words were there.

"See you?"

"Without glamour. I can try to remove it for you." He grinned. "Or we can get drunk. I have some wine."

"Um…" She met his gaze in the mirror.

"Come on, live a little." He gave her his most disarming smile, questioning why he bothered. He didn't *want* to show her, did he?

She arched one eyebrow. "From what I understand, I'm nearly immortal. I don't think I have a choice."

"It'll be easier if we drink." He meant it'd be easier for *him* if he drank. "Just a few sips. Promise." He saw Callie's resolve wavering.

"Maybe we should just go to bed."

He couldn't help himself. His eyebrows lifted and he glanced at his mattress. "Oh, yeah?"

She sighed. He sensed victory.

"Okay," she conceded.

Rowan went to the cupboard and retrieved a clear, long-necked bottle with a bulbous bottom. The brew fizzled when he uncorked it, emitting violet sparks like a mini firework. He took a swig, not bothering with a glass. The semi-sweet flavor of berries and flowers lit a fire down to his belly leaving a honey aftertaste.

"I can't believe I'm doing this," she said when he handed her the wine. She took a sip, and then a longer drink. Rowan watched her throat work as she swallowed. What it would taste like if he pressed his lips there. Flowers? Vanilla? Honey? When she was done a bit of the bright concoction dribbled from her mouth and Rowan nearly groaned. Already the drink was making his limbs warm and his thoughts fuzzy. It wouldn't take long for his inhibitions to disappear. He took the bottle back and gulped.

Two weeks, Rowan thought. How could he fit an eternity into fourteen days? And how would he survive if she didn't leave with him?

He'd find a way to come back, he decided. He couldn't leave her. No matter what.

Rowan gathered Callie against him, surprised when she came willingly. She felt small in his arms as they spun around the tiny cottage. His hands were in her hair, pressed against her shoulder blades, curved around her hips. Callie threw her head back and laughed, and though they hadn't had much to drink, Rowan wasn't sure if she'd remember in the morning and why it bothered him if she didn't. There was no music, but they danced slow, bodies fused together like lovers, they danced fast, their feet barely touching the floor.

Rowan had never felt more alive. Here, where it didn't matter that he was unimprinted and unimportant. Here, on the eve of the rest of his life, he wanted to tell Callie everything.

It terrified him, even when he was full of liquid courage. So when they stopped moving and stood, arms tangled, sweating and breathing hard, panic closed his throat. There was a second bottle of wine above his sink and he debated another gulp for good measure, but knew if he did, he would forget this night, and it seemed important somehow. Instead, he slid his hands from Callie. She glowed now, the blue of her skin a beacon in the darkness. The warmth of her cheeks turned the color slightly purple. Her hair hung in loose waves that framed her face. Her eyes were bright.

He stepped away. "Ready?"

Callie closed the careful distance he'd put between them. She touched his cheeks, smoothed damp strands of hair from his face. He could see himself reflected in her eyes.

"Promise you won't be afraid." The words sounded small. Embarrassed. The scars should've been the hard part. They were visible now, crisscrossing his flesh, marking him for what he was, reminding him of what he'd done, of the life he'd taken.

"I promise," Callie whispered.

෫ ♦ ౪

Rowan slipped away from her, moving closer to the fire. She felt the absence of him in the cool air that slid against her sweaty skin. The intensity of her glow was difficult to look at, like staring at the sun after walking out of a darkened movie theater. It wasn't so bad, she decided, liking the way the blue energy twisted inside her like a kaleidoscope.

181

He met her gaze from across the room, backlit by the blazing fire. She was drunk, too warm. Everything felt sloppy, loose, disconnected.

Why were her fae markings so obvious when Rowan's continued to hide even after the wine had stripped away their glamour?

"You sure?" he asked, as though sensing her unease.

Her focus went from his scruffy, too-long hair, skipped across the scars on his chest and stomach, and lowered to his dirt-caked toenails. Callie searched for any remaining worry over Hazel's thoughts. She found none, but it was always that way with Rowan, as though he scattered her judgment and overshadowed her worries.

Callie nodded. Her heart thundered against her ribs, wishing to be independent of its bindings. She flattened her hand there, in case it managed to escape. What was this warmth inside of her? She was still dizzy from dancing, her skin layered with a light sheen of sweat. She hoped this night never ended. Tomorrow, when she was sober, everything would come crashing back.

But right now, she was Rowan's, and he was hers.

Rowan lowered his head.

A strange sound filled the room, that of tearing flesh and rustling fabric. Rowan shook his shoulders, as though fighting a chill. Callie held her breath.

He exhaled and massive wings rose behind him. They were oily, feathered, and intense, almost absent of color, and hurt her eyes as though she stared into absolute darkness. They grew, unfurled, stretching larger and larger until they finally stopped just before the tips reached the ceiling. The feathered points draped the floor. She couldn't fathom how he carried them on his back. She couldn't look away, couldn't breathe. Couldn't speak. Callie was intrigued, horrified, and a million other things she couldn't name. Blackness threatened the edges of her vision, or maybe it was just Rowan's wings. They seemed to suck all the light to them and blot it out.

Rowan waited, impossibly still.

"Can you fly?" she stammered eventually, mortified at her choice of words. They were just so... *huge.*

He stretched, opening his wings until he resembled a bird of prey in glorious flight. They spanned the entire length of the cottage. Rowan was a fallen angel, dark and dangerous; yet so beautiful that she couldn't look away.

"Yes," he said quietly, "I can fly."

"That's—" She nodded frantically. Swallowed. "That's…it's…whoa." Callie stumbled backwards. "I need to sit down." The floor rose up to meet her and Rowan's gaze followed her descent. She buried her face in her arms and took deep breaths.

Rowan had wings.

Rowan could *fly*.

When she finally looked up, he hadn't moved but continued to stare as though he expected her to run. He took a tentative step, and then another, watching her cautiously. His wings hovered like a shadow behind him, ominous as a thundercloud.

He was magnificent.

Up close, the exquisiteness made her throat hurt. He pulled the length closer to his body, but even tucked against his skin, their sheer size didn't diminish. He was scarred, dark…*beautiful*. And like a horrific car accident, Callie stared.

He knelt, eyes on the floor. She took in the soft curve of his wings, the delicate skin at his throat where his pulse thrummed, the roadmap of scars.

"Touch me," he whispered.

She couldn't fathom her thoughts into actions. Callie's muscles had turned to stone.

"Please," Rowan begged, *"please."*

Callie wanted to cry.

He was Rowan, and at the same time, he wasn't. Gone was the strong, certain boy she'd come to expect, with his razor tongue and careless actions. Gone was the cockiness. The wall he hid behind. On his knees before her, he was raw, exposed.

She'd read the books in the library. There was a word for faerie markings like his. *Predatory*.

The fae who chose to inhabit Fraeburdh have mostly animalistic markings, which favor predatory beasts, such as wolves, cats, and birds of prey. Some have the ability to hide their faerie form, making it easy for them to move amongst humans and other fae unnoticed.

It didn't matter where he came from, she decided. She never wanted to be without him.

Callie raised her hand, surprised to see it fill the charged space between them. Her energy cast an eerie blue glow, which his wings absorbed, as if they stole her power. Rowan caught her wrist just before her fingertips grazed his left wing. He swallowed, released her, and looked away. Her fingers delved into the soft spray of feathers. They felt impossibly light, much thinner than any feather she'd held before, glossier, and softer than silk. She slipped her fingers between them, feeling a delicate web of fragile bone and gentle counter pressure of tissue underneath. He smelled dark, like the earth beneath an ocean, mixed with salt and faerie wine.

Rowan made a sound low in his throat and Callie withdrew her hand, startled. "Am I hurting you?"

The shadows in the room had grown long, and Rowan's eyes were black as pitch when he shook his head and returned her hand to his wing. She stroked it again, higher and higher, pushing to her knees so she could see where they joined his back. The wings rose from the space between his shoulder blades, arcing gracefully from beneath a thin layer of down. He was scarred here, too, as though someone had tried to hack off his wings with a handsaw. She traced the curving scars, splayed her hands across the wing bases.

Slowly, Callie became aware of how close they were. She had both arms around him where he knelt, the side of her breast pressed against his cheek. Her pulse jumped. She sat back, embarrassed by her unbridled curiosity. Heat crept up her neck and into her face as she struggled to control her breathing, which was too fast, as if she'd run a marathon. Her skin felt tight, itchy. Her head buzzed.

"Becoming Fallen doesn't stop you from assimilating into the human world," Rowan said, looking away, expression impenetrable. "My foster father was exiled from a faerie city—I don't know which one because I didn't put it all together until I came here." He reached for her hand and held it tightly, as though drawing courage.

"He had so many foster kids over the years, and then one day, he got lucky. I discovered my healing power a few months before my eighteenth birthday. It was an accident—" His eyes were far away now. "My foster mom cut her hand making dinner. It was bad…and when I went to wrap it in a towel, it just happened. The cut disappeared. Of course, she was freaked out, but my foster father got this wild, greedy look. That night he tried to kill me."

Callie shuddered and Rowan squeezed her fingers before continuing.

"Back then, I didn't know that he wanted to be Immortal, or even that the fae existed. I'll spare you the details because you've seen the scars, but he tried to drain my blood. Almost succeeded, too. I remember lying there thinking, *this is it*. But then my foster mom found us." He swallowed hard and when he met her gaze, his eyes were wet.

"She opened his skull with a golf club, but not before he stabbed her." He pressed a hand to his an invisible wound in his stomach. "She pulled herself over to me and we lay there, helpless, bleeding out together. She kept telling me I'd be okay, it'd be okay. When she took my hand," his voice broke, "I didn't know what I was doing. Her energy just came to me. The cuts started healing and the pain eased. I could've healed her, but instead, I stole her life…her energy. I killed her so I could live."

Rowan swallowed. "I'm no better than him. She was always so good to me, and I just watched her die."

Callie couldn't read Rowan's expression. The urge to say something important overcame her, but she had no idea what that something was. She rubbed the goosebumps on her arms, licked her lips, tasting salt. "It wasn't your fault," she said finally.

Rowan exhaled, the scent of his breath sweet on her face. "Tell me."

"Tell you what?" she whispered, even though she knew what he wanted. He'd exposed everything, right down to the very core. She couldn't remember a more honest moment in her life.

"What happened to you. I saw some of it in your memory, but…"

"I can't," she said, nausea turning her stomach.

"Can't or won't?" Rowan asked.

"Both."

"Liar." He flattened his palms on the dirt floor, curled his fingernails, making angry gouges there.

"Can't," she said. "Can't lie."

"Oh Callie," he whispered, finally looking up. She felt as if he saw right through her. "Lying is as easy as breathing."

"I'm drunk."

"You're not drunk."

"I am."

Rowan sighed and stood.

Callie forced herself to watch him. "I'm not drunk enough," she amended. She knew this was one of those situations where two people opened up to one another and then had life-affirming sex. She'd read enough books to know how it worked. But sex would never be life affirming to Callie—if she had her way, sex would never be anything to her.

She could tell him, just let it all pour out of her until she was empty, but then he would feel the same way about her as she felt about him. There would be pity in his eyes when he looked at her, a hesitance to his touch.

She couldn't do it.

Rowan held out a hand, shoving it annoyingly close to her face, until she had to either take it or bat it away. He jerked her to her feet, too hard. She stumbled against him. He caught her, and for a brief moment, they embraced. Rowan moved away quickly.

Callie reached for the bottle of wine, disappointed to find it empty. Rowan plucked it away, setting it with a thud of finality on the table. "You've had enough, anyway," he said.

She frowned, hands fluttering like nervous birds. "I haven't had enough."

Rowan chuckled. "We're going to bed."

Callie's eyes wandered to the bed, lingered there as she imagined all the ways they could lay there together. The words were out before she could stop them. "Where are you going to sleep?"

"In a tree, obviously."

"What?"

"I'm kidding." He pushed her toward the bed with gentle hands. "Go to sleep."

"Okay." Callie lay on the bed. Rowan's scent surrounded her. She rolled, pressing her face into his pillow, inhaling him. If she weren't drunk, or shocked, she would've been mortified.

ಹ Fourteen ೧೩

CALLIE SLEPT, FACE hidden beneath Rowan's pillow. Her unconsciousness was absolute, like that of an infant napping in a crowded, loud room. He knew she must be exhausted after the long day combined with the faerie wine. Fatigue filled his body, but Rowan ignored it. He'd stood vigil, watching her first from the kitchen table, and later, next to the bed. He kept thinking she'd wake and notice him, but she slept soundlessly through the remainder of the night.

Though it was childish, Rowan worried how Callie would react to him when she woke. The effects of faerie wine were unpredictable, and if you drank enough of it, comparable to the lurching insanity of a bad acid trip. He hoped he wouldn't morph into some giant, disfigured beast in her mind. The apt description had Rowan's gaze sliding to her again. God, he was an idiot, telling her all that. What had he hoped to accomplish? Maybe he thought Callie would sympathize with him. Maybe he thought his scars wouldn't frighten her, but draw her closer to him.

He was so stupid.

She'd never want to leave with him. Especially not now, knowing that he carried markings from the City of War.

Rowan knew his path—his inevitable departure from *Eirensae*, but was more concerned with Callie. He didn't think he'd sleep easy until she made her decision to stay or go, though after she made it, he might never sleep easy again.

When the first strains of daylight crept through his windows, the sound of nearly silent footsteps ghosted into the cottage. *Ash,* he thought, recognizing his best friend's movement even before he knocked. Rowan slipped the wood plank out of the door and let Ash inside.

Ash looked terrible, tired, face pinched with worry, the angry bruise from Rowan's fist darkening his jaw. Rowan imagined he didn't look much better. Ash's gaze went to the bed. Rowan told himself he didn't resent the propriety he saw in the other boy's face. He lifted a finger to his lips and gestured that they should go outside, leaving the door open a crack just in case she woke.

"I spoke with Hazel this morning," Ash said, sitting on the grass, combing through the long strands with his fingers. He wore the same clothes from yesterday, the wind picked up the tattered fabric, which flapped like flag of surrender.

The sun was barely a burning slice over the horizon but the brightness hurt Rowan's eyes. A headache throbbed in the center of his brain. "And?"

Ash lifted a shoulder. "She's only concerned with Callie. She doesn't care that the city is falling apart. She ordered me to keep an eye on her." Ash met Rowan's gaze. "And you."

"We can't trust her," Rowan muttered. He didn't buy her lazy attitude or the way she regarded problems as non-issues. For the leader of a city, she was too passive, standing up only when someone questioned her status, content to remain hidden in *Eirensae* behind the wards that protected her. He'd never seen her step foot outside the city.

She had something to hide. Then again, who didn't? Rowan wasn't exactly forthright with everything he knew, either.

"She's our leader, Row. If we can't trust her, then who?"

"Sapphire," he said, glancing around to make sure they wouldn't be overheard. "She knows more than she's saying, and I suspect she hasn't told Hazel."

Ash went still.

Rowan stopped him before he could say anything. "All I know is that Callie and I are involved up to here in it." He held his hand at eye level, meeting his friend's gaze. He almost told Ash about Sapphire seeing Callie as the catalyst for the impending war. He just couldn't make himself say the words. "And I'm leaving. Two weeks," Rowan supplied when Ash looked surprised. "Don't pretend you didn't know."

"There's still time to find your amulet. You're going to give up? I can't believe you." Ash shoved to his feet, glowering down at Rowan. "I thought you were better than that. Ever since Callie fell through the pond, you've changed. I don't know what's wrong with you, but the Rowan I know wouldn't give up. Not ever."

"I'm not giving up, I'm accepting my fate. Besides—" He swallowed, not wanting to say the words aloud. *'Besides,* Sapphire told me that I don't belong here. As in, I *do* belong somewhere else. Another city, I guess."

"That's crazy and you know it," Ash said, voice rising.

Rowan jerked his thumb angrily at the still open door and Ash quieted down.

"You came through the wards. You know how it works."

"Are you telling me Sapphire's wrong?" Rowan asked. Ash didn't have an answer to that so Rowan continued. "There is war coming, and the city will never survive with Hazel leading it. When Joshua died, we lost our strategist, and Hazel wasn't smart or effective enough to carry on his practices. We're defenseless, against the City of *War,* against *Immortals,* Ash. Don't you get it? The child that died? Someone used her to create an Immortal. Even I don't know how to kill one of those. Guess who else can be used to create an Immortal? Callie. She's not safe, Ash. Not here, and certainly not on the outside."

Ash went pale as the enormity of Rowan's words finally sank in. "Then we have to find your amulet."

"I already told you. My amulet's not here."

"You know when you're leaving?" Callie said from the doorway, interrupting their argument.

Rowan flinched and dropped his head into his hands. Maybe he'd wanted her to overhear. They hadn't exactly been quiet. Her face was carefully composed when he finally got the courage to turn. Callie's clothes were rumpled; a red imprint of his pillow still marked her cheek. She'd pulled her hair into a messy bun on top of her head. She looked soft, so soft that he wanted to take her into his arms and make promises.

"Where will you go?" she asked quietly when he didn't answer.

"I don't know," he said, honest. He'd survive. He'd survived worse, after all. At least he'd be of age this time, no longer a target for the Fallen.

Unlike Callie.

She folded herself next to Rowan on the step, keeping her gaze on him. A moment of unspoken words passed between them. Callie pushed loose strands of hair behind her ears, eyebrows furrowed with thought. "Then teach us to fight. All of us," she said.

"Hazel will never—" Rowan interjected.

"Forget Hazel. You didn't see her last night. She's in bad shape, not fit to dictate what any of us does." Her voice took on a hard edge. "Ash and I will gather anyone who's interested and meet you in the forest in an hour." She touched his arm with a bed warm hand, a million emotions swimming in her eyes, the most prominent of which was trust. "Please, Rowan. We have to teach them how to protect themselves."

Slowly, Rowan nodded, enjoying the answering smile on Callie's face. He didn't know how the tiny fizzle of hope inside of him would pan out, but at least it was there, and at least it was burning.

ଛୀ✦ଔ

Callie and Ash divided and conquered. Most of the fae were up early, helping clear rubble. The palace huddled, a fallen giant in the center of the city, occasionally belching clouds of smoke and rumbling as the fae depleted the remaining structure.

Callie hadn't really considered Rowan's departure, despite his days dwindling down like grains of sand in an hourglass. He was too big, too permanent—too *alive*. She tried to imagine him as human, wingless, *powerless,* it stripped Rowan of everything that made him, like applying turpentine to canvas. He was fae, from the glimmering black energy beneath his skin to the thundercloud wings rising from his back. He simply couldn't be undone or unmade. They couldn't steal his future based on ancient, worn-out rules any more than they could dictate Callie's because she was a child. She refused to be controlled. They were the same in that way.

She'd finally decided that she would leave *Eirensae* with Rowan. The how still eluded her.

In the end, they gathered a meager group of fourteen for training, though the city's population was well into the hundreds. Callie appreciated the familiar faces, Cypress, Sai, Willow, Chicory, and Ash; though she wished Sapphire could've come. Callie missed her sister, and more, she was afraid for her. But if Callie stayed, Hazel could use Sapphire against her, or force Callie to use her powers on Sapphire. Callie wouldn't risk her sister, and she hoped the rest of the city would protect their prophetess if it came down to it.

Rowan didn't seem impressed by the assembly, but he was a thorough instructor nonetheless. By the end of the training session, Callie's muscles were sore and sweat beaded in her hairline. She'd fought Ash and Willow, tried her hand again Sai—who'd already trained as a warrior. She'd allowed Rowan to toss her around like a boneless doll to demonstrate falling.

Ash threw himself into the training, determination in every step, dragging himself from the ground so many times that Callie knew he'd have trouble walking home. Willow had looked bored and offended that she was required to get dirt under her nails. They practiced for one hour, and agreed to meet again the following day.

Time, though nearly endless for the fae, had made its presence known. How far would the training take them in two weeks? Callie didn't want to leave her friends unprotected. She also couldn't let

Rowan wander into the human world alone. He was only one who could protect her on the outside.

A hard ball of dread wedged itself in her stomach. What would life be like out there? Where would they go? Callie shoved the thoughts away. One step at a time.

She stretched, wincing. "I need a shower." She twisted her arm to inspect a growing streak of midnight, a memento of Rowan's quarterstaff. Ash encircled her bicep, and lowered his lips to the bruise. Callie's eyes widened and shifted to Rowan. Her mouth tightened when their gazes collided.

"I'm going to the library," Rowan said, flicking his sweat soaked hair from his forehead. His eyes followed Ash's hand as it slid into Callie's before moving to her face. She wished she could read Rowan's expression and that he hadn't rebuilt the walls they'd torn down the night before.

Self-conscious, she slipped her hand from Ash's and rubbed a sore spot on her shoulder, but Rowan had already stalked off, following the path the others had taken. Callie watched his retreating back, trying to see the wings he so carefully concealed. A headache formed between her eyebrows and she gave up.

"Should we study?" Ash asked. He kissed Callie's cheek and she smiled, though the movement felt forced and unnatural. Rowan had disappeared into the trees and Callie's fear bloomed into terror. What if Rowan just vanished? What if he changed his mind about protecting her and the last time she saw him it was with disappointment written all over his face? Ash caught her hand again and Callie jerked it away.

"I can't do this."

"Study?" Ash said, confused.

"No." She held up both her hands, palms to Ash and focused on a spot of bark behind his head to avoid the hurt that spread across his pale face. When the words didn't come, Callie dropped her hands and swallowed hard. All she could think about was Rowan, and the distance between them, and how it felt like miles and impossible miles.

When Ash spoke, his voice was hesitant. "I know you're hurting—I've known it since the day you arrived. I wish you trusted me enough to tell me." He moved closer, touched her face.

Guilt closed Callie's throat and she swallowed hard.

"I'll tell you something instead." Ash moved closer so that all Callie could see was the endless green of his eyes. "There is so much change happening in *Eirensae*. Things that we never thought would come to be." He glanced away, briefly, and Callie knew he was thinking of Rowan. "I'm scared," he said. "I'm scared for us, and for you, and what will happen."

"Ash—"

"I've never cared much for myself. When I found out that I belonged to the fae, things finally made a bit more sense. Here, I fit. But there are days, especially lately, that I wonder if I'm not serving my purpose. I know my amulet dictates my status and future, but that route feels empty. With you," he paused here, searching her face, "with you, things make even more sense. What scares me most about all the change—you know, the Fallen and the deaths—is that it could've been you. I'm nothing more than a teacher. I'm not a warrior; I have no training, and I'm so *terrified* that—"

"Ash," Callie repeated, pressing her hand to his lips. They were velvet beneath her fingers. The lump in her throat grew from a walnut to a grapefruit. Callie cared for Ash more than she wanted to admit—more than was fair, to either him or Rowan. "You can't feel like that—like *this.*" She tugged his hand gently from her face, keeping it cradled in both of hers. "I'm not good for you. I'm sorry that I let you think that...that this could somehow work. But I have to figure out things for myself and—"

"What are you saying?" Ash interrupted, suddenly cold as stone.

Callie released his hand. "I'm sorry."

"I get it," he said, backing away and shoving a hand through his hair, making it stand on end. "It's fine." He shook his head, so slowly that Callie didn't think he realized he was doing it. "Really. It's fine." He made a disgusted sound, something between a snort and cough, and turned away. Callie watched him weave between the trees, much as

Rowan had. Her two lifelines, pulling her in opposite directions, tighter and tighter, until nothing remained but the impending snap.

She wished she could talk to Jack, but even he was gone, out retrieving the body of the child they'd lost.

℥◆℞

"Shouldn't you be with Callie?" Rowan barked when Callie slipped into the library a short while later. He glanced up from the leather bound book in his lap. "Oh. It's you."

Callie stood frozen in the doorway, suddenly feeling like an intruder. From this angle, she couldn't see the title of his book, but judging by the sketches of swords, it had to do with weaponry. Rowan watched her carefully, as though he expected her to make a sudden move.

"Thank you for training everyone today." The words gusted from her mouth and she used them to propel herself into the cool green of the library. The midafternoon sun sent rainbow prisms of lights onto the books and floor. One of them glinted off Rowan's hair, turning it oily as a raven's wing.

She needed to tell him her plan. That she wanted to go with him when he left the city. She needed his help to figure out how to remove the binding spell.

He grunted and slammed the book shut. The title was in Gaelic, but she recognized one of the words: *Fraeburdh*. Rowan tossed it onto the broad surface of the tree stump table. "What do you want?"

Callie stilled again, a deer caught in the twin beams of headlights. Last night, Rowan's arms had been around her, the length of their bodies fused like moss draping a branch. Just this afternoon his hands had encircled her throat as they demonstrated how to escape a chokehold and she'd felt strong and safe.

Now, however, she needed twenty hands just to keep hold of all the strings. Rowan waited for her to answer, mouth pressed tight, one eyebrow lifted. "Well?" he prompted. What had caused the sudden change?

"I broke up with Ash," Callie said, forcing her legs to take her between the stacks. She *had* to tell him. Even if he scoffed her, even if he made her feel stupid. "I mean…we weren't together. But…I just—"

"Last night was a mistake," Rowan said, standing. He returned his book, nestling it between two leather hardbacks on the living shelves. "I shouldn't have told you those things—*we* shouldn't have…" he trailed off. "I'm not trying to persuade you to leave with me. I know that's what it looks like, but it's your decision, Callie. I never—"

Callie moved out of Rowan's view. She heard him return to the table and sit again. She slid a book from the shelf. Inside, her amulet nestled against the pages, brilliant blue against pale cream. She picked up the leather cord carefully and returned the tome to its place.

With the amulet swinging in front of her like a talisman, she carried it back to Rowan and dropped it on the table in front of him.

Rowan's mouth opened then closed again. "Is that?" he whispered.

Callie pressed both palms to the smooth, worn table and leaned close to Rowan's face, emboldened by finally making her choice. "I'm going with you." She held up a hand before he could speak. "You didn't coerce me. Last night was…special and I'm glad you trusted me with your past." Callie shook her head, trying to dislodge the emotion in her throat. "For my entire life, I've been told what to do and where to go. I've been part of a flawed system that hurt me more than helped me. But I'm not helpless anymore. I'm strong, and last night you helped me realize that I don't just have to accept what everyone has told me. I can make my own way, and that's what I'm going to do."

"Callie—" Rowan started.

"No," she interrupted. "I'm not done. I don't know what we'll find out there, but you've promised to protect me and I believe you. But I need another promise from you. I need to know that we will try to find a way to get Sapphire out of this. I can't leave her behind without it."

Rowan touched the edge of the blue stone, thoughtful. Finally, he nodded. "I can promise you that."

"Good," Callie said. "Now I need to go work off some anxiety. You up for more training?"

℘✦ℭ

196

Rowan slammed the quarterstaff into the soft ground next to Callie's face. "Dead," he muttered, rising from a crouch. Callie groaned and rolled to her feet, slow to stand. Rowan attacked before she could get her balance. The clack of the quarterstaffs resounded across the city.

Every movement radiated his mood. Rowan was pissed, though he wasn't sure if he was angrier with himself or with Callie for breaking up with Ash. What had she expected? He'd known this would happen the second he opened up to her. Love was a two-way street, after all, and still, he hadn't stopped himself.

She'd given up her amulet for him, her life inside of *Eirensae*. And even though it was what he wanted, it didn't sit right.

Rowan wiped sweat from his brow and circled Callie, staff ready. She glowered, mouth pressed into a tight line, eyes narrowed. He could tell she was trying to focus on training, but she was distracted by their impending plans. He gave her credit, though. She had guts.

Rowan feinted right and Callie overcompensated. His staff slammed into her side and the answering rush of air from her lungs washed his face.

Callie gritted her teeth and remained standing. Rowan took that as a challenge and swung low, aiming for her shins. She attempted a block, but it was too slow. Her knees buckled.

"Damn it, Rowan," she cursed, breathless, scowling up at him from the ground.

He smirked. Callie's eyes narrowed to furious slits. Suddenly, his quarterstaff jerked from his hands and landed in the grass thirty feet away, though Callie never touched it. Before he could voice his surprise, Callie was on him. Her shoulders connected with his shins and they tumbled, a flailing tangle of limbs, into the grass. Callie wiggled until she was on top of him, knees pressed into the softest part of his thighs, just below his groin. She held his wrists over his head, a perfect pin, but he'd stopped fighting long ago. She smiled now. He felt exhaustion shaking her muscles.

She made a disgusted sound and climbed off of him. Always one to get the last word, Rowan caught her ankle and twisted, rolling out of the way as she fell so that he could mirror her pin. She went limp beneath him and he pressed his forearm to her throat. Her pulse pounded against his skin.

Callie's knee connected with Rowan's groin and he yelped. Steeling his jaw, Rowan caught Callie's arm and twisted it behind her, holding the length of her body against his. She struggled, but he hadn't taught her how to escape this hold and she was too tired to wriggle away.

"You're fighting dirty today," he said, lips pressed to her ear.

Instead of answering, Callie snapped her head back. He felt his nose flatten beneath her skull, and a few seconds later, blinding pain. Fireworks splattered across his vision like splotches of paint on canvas. Callie rammed both elbows into his belly. He managed to catch one of them and wrestle her to the ground. She resisted, but eventually went slack.

"I give," she huffed.

Rowan slid off of her and rolled to his knees, sweeping a hand under his nose. It came away covered with blood. She'd broken his damn nose and he had an ache that shot straight from his groin into his stomach.

Callie pushed herself onto her elbows, grimacing. "You're a real asshole, you know that?"

"Yeah," he breathed, "I've heard that once or twice." Rowan glanced at her. She had her arm lifted where three parallel gashes welled with blood. If Rowan looked, he'd probably find her skin beneath his nails. The thought made him faintly nauseous. "I don't know why you bother with all this when you could just explode people's brains, or send them flying. Does anyone else know you can do that?" Last he knew, Callie only had four powers, fire, water, the brain exploding thing, and the ability to see inside people's heads. Nobody needed five powers. Hell, nobody needed more than one. It didn't sit well with Rowan that Callie could move things with her mind. It was a powerful, coveted ability.

Callie looked up, expression shuttered. "Just Jack."

"Good. Keep it that way. You're already scary enough with the explosion thing. I think maybe we should quit training, before your hands turn into weapons of mass destruction."

Callie worried her lip. "It's not about being able to explode someone's brain. It's about controlling my life. My powers seem passive." She waved an arm with a frown. "That's not accurate, I know, but looking at someone and blowing up their brain is not the same thing as physically defending myself." Their eyes met and Callie sucked in a breath. "You've given me more than you know," she said quietly. She reached out, gently wiping the blood from beneath his nose. "I'll help you heal that."

"No," he said immediately, voice flattened out and odd.

"Don't be an idiot."

"Let me heal yours, then."

"I'm *fine,*" Callie insisted.

"Me too."

"It looks broken."

"It's not."

Callie sighed and Rowan felt a smile tug the edges of his mouth. Somehow, they would be just fine.

౸◆౬

Though they'd broken up, and Callie wasn't sure if it was a *real* break up, as they'd never officially started dating, she still expected Ash to show up at her door laden with study material. As the afternoon wore into evening, Callie realized he wasn't coming. It was better this way. Maybe he'd be less heartbroken when she left with Rowan.

She'd returned her amulet to the book inside the library, where magic had kept it hidden for her. She didn't trust herself to leave it anywhere else. What if she got scared and decided to bind herself to the city? She thought of the cauldron, hidden in the caves, which stored the combined energy of *Eirensae*. The magical object connected to each imprint, gleaning a small amount of energy from every faerie, which powered the wards surrounding the city. In exchange, it protected the members and bound them together. Belonging to a city was permanent, and once Callie put on her amulet, the change to her skin and magic would remain forever. With it came the agreement of loyalty to *Eirensae* and willingness to follow the leader of the city.

Hazel.

The permanence of the decision frightened her, and even if she didn't know Hazel's plan, it would be a terrifying choice.

Callie was powerful—so powerful that Rowan had been surprised when she'd easily tossed his quarterstaff away with her mind. Even Ash didn't know she could do that. Callie hadn't forgotten Hazel's hungry gaze when the older woman had said Callie was destined to stand beside her.

Without conscious decision, Callie found herself in the walls of the city. The tall buildings rose like sentinels, casting the early evening in shadow. A few people greeted her by name and she smiled at them, amazed that despite everything, *Eirensae* had become her home. She passed the ruins of the palace, now just a scorched, flattened bit of earth, and felt bittersweet nostalgia for the wreckage. Smiling, she remembered the strength of Rowan's hands as he'd pulled her back inside the window when she'd tried to escape, and dancing with Ash and Jack at the welcome ceremony. Callie remembered the joy on Sapphire's face when she became prophetess and the night she'd spent in the hospital with Rowan.

Her time in *Eirensae* wasn't long, but the memories eclipsed those she had of the human world, and obliterated the few happy ones she'd managed over her seventeen years there.

Leaving the newer part of the city behind, Callie wandered into the old section. She'd been here a few times when she was allowed out with Jack to search for her amulet.

Vines and moss covered the stone houses, broken only by the glass panes of small windows. It seemed that the buildings grew straight from the earth. Many of the vines bloomed, and the scent of flowers was stronger here on the narrow path.

She'd never been to Sapphire's new home but had seen it in Rowan's mind. It was supposed to be secret, as Sapphire's duties did not lie with the individuals but with the whole of the city. She was not a fortuneteller and didn't hand out prophecies for amusement. But more than prophetess, she was Callie's sister, and she deserved to know that Callie was leaving.

The low building came into view. There were flowers everywhere. They spilled from the creeping plants that covered the exterior of the small cottage and lined the dirt path to the door. The foliage concealed the roof so that the house resembled a small hill, where a flower patch had taken up residence with flourish. An arched wooden door hid among the vines, adorned with a small brass knocker in the shape of a tree. There was no doorknob or hinges.

Callie blew strands of hair from her face, nervous, and lifted her hand. What if Sapphire turned her away? She knocked; the sound rang around her, sharp as the crack of a rifle.

What if Hazel found her here?

It was oversight, Callie was certain, that she walked freely at all. With Hazel injured and the guards sent on a mission, there just wasn't anyone for Callie to report to.

Sapphire opened the door, smiling. She wore a simple yellow dress covered by a stained apron. Her hair was tucked into a bun on top of her head and she carried oven mitts in one hand. "I've been waiting for you," she said, and then she hugged Callie, pulling her over the threshold and into the open cottage, which smelled of baking berries. When Sapphire pulled away, she gestured to the assortment of jars lining the table. "I'm making jam. You can help."

Callie stared at her sister, bemused. "Jam?"

Sapphire nodded and ran a hand over her forehead, leaving a streak of scarlet. "Yes, jam."

Callie laughed and hugged Sapphire again. "I just thought," she said into Sapphire's neck, "I don't know. I thought Hazel would have you locked away in a tower. That you'd be surrounded by notebooks and sketchpads. That you wouldn't be," she leaned away and searched Sapphire's face, "well, *you.*"

"I think," Sapphire said, returning to the roiling pot of red liquid on the stove, "that you have a fairytale fetish. Besides, there's no towers in *Eirensae*. Princesses, either, though I have heard rumor of a prince." She winked, and Callie got the impression that the gesture was more conspiratorial than it should've been.

"How's Rowan?" Sapphire thrust a ladle into Callie's hand and directed her to the table, where a pot of cooling jam waited.

"I broke his nose today."

Sapphire froze, and then chuckled. "Good for you." She picked up a second ladle and began to scoop the hot mixture into jars, her hands moving with practiced deftness. "What has he told you?"

"He's leaving." Callie swallowed the hollowness in her throat. "Two weeks from now." She palmed the giant spoon, but didn't move to help Sapphire.

"And you want to go with him."

"Yes," Callie said, surprised at the fervor behind the word.

Sapphire nodded slowly. She dropped the ladle into the empty pot and folded herself into the chair opposite Callie, reaching for her hands. "I think it best if the two of you stay together, though I'll never admit I told you that."

"What did you see?" Callie demanded, curiosity winning out over fear.

"When you were little, did you ever read those 'choose your own destiny' books?" Callie nodded and Sapphire continued. "What I see is a lot like that. There are all these different decisions to be made, but unlike the books, there isn't just one reader. There are hundreds of readers, and they're all choosing independently of each other. Though their stories will intertwine, they aren't accounting for anyone else in their decisions. It's impossible, at this point, for me to discern anything. I can only rely on instinct, and instinct tells me that you should trust Rowan."

"I will, I mean, I do," Callie said after a while.

Sapphire arched one eyebrow.

"I do trust him, with everyone but himself, which is why I have to go. He's not afraid of anything, and he's reckless to his own ruin."

"Oh I think there's one thing he's afraid of," Sapphire said, pulling her hands from Callie's.

"Mm," Callie said, noncommittal.

"He's scared for you."

"Mm."

Sapphire slapped the table, clattering metal lids and rings. "He cares for you. I'm prophetess, Callie, not some oblivious bystander," she broke off with an angry noise. "And your sister, at that. Even if I hadn't witnessed it myself, he's told me. Go ahead," she encouraged with a wry smile, "tell me it isn't so. *Lie*, Callie. Tell me that Rowan doesn't care for you. Tell me that *you* don't care for *him.*"

Callie's face reddened and her lips remained shut.

"You two are good for each other, despite how hard you fight it. Besides, you can't stay here. I always knew you would leave. Being under Rowan's protection is the best of all the worst situations. You're being selfless, Callie, and that makes me so proud of you."

"You know what Hazel plans for me, don't you?" Callie whispered.

Sapphire took a deep breath and nodded. "You can't let it happen. You have to get away from her and *stay* away from her. All you need is a way to break the binding spell."

Callie looked up sharply, ignoring the burning dread in her gut. It was true, then. "You know how to break it?"

Sapphire shook her head. "No, but I know someone who does."

"I'm scared," Callie admitted.

"I know you are. But I'll be okay here. Hazel controls me, and she trusts that control. All you need to worry about is yourself." Sapphire smiled. "And keeping Rowan in line."

Callie groaned.

"Open up to him, Callie. You might be surprised by what he offers. He did save your life, after all." Sapphire stood. "You have to get going now." She edged around the table and caught Callie in a tight hug. "I love you, sister."

Callie felt tears threaten her eyes. "I love you, too."

Though it wasn't a goodbye, at least not yet, it felt as permanent as one. Callie made it out the door with the directions to Gardenia's and tears spilling down her cheeks.

Callie hesitated on the doorstep. Creepers crawled up the worn stone stairs and were soft under her bare feet. Though Rowan had healed the gash on her palm from Hazel's blade, Callie still felt the sting of the knife and the unsettling weight of the binding spell. She would be glad to be rid of it, yet the thought of being *free* worried Callie. She hadn't been in *Eirensae* long, but the human world felt far away, wispy, like the clinging fog of a dream. It terrified her to go there again.

Shaking off her nerves, she rapped on the doorframe. Gardenia answered immediately, as though she was standing on the other side just waiting for Callie to knock. Gardenia's smile deepened the fine filigree of lines beside her eyes and mouth, belying the youthfulness of her gaze. "Calla Lily, please, come in."

Gardenia's house was small, the space cramped with pots and jars and drying herbs, but clean and neat as though she took great pains to make the tiny rooms presentable. Gardenia went to a dying fire and added a log, sliding a teapot over the flame once it leapt to cheery orange and yellow. The older woman was petite, her head reaching just below Callie's shoulders. Her hair was gray, shot through with streaks of pure white, and she wore it long and loose over an ocean blue gown that matched her eyes.

"Sapphire told me you'd come," Gardenia said, leading Callie to the table and gesturing for her to sit. "Seems you've become the most pivotal piece to *Eirensae's* survival. Can't say that I'm surprised, with all that energy you carry around." Gardenia chuckled and busied her hands preparing tea. "Sapphire didn't tell me your plans, just that she believes you will save our people." Gardenia looked up, pursed her lips, as though she hoped Callie might enlighten her to the details.

Callie lifted a shoulder. The worst, and possibly best, part, was that Callie had no idea what was going on, either, just that she would refuse Hazel and follow Rowan when he left.

"Suit yourself, then, dear." The teapot whistled and Gardenia hurried to retrieve it. When they both had steaming mugs of fragrant lavender tea in their hands, Gardenia continued. "I've witnessed the ebb and flow of the fae, much like the tides of the ocean, for over two millennia."

Her seventeen years felt like a tiny blip on the map of time, hardly discernible at all, and yet Gardenia trusted Callie with the fate of her beloved city.

"I can feel the night settled over *Eirensae*, dark as the forest under a new moon, hovering, as though the entire city is hanging from a precipice just waiting to fall. I've seen the blackness in the prophetess's visions, and the fear that she carries in silence. I've also seen hope, and I see it in your eyes, *a stoirin*." Gardenia stroked the back of Callie's hand where it lay on the table between them.

"To fear the unknown is to borrow trouble. We must not fear the future, child, only the failure of the weak to act. You are not weak, so there is little to fear." Gardenia patted Callie's hand and sat back, lifting her mug to her lips. She sipped the tea thoughtfully.

Their gazes met and held. Callie swallowed hard.

"Your life is tangled in things that will be difficult to escape, but you are smart, and strong, *so* strong. You have a pure heart, Callie, and you honor us with it. You are far too young for the tasks set before you."

"Tasks?" Callie murmured, riveted. The words were lyrical, the twisted refrain of a story that Callie couldn't unravel to fit her life.

"War, death, fear, it will overcome our people. Many will die from cowardice; others will die defending things that never belonged to us. The way of our people is stagnant. *You* will change that, either to our success or peril."

"I...I—" Words formed in Callie's mouth, but none broke the surface. A knot formed in her stomach, weighted heavy with terror and guilt. She never planned to save *Eirensae* from some impending war. The city was her home, her family, but how could she alone defend it?

"Know that we will stand with you to whatever end may come," Gardenia said. "Now, for the binding spell." She held out her withered hand expectantly and produced a knife from the pocket of her dress. The handle was bone, worn smooth from years of use. The blade curved and tapered to a wicked point. Ceremonial markings etched the sides, four looping symbols that Callie did not recognize. "Your palm," Gardenia prompted when Callie remained frozen.

The cut barely stung and soon a pool of blood collected in Callie's hand. Gardenia chanted, voice as steady as the hands that held Callie's. Warmth rose under Callie's skin, seeming to come from all over as though the sun had scorched her. The heat drew to a high point in her upturned palm and the fresh cut sealed, leaving a puddle of crimson which Gardenia wiped away with a towel.

"Hazel's blood," Gardenia said, closing Callie's fingers into a fist. "You're free." The old woman squeezed Callie's hand. "Promise me that you will be careful. Don't be afraid to follow your heart, it often knows more than your head."

"Hazel will be mad at you for doing this," Callie said.

Gardenia laughed. "You leave Hazel to me." She pulled Callie into a soft, violet scented hug. "Trust yourself."

ℰᴑ Fifteen ᴼᴆ

ROWAN GLANCED UP when Ash strolled into the library later that evening. A deep scowl twisted Ash's face and his eyes widened when he saw Rowan. "What happened to you?"

Rowan grimaced and touched his nose gingerly, feeling the soft give of crushed bone from sparring with Callie. He'd made the mistake of looking in the mirror after his shower. Bruises darkened the skin beneath his eyes and the bridge of his nose had a bumpy ridge that hadn't been there before. Strangely, the imperfection didn't bother him.

"It was the same thing that made you so chipper. Or should I say, same *someone,*" he said.

Ash sprawled into the chair opposite Rowan and grinned. "She's breaking hearts and noses? *Classic.*" Ash slid the book Rowan was reading toward him, eyes narrowing as he read the foreign words. "You're researching the markings of *Fraeburdh?*"

Rowan lifted one shoulder, feeling the amusement drain out of him. He could deny it, tell his friend that he was simply curious about the other city, but Ash wasn't stupid. Everything about *Fraeburdh* fit Rowan like second skin. The fighting, the knowledge, the anger, the absolute *blackness* of his energy. His *wings.*

Ash scanned the pages for a moment, flipping back and forth. He stopped when he came across a drawing of a faerie with sharp wings hovering above its back. The points ended in talons that dripped crimson. A snarl warped the man's lips, revealing rows and rows of feline teeth, pointed as needles. They, too, were covered with blood that spilled over his lips and dribbled from his chin. His body was emaciated, ribs visible, collarbone protruding. Ash scrutinized the drawing and then searched Rowan's face. "I see the resemblance."

"Ha ha," Rowan said, snatching the book back.

"You can't honestly think you belong there."

"Look at me, Ash, and look at the fae from *Fraeburdh*. They love to fight, they have dark colored energy and animalistic markings." Ash held up a hand to stop Rowan's rant, but the words spilled from Rowan like water tumbling over a cliff. "*I* love to fight, *I* have black energy, *I* have wings. It's like looking in a damn mirror." He slammed his fist on the open page, making it jump.

"*I* have animalistic markings," Ash said, lifting his hands, where Rowan knew webbing connected the other boy's fingers.

"Yes, but yours are *benign*, Ash. A frog...*a frog!* I'm a bird of prey! Tell me what's benign about a crow, or a raven, or, I don't know, a goddamn vulture." Rowan was shouting, he couldn't help it.

"A vulture?" Ash smirked.

"Vulture, scavenger, carrion, as in, *I want to sustain myself off the flesh of others.*"

Ash stared at Rowan, face tight. Rowan knew the other boy was trying not to laugh.

"Do you," Ash asked, swallowing laughter, "want to eat the flesh of others?"

"What?" Rowan said, disgusted. "Of course not." Bitterness burned his tongue and throat, and though he hadn't thrown up in years, Rowan thought he might. He jammed his hands into tight fists until his nails dug into his palms. His jaw ticked. He wanted to kill something, which was *exactly* what a fae from *Fraeburdh* would want to do. How could he protect Callie when he had such hatred inside of him?

"Well, good, you had me worried for a second." Ash shut the book carefully, pushing it just out of Rowan's reach. He ran his hands through his hair and sat back in the chair with a sigh. "Here's what I think."

"Don't you dare say that my amulet's here," Rowan said through gritted teeth.

Ash snapped his mouth shut and swallowed the words on his tongue, reconsidering his argument. "You're my best friend," he said finally, quietly, as though the admission hurt to say aloud. "Do you think I want to idly sit by and watch you run away from home? If you say it's not here, fine, I'll believe you. But *Fraeburdh?* Come on, Row. You're nothing like those...those—useless assholes." He made a wild gesture. "What about *Macántacht?*"

"The City of *Honor?* You've got to be kidding." Rowan couldn't hide the scorn in his voice, though he was pleased that Ash thought that highly of him. The fae of *Macántacht* were known for their strict belief in right and wrong, just as *Fraeburdh* was known for war and *Eirensae* for fertility.

"Your self-loathing is delightful," Ash pointed out.

"I always thought it was one of my best features. The ladies love a tortured soul."

Ash's expression turned serious. "Please don't go."

"I have to. If I stay, Hazel will strip my powers...my existence. I *won't* become Fallen."

Ash hesitated. "I could come with you."

"You can't," Rowan insisted, touched by his friend's loyalty. "Who would protect the city?"

"Callie, of course. Isn't that Hazel's plan?"

Suddenly Rowan felt the huge wedge that had come between them. They were both in love with the same girl, and though Rowan would deny his feelings until he ran out of breath, Ash *had* to know. They always stepped so carefully around her, and they never talked about her, at least not in any depth. Rowan was fiercely protective, but then again, so was Ash. Rowan should tell Ash that Callie planned on leaving with him, but he couldn't bring the words up from his chest. It would devastate Ash.

"You love her," Ash said. It was a statement, not a question, but Rowan answered anyway, surprising them both.

"Yes."

Ash nodded and pressed his lips together, looking exhausted. "Me, too."

Rowan sat back in his chair and the two boys eyed each other, the enormity of each admission heavy between them. It wasn't news, but at the same time, everything became more real. Was it loyalty that sustained their friendship? Ash had never judged Rowan, never given up on him, not even when the rest of the city had turned their backs. Rowan wasn't certain what he gave Ash, except maybe that Rowan understood what it was like to want something you couldn't have.

Callie appeared in the doorway of the library as though summoned by their conversation. Her eyes lit on Rowan's face and she winced, then they traveled to Ash's, and her expression darkened. She hesitated, looking panicked. Her hands twisted in the fabric of her shirt. "I didn't realize you two were here," she said, breathless. "I'll just, uh, study some other time." She took a step backwards and then another, disappearing into the tunnels.

Both Ash and Rowan stood. Seeing this, Rowan made to sit down again, to let Ash run after her.

Ash sighed and plunked back into his seat. "You go. She doesn't want to see me right now."

Rowan looked at his friend. Misery made Ash's features harder and more pronounced. Ash truly loved Callie, would give anything for her to return that love. And Rowan, who'd been nothing but himself, bitter, rude, and abrasive, had somehow caught her attention. As Rowan moved toward the doorway, he wished he were a bit more like Ash and a little less like himself.

"Callie, wait," Rowan called, pounding through the passage. Callie's hair streamed behind her, billowing like the golden sails of a ship, but she didn't slow or even turn her head. He chased her through the portal room where the glamoured night sky stretched above them, and into a different tunnel. He knew she'd have to stop eventually, as this path dead-ended. Callie kept up the pace until the shimmering cauldron appeared before them. She stopped just before she hit the invisible barrier, flattening her palms against the ward.

Rowan stayed a few feet away, breathing hard from running. Callie's shoulders shook and she banged her head lightly on the see-through wall. "Go away, Rowan," she said, but the order carried no force.

"What's wrong?" He moved closer now, touched her shoulder. She shivered under the weight of his fingers.

"How can I leave her?" Callie whispered. "How can I just go? Where will we go?" She bit her lip and Rowan saw a tiny line of blood well there.

"I don't have all the answers, but I think we should tell Ash. He deserves to know."

Callie shook her head. "No. I can't handle another goodbye." She held up her palm. A thin scar traversed the flesh there. "The binding spell is gone." She lifted her chin and he saw tears shuddering on the edge of her eyelashes. "I'm ready when you are." She wiped her eyes. "Go spend some time with Ash."

Rowan wanted to comfort her, somehow make everything better. It was going to be a long two weeks until they left. "Come with me," he said. "You don't have to avoid him because of what happened between the two of you."

Callie swallowed hard. "He's your best friend. I'm just a girl." She flashed a quick smile. "I'll be okay."

౬౦✦౧౪

"Here," Ash said, pointing to the yellowed page. The script was cramped and slanted, written in Gaelic. "It says *Immortal.*"

Rowan looked over Ash's shoulder, squinting to make out the handwritten words. The scrawl covered the entire page, margin to margin, as though the author was afraid they'd run out of paper before they ran out of words. "It's a poem," Rowan said, translating the language. "It says to kill an Immortal, discharge the power of four." His lips moved as he struggled with the rest of the words. "It mentions the four treasures, but I can't read the rest."

"The power of four," Ash repeated. "What does that mean?"

211

Rowan shrugged. "Hell if I know. Maybe the four treasures, the four cities? In all my research, I've never heard of someone actually destroying an Immortal. They're too strong." He scanned the text again.

"Forgive me for questioning your renowned battle skills, but you aren't going to seek out an Immortal, are you?" Ash stared at the page as he asked.

"I don't know. Maybe. Whoever killed the child deserves to be destroyed, it's faerie law," he reminded Ash. Not that he intended to fight an Immortal. He just needed to consider every possible situation. He didn't know what would happen once he and Callie made their way into the human world and he'd made her a lot of promises. He was terrified he wouldn't be able to follow through. They were the best of both worlds, with his healing ability and her offensive powers, but Sapphire had told him Callie wasn't invincible. He had to gather as much knowledge as he could before they left, especially with the possibility of Elm being an Immortal. Then there was the Fallen and *Fraeburdh*. And he knew with certainty that Hazel wouldn't let Callie go without a fight.

"I think I found something," Ash said a while later. "I keep coming back to the power of four. When the fae lived as one, before the Great War, all of the treasures were kept together and the fae were bound to them. If an amulet was made to bind the wearer to the four treasures, they would be stronger than any single fae bound to a city," he said excitedly. "Maybe stronger than an Immortal."

Rowan nodded, thoughtful. When the fae divided, each faerie chose a home and a new city. But the war did not end and the divergent fae rose up against each other. *Cloch* fell to *Fraeburdh* and the stone of truth was lost. One couldn't be bound to all four treasures when one was missing. He said as much to Ash.

"That's why no one has ever defeated an Immortal," Ash said. "The fae swore allegiance to one city, and their bindings to the other three were stripped. Without all four treasures, including the stone, none of us can defeat an Immortal."

৪১◆৫৪

Two days passed before Jack and Hawthorne returned with the body of the child. They carried her into the city through the northern gate. Orbs lined the path through the forest, casting pale blue light onto the trees and the newly bloomed flowers that sprang from the earth as though anticipating the child's homecoming. The fae of *Eirensae* stood vigil on both sides, dressed in green. Only their tearstained, pale faces shone from the darkness. The delicate, sorrowful melody of a pan flute drifted on the night air and slid against the mourner's skin, providing comfort.

Callie stood between Rowan and Willow, close enough that Rowan's earthen scent mixed with Willow's heady jasmine and the light fragrance of the blossoms they held. Ash was across from them, face downcast. Every so often, Callie would catch the movement of his head as though he kept peeking at her. The three of them had spoken little since she'd decided to leave. Callie made excuses and spent a lot of time with Willow, though the girl usually drove Callie crazy with her triviality. She'd hardly seen Ash, who'd thrown himself into research alongside Rowan. Rowan, however, had resumed his role as Callie's personal protector. He'd stationed himself outside her cottage door, and could be seen there at all hours. He wore his black eyes like badges, though she suspected he'd let someone heal his broken nose.

Jack came into view first, expression somber as one of the four bearers of the linen pallet that carried the child. Callie had helped construct the deathbed, anxious for something to do. The long, sturdy piece of bleached fabric attached to four thick branches with ropes of hemp.

Hawthorne walked beside Jack, just as slow. Though they'd seldom spoken, Hawthorne's eyes met Callie's, and he smiled. The smirk remained as the group came closer, until uneasiness spread through Callie's gut. Sai followed in the rear, along with a young faerie she didn't recognize.

Rowan shifted and his fingers brushed Callie's. Their energy connected and crackled, drawing her attention from Hawthorne. A brilliant blue lit between Rowan and Callie, and Rowan jerked his hand away, cursing under his breath. Ash's head snapped up, but then the procession slid between them on the path. Callie shook off the shock of Rowan's touch and tossed her flower onto the pallet, where it joined a growing mound of blossoms.

The child, who was a few months older than Callie, was beautiful. She had long, dark hair, just discernible beneath the blanket of flowers. They'd draped her in green, the color of death. Her skin was glamoured, angular cheeks rosy, eyes painted dark with kohl. Callie wondered if her irises were blue or green, and if she would've felt at home in *Eirensae*. Callie would've been the one who prepared the child for the welcome ceremony. Now that Callie was leaving the city, she'd never get a chance to lead another into their new life as fae.

The realization felt finite, and tears burned streaks on Callie's face. She felt Rowan's gaze on her, warm as fingertips and soft as silk, as though she could wrap herself in it. She worried what it would be like on the outside.

Rowan's hand touched hers again, this time with purpose. He stroked the tension of her fist until it unfolded like the petals of bud. Their fingers skated over one another, searching, *searching*. Finally, they linked. The rush of his energy, black and boundless, exploded into Callie's veins. It pulsed beneath her collarbone and skittered across her stomach. It filled her mouth with sweetness. Security. Callie's eyes fluttered shut, sending fresh tears onto her cheeks. Rowan's grip tightened, and Callie hoped that meant he wouldn't let her down. She wasn't sure she could do this without him.

❧ Sixteen ❧

WITH UNEASINESS ROILING in his belly, Rowan watched the child burn. Callie's hand remained in his, their energy connecting like fireworks.

They would leave tonight, he decided. It'd be a cleaner break if it weren't announced. If they just snuck away and disappeared. Callie squeezed his hand and Rowan glanced at her. The colorful flames reflected in her eyes.

Rowan caught Ash's gaze from across the pyre. Ash wore his jealousy like armor. It blazed in his eyes and rode heavy on the downward turn of his mouth.

A cleaner break, Rowan thought.

As Rowan walked Callie back to Sapphire's cottage, he remembered the last funeral they'd attended, and how Callie had nearly died. She was quiet as the left the others for the solitude of the cottages. He wondered if she was thinking about the same thing.

They'd wait until the city was asleep, and then they'd go.

He'd find a way to protect her. He'd give up everything, his claim to another city, being fae, *everything,* to keep his promise.

Rowan closed his eyes, remembering the slide of his foster father's knife against his skin, and the answering flood of pain. He couldn't let that happen.

They stopped at the foot of her stairs. Callie released his hand and hid both of hers behind her back. "Thanks," she said.

"Usually they thank me the morning after." Rowan smirked, but he didn't feel it in his heart.

"I'm sure," Callie said.

"So you're not going to invite me in?"

Callie paled.

"I'm kidding." Rowan shoved his hands into his pockets.

Callie took a breath. "Where will we go first...you know, after we leave?"

"We'll go into hiding. I know some places."

"And if nothing happens?"

Rowan turned his face upward. A full moon presided over a star filled sky. "Maybe I'll go to medical school. I don't know. We'll figure it out."

"You aren't—" she hesitated, drawing Rowan's gaze back to her face. "You aren't scared?"

Rowan grinned. "I love adventure. What's there to be afraid of?"

"Being alone. Won't you miss this?"

"I've been alone my entire life, Callie. Whether I'm here or out there hardly matters."

Callie's cheeks reddened. "That goes both ways, Rowan. Maybe you don't need anyone, but there are people who need you. I hate that you act like it doesn't bother you to leave."

Rowan drew a deep breath, regretting walking her home. They'd have plenty of time to argue once they got outside. He should've let Ash do it, or Jack, anyone else. He put his hands on her shoulders, and for once, she didn't immediately pull away. "You think you know who I am, but you have no idea. Whatever it is you think you feel for me, it isn't real. I'm not Rowan of *Eirensae*. I'm not some good faerie who heals people. This is all a product of my situation, but it's not me. You're trying to make me into the hero."

Callie looked up, eyes furious. "Why do you do this?" She shoved his shoulder. "You let people in just to push them away. The other night—" she broke off and waved a hand. "The other night I saw you, Rowan, and I saw *all* of you. I know what you are and I'm still here. You keep pushing and pushing, but guess what? I'm pushing back. All that doesn't matter to me. I'm going with you, but you're not making it easy on me."

Her face was inches from his, her eyes narrowed and pale blue in the moonlight. He could feel her heartbeat and the intense tingle of her power sizzling along his skin. He told himself not to, but his hand lifted, caressed the soft angle of her jaw.

Callie inhaled sharply. Closed her eyes.

"I push because I want to keep you safe." He slid his hand to her neck. "This," he pulled her closer, until his lips grazed her ear, her cheek, "isn't safe." Her pulse leapt beneath his hand.

His nose skimmed along her cheek as he moved back. Callie's eyes were open now, luminous and wide. He cupped her face, slipped his hands into her hair. He knew she would pull away at any second. She was terrified. He felt it in every sharp breath, in the way her hands fisted at her sides. He saw it in her eyes.

Stop me, he thought, as his head dipped.

The kiss was leaping off of a five-story building. It was the sunset over the ocean on the longest day of the year. It was holding someone too tightly so they couldn't let go.

Callie's mouth was warm beneath his, her lips pliant. She didn't lift her hands to his neck or pull him closer, but she didn't push him away, either. Rowan kept it gentle, though the urge to drag Callie against him pulsed beneath his skin.

Her energy was fathomless against his lips. Strong as faerie wine, Rowan was drunk with it by the time he pulled back to catch his breath. Callie had her eyes squeezed shut, her hands stayed balled into tight little fists. Rowan stroked his thumbs over her face.

"Hey," he said gently.

He watched her throat work. Her eyes were wet when she finally opened them. She unclenched her hands and lifted her palms. Each hand had four bright red crescents where her nails had dug in.

Callie blinked, spilling tears, and looked away. "I'm sorry."

"God, Callie," Rowan breathed.

Heat rose in her cheeks. She swiped at the wetness there. "I'm sorry," she repeated.

Rowan caught her hands. He forced her to look at him. "For what?"

She swallowed hard.

"Tell me what you're sorry for," he pressed.

Callie's eyes widened. Her body went still, even the pulse of her energy against Rowan's skin stuttered. He turned, following her gaze.

Flames rose from the city like a rainbow of destruction. The sight was so wrong that Rowan could only stare for a moment, derailed.

Eirensae was on fire.

His fingers tightened on Callie's hand. "We've got to go."

Callie remained rooted to the spot, the flames dancing in her eyes as they'd done earlier at the funeral. "Sapphire," she whispered.

Rowan pulled harder. People were beginning to spill from between the tall buildings. From this distance, Rowan couldn't tell who they were. Panic fizzled into his veins. "We have to go." He shook Callie's arm until she looked at him.

Her expression was a mix of horror of disbelief. "I can put out the fire," she said, trying to pull away from him.

Screams came from far off. Rowan's gut clenched. He may not belong to *Eirensae,* but he never wanted to see it destroyed. "Listen to me." He caught Callie's chin between his fingers. "They are coming for you." He didn't know who it was, whether it was the Fallen or *Fraeburdh,* but this was what Sapphire saw. This was the beginning of the end. "You have to get out of here and we have to go, *now.* Remember what Sapphire told you."

Callie opened her mouth to protest, but Rowan pulled her toward the caves before she could speak. She may have been magically stronger than him, but he still had the advantage when it came to physical strength. It didn't take long for her steps to match his.

He didn't let go of her hand as they raced along the cottages. They passed a few fae stumbling from their homes, the fire lighting their faces. They all shared the same expression. Disbelief. Fear.

They were supposed to be safe, hidden away beneath the pond.

Hazel had promised.

There was no relief when they passed through the portal to the caves. Callie gasped beside him and pressed a hand to her side. Voices bounced through the passages, reverberating off the walls until Rowan couldn't tell which direction they'd come from.

Callie's eyes went wide. Rowan held a finger to his lips and pointed to the opening that led to the library. If someone was lurking around *Eirensae,* they probably weren't looking for books. They slipped into the tunnel and pressed flat against the wall just as two men emerged from the far side.

Rowan's insides sank.

"Perhaps we should thank Elm for making it so easy to sneak in with the child," the taller one said. His accent was thick and unfamiliar.

The shorter boy, however, Rowan recognized instantly.

Hawthorne had both arms wrapped around the cauldron. His muscles bulged with the effort. Sweat beaded on his forehead and upper lip. He grunted.

"Father may be disappointed with the loss." The taller boy tilted his head. A shock of black hair slid over his face, covering one eye. He tossed it away. "Would you like me to carry that burden for you? It seems…difficult."

"Oh, shut up, Coal," Hawthorne said, thrusting the cauldron into the other boy's hands. "King Arol will have plenty of faeries to choose from. I still can't believe it worked."

Coal chuckled, lifting the cauldron easily under one arm. "They will flee like sheep headed for the slaughter and we will capture them up."

Next to Rowan, Callie's breath caught.

Hawthorne and Coal froze.

"Who's there?" Hawthorne called.

Rowan let go of Callie's hand. He felt her fingers brush against his as she searched for it again. He stepped out into the open and prayed that Callie would stay hidden and not do anything stupid.

∞◆∞

Callie bit her lip to keep from calling Rowan back. The knobby wall pressed into the back of her calves, her shoulders. She was afraid to close her eyes, even for a moment. They were stealing the cauldron, and with it, all of *Eirensae's* power.

Hawthorne's eyes widened as Rowan moved for the open space. "Rowan? This is excellent." He clapped Coal on the arm. "Look who it is."

Coal's face transformed as a grin spread across it. "Brother!" he boomed.

Rowan's back was to Callie. She saw his shoulders tighten. "I'm gonna have to take the cauldron back," he said.

Coal's grin dropped into a frown.

Hawthorne smirked. "Go ahead and try."

Callie stared at Coal, feeling a snap of realization rise in her mind. He had black hair, and even in the dim light, the blue of his eyes was striking. They reflected like an animal's, casting two dancing beams wherever his gaze landed.

He was taller, more muscular with broader shoulders, but he looked just like Rowan.

Nausea filled her throat.

"Brother," Coal repeated, quieter this time. "I have always wondered what our first encounter would be like. I assumed we would forgo the fighting. It is destined for *Fraeburdh* to have the cauldron."

"I'm not your brother," Rowan said.

"You cannot deny genetics," Coal said. "We have our father's look. Surely you must have noticed."

Rowan moved so fast that Callie almost couldn't follow as he slid around Coal and landed a debilitating blow to the bigger boy's shoulder. The cauldron hit the floor with a muted thunk. Hawthorne swore.

Coal laughed. "Fighting it is, then." He swung his arm, catching Rowan across the throat and throwing him to the ground.

Hawthorne waded into the fray only to drag the cauldron out of the way. He made for the tunnel that led to the pond, hefting the cauldron into his arms.

Rowan leapt to his feet to counter Coal's next attack as Callie stepped out into the open. She couldn't let Hawthorne get away.

Her sudden appearance distracted Coal long enough for Rowan to get a jab into Coal's throat. Rowan dodged Coal's kick. "Run, Callie."

Coal was grinning again, a wide, maniacal smile that lifted the hairs at the back of Callie's neck. Coal slid his arm around Rowan's throat. Callie saw Rowan's eyes widen as he struggled to get out of the grasp. Callie knew he would, he'd taught her how to escape it, after all.

She hesitated. She didn't want to leave him.

Coal's eyes were heavy on her like a touch. The reflecting beams of light traveled from her face, over her chest, her belly, her legs, before returning to her face. "Who is this beautiful creature?" he asked, his face pressed against Rowan's. "The infamous Calla Lily? Hawthorne did not do you justice."

Her stomach soured.

Rowan's face darkened. "Go," he mouthed.

He was stalling, she realized, giving her time to get away. Heart pounding, she turned from Rowan and hurried after Hawthorne.

The sound of a body hitting the floor came from behind her.

She flinched, instinct telling her to turn around and help Rowan, but she kept her feet moving forward. Hawthorne couldn't have gotten far and Rowan would catch up. She ran, flinging herself through the tunnel at breakneck speed, gathering the energy beneath her skin. She'd never attacked someone on purpose. Today, she would learn how.

All at once, it went dark, as though someone had flipped the light switch for the orbs. Callie stumbled, missed a turn and slammed into rock. She bit her lip to keep from crying out, fingers scrabbling for purchase on the slick, vine covered walls. Her knees throbbed in time to her racing pulse.

Silence. Callie reached into the blinding darkness, stretching her fingers along the wall, searching. Carefully, she took a step and then another, holding her breath. When she grew dizzy, she allowed herself a tiny bit of air. The sound was loud in her ears. Petals caressed her cheek, silky, like gentle hands. She shuddered.

She drew another shaky breath, wincing at the noise. Her progress was slow, the darkness so complete that it relegated her to molasses speed. The caves seemed to press against her, heavier and heavier until she thought she would suffocate.

Callie forced herself to breathe slower and calm her heart rate. She needed to remember everything Rowan had taught her. In a fight, she was nearly invincible. She could explode brains. There was nothing to be afraid of. If Hawthorne or Coal attacked, she would disable them. Callie relaxed a fraction. The vice on her lungs eased.

Something soft scraped the ground to her right. She froze. A footstep? It came again from her left. Callie closed her eyes, the insides of her eyelids as black as the tunnels around her, and listened. *Nothing.* She strained until the thundering of her heart was deafening. She moved on, ignoring the numbing terror.

Suddenly the wall disappeared beneath her hand and she found only empty air. She took a tiny, hesitant step, and her glamour disappeared. She lit blue, and in the sudden light, she saw Hawthorne's grinning face.

Hawthorne dove for Callie and she leapt out of the way. He was on her in an instant, heavy weight throwing her down. Callie's jaw smacked the ground with bone crunching force and bright sparklers burst behind her eyes. She felt each contact point acutely, her knee, shoulder, elbow. Hawthorne straddled her waist. The iron hard muscles of his thighs pressed painfully against her hipbones. Callie thrashed beneath him, blindly, without direction, feeling sick satisfaction every time their flesh connected.

He captured her wrists, which still glowed with iridescent blue energy. Callie glared up at him, struggling.

"I told Coal you'd be a problem. You're too strong and too stupid to realize where your loyalties should lie. It would've been a mercy if Elm killed you."

Callie twisted her hips back and forth but Hawthorne hardly moved. He weighed much more than her, his body layered with muscle.

"The cauldron is only the beginning," he said with a grin. He trapped both her wrists in one hand and stroked her cheek. "So much power and beauty. Such a shame to waste it."

Callie ground her teeth together; Hawthorne's touch awoke an immeasurable fury inside of her. The second she wriggled an arm from his grasp, she jammed her palm into his groin. Hawthorne yelped and she bucked until he rolled off of her. Hauling herself to her feet, Callie rammed her knee into his lower back and Hawthorne sprawled, face first, onto the floor.

Callie wheeled around to find a grinning Coal behind her. He seemed completely at ease where he stood, vibrant gaze on her. He rocked back on his heels and lifted on eyebrow. "My lovely, lovely Calla Lily." He took a step forward.

Callie stood there stupidly frozen in his gaze. "Where's Rowan?" she demanded.

"How beautiful you are." Coal raised a hand as though to caress her face.

Callie made a disgusted sound and whirled. His fingers caught the strap of her dress and the fabric snapped as she bolted.

Her knees and hips protested, pain firing up her legs with every step. She glanced around the tunnel, disoriented. She couldn't remember what direction she'd come from, every craggy rock looked identical to the last craggy rock. "Shit," she muttered, ignoring the footsteps pounding behind her. One of the tunnels *had* to lead out. She'd find Rowan.

Callie burst from the passageway into a dim room, and gasped. The reflection pond swayed above her. Callie skidded to a stop, dumbstruck. The room had no doors. Even the tunnel she'd come from had disappeared into the stone wall. She spun in a tight circle, air wheezing from her lungs as she tried to catch her breath. When Callie completed the rotation, both Coal and Hawthorne stood in front of her. The clunk of Coal setting the cauldron down resounded with finality through the small room. He watched Callie, smile glittering.

"It seems you have reached the end, my darling," he said.

The words sent a shiver up Callie's spine.

"Don't kill her," Hawthorne said with a dismissive wave of his hand. He pulled the cauldron closer to him and leaned against the wall, recovering, eyes narrowed, arms crossed.

"I have no intention of killing her," Coal said, stepping toward Callie. His expression softened, but his eyes remained hard as cobalt diamonds. "You shall return with us. You amuse me, and I know you will delight Father."

She didn't wait for Coal to finish his speech. Closing her eyes, Callie called upon the power inside of her. She imagined Coal's ears bleeding, him falling, clutching his head.

Nothing happened. Her energy, usually an endless inferno inside of her, fizzled like a dying match in a bowl of water. Her eyes opened.

"You can come with me," he pressed his lips together, seeming to search for the right word, "voluntarily." He was closer enough now that Callie smelled the familiar-foreign scent of him. Like Rowan, but darker.

Rowan's words, unbidden, filtered into her mind. That first day she hadn't understood, now, she did. *This is the antechamber; you know your charms are stripped here.* Nauseous realization tore through her. She couldn't use her powers. Resigned, Callie set her feet, ready for the impending fight. A vicious sense of satisfaction wound through her and she was glad for her hand-to-hand training.

Coal was a much stronger fighter than Hawthorne, maybe even stronger than Rowan, and he immediately gained the advantage, winding a hard arm around her throat. Callie went slack under the hold and tried to let her body weight free her, but Coal was too strong. She clawed at his eyes with no luck.

Mere seconds passed before Coal had Callie pinned beneath him, massive, choking hands curled around her throat. Callie wheezed. Her pulse pounded against Coal's fingers like the incessant thunder of a steam train and echoed in her ears. Coal grinned and pressed harder. Callie's peripheral vision darkened at the edges and everything in front of her came into crystalline focus. She saw each strand of Coal's jet black hair and the diamond droplets of sweat that collected on his forehead. His teeth behind his stretched lips were bone white, and set in perfect, straight rows. His breath smelled of dank earth and iron.

Callie felt herself go still. Coal's voice came, as though from underwater during a thunderstorm. "She is a valiant fighter."

"Rowan taught her," Hawthorne said.

Coal's eyes widened and he glanced at Callie, amused. "Did he now? *Eirensae* is full of wonderful surprises. I expected him to be weaker. Father will be happy that our mother has not influenced him overmuch."

The hands at Callie's throat no longer hurt. The pressure felt like a sodden blanket, pushing her under, holding her down, heavier and heavier. Her vision was nothing more than pinpricks. Callie closed her eyes. *Be patient,* she told her panicked body. *Relax.* She had to make them believe she'd passed out. Her lungs begged for breath, contracting inside her chest, shuddering like beached fish. The pulse in her ears slowed, became sluggish. *Patience, patience, patience.* She wouldn't let her fear win.

She lost track of how much time passed, minutes, hours, each moment stretching out into an agonizing, infinite forever. Finally, Coal's hands lifted from her neck. Though she wanted to gasp for breath, gulp in the air until she burst, she allowed herself only one, tiny breath. The room spun around her, even with her eyes closed, even lying still and flat on the floor. She tumbled round and round, as though trapped inside a kaleidoscope.

Patience, she thought.

"She is unconscious," Coal said. She heard the rustle of fabric as he stood.

"Those bruises are nasty. You sure you didn't kill her?" There was a pointed pause.

"Bring her," Coal said. "It is the only way to keep her from Hazel."

Callie let her body loll when Hawthorne's hands found her though she wanted to smash in the side of his head. His fingers slid beneath her back and knees, almost gently.

"Hurry," Coal ordered, though his voice remained genial. "We have lingered here far too long. She was an entertaining, yet time-consuming distraction." A distinct scrape of metal told Callie he'd picked up the cauldron.

"*Ealaithe,*" Hawthorne said.

Nausea bloomed in her stomach when Hawthorne lifted her and she worried she'd give the entire ruse up by vomiting on him. She bit the inside of her lip until she tasted blood. When she was finally cradled against Hawthorne's chest, she opened her eyes. Hawthorne made a surprised squeak just before Callie jammed her thumbs into his eyes. She felt the soft, hard-boiled resistance, tissue and blood. Hawthorne screamed and dropped her. The floor rushed up in greeting and Callie smacked unceremoniously into it, body slack as a sack of potatoes. She rolled to her feet. She hurt everywhere. Her head whirled, the room felt like a ship at rough sea.

Hawthorne screamed again. When he lifted his hands from his face, blood trailed his cheeks and smeared his fingers. "You *bitch.*"

Coal frowned from across the antechamber.

"Control yourself, Hawthorne," Coal ordered.

Callie saw Hawthorne's jaw grind.

Coal's gaze returned to Callie and he smiled. "You are a constant amazement. Rowan has taught you well. I will admit I am impressed with your skill and determination. You will make an excellent warrior."

Callie knew she had one chance to escape. Behind Coal, a winding staircase disappeared into the reflection pond. Much like the library, the steps were made of a fine filigree of branches and roots. Vines spiraled over the banisters, dripping flowers as pale and bleached as fine china.

"I'm already an excellent warrior," she said.

Adrenaline flooded Callie's blood as she moved toward Coal. He still smiled, as though he was never worried during a fight, as though he was never outmatched. She knew she was no competition for his brawn and muscle, but she hoped she could at least outsmart him. At the last second, just before his hands collided with her, she rolled, fingers wrapping around the heavy, solid weight of the cauldron. When Coal whirled, the cauldron struck the side of his head with a sickening crunch. The impact ricocheted up Callie's arms and the magical object clattered to the floor where Coal had fallen.

Beneath the close crop of his hair, Callie saw splinters of bone and scarlet blood. From his knees, he grinned up at her. "Run, little Calla Lily. Run, but know you will come to us. Rowan's life depends on it."

Callie spared a glance at Hawthorne. Bloody hands covered his face and he said, "What's going on? Coal? *Coal?*"

She stumbled for the stairs, taking the spiral steps two at a time. With a gasp, she exploded into the cool, damp night of Lisburn. The stairs deposited her on the bank and immediately disappeared. Callie collapsed in the dry, brittle grass, gulping the metallic, bitter air. Above her, the black slash of Pennsylvania night sky coalesced, sprinkled with dimly flickering stars. The scents were the worst, rotting garbage, iron, *humanity.* She'd forgotten what the human world smelled like, or maybe she'd never realized it had a distinctly decaying scent. Already she missed the floral safety of *Eirensae,* of home.

Callie rolled and shoved to her feet. Her heart pounded everywhere.

She took a deep breath. Coal and Hawthorne would come through the pond. They couldn't go back through the city, not with it on fire and Rowan waiting for them.

Her insides swung uneasily. Rowan was okay. He was fine.

She couldn't go back after them, she wouldn't be able to fight off both Coal and Hawthorne. Not without magic. Here, in the human world, her powers weren't stripped. Here, she could take anyone down with a single thought. Callie wiped the sweat out of her eyes and settled on the bank. She would wait them out.

The minutes passed, interminable to Callie as she stared into the place that'd started it all for her. Her foster home was only a block over. Next to that, Nate's house. She dug her hands into the rocky dirt surrounding the pond.

She thought of what Cypress had told her on her first day in *Eirensae.* Calla Lily means resurrection. Across the pond, that dingy city, that was her old life. She didn't even miss it, now.

Callie pushed to her feet. *Where were they?*

A dog barked in her old neighborhood. A single car rumbled down the street.

Maybe they were waiting for her beneath the pond just as she was waiting for them above it. Maybe they were too cowardly to face her when she had her powers.

The stones along the pond dug into her feet as she debated. She knew Rowan would tell her to wait.

Callie curled her hands.

Before she could step into the water, the stairs appeared and a shape came hurtling off of them. It crashed into her with bone jarring force. Her head bounced off the ground and her teeth snapped together.

She tasted blood.

Callie glimpsed black hair and a flash of blue eyes as she struggled to throw her attacker off.

"Callie?" he breathed.

She shoved to her elbows.

Rowan crushed her to him. "I thought they took you. I went through all the tunnels. You were gone." Somewhere along the way, he'd lost his shirt. He had deep, bloody gouges on both of his sides.

"I came through the pond before them. They never came this way. I was waiting." She could hardly breathe, he was holding her so tightly. She hoped he never stopped.

"There was so much blood," he said between breaths.

Callie smiled against Rowan's neck, feeling his pulse thundering there. "I might've done a little damage." She pushed him away, searching his face. He looked tired and sweaty. A bruise spread across his forehead. "We have to go back. The city—"

Rowan shook his head, still catching his breath.

"Yes, Rowan. My sister is there. Ash is there. We can't just abandon them." She stood and moved toward the pond.

Rowan climbed to his feet more slowly.

Callie stepped into the water. It was cold and slimy as it soaked the bottom of her dress. The bottom was sandy and full of plants. She waded to the middle. The first time she'd been in the pond it was warm and silky.

She lit bright blue.

228

Rowan shoved his hair away from his face and Callie saw his wings rise behind him, graceful and magnificent. Their glamours had disappeared.

Callie shivered. "I don't understand."

Rowan stooped and ran his hand through the water. His fingers combed through weeds and pieces of garbage. "The portal is gone."

Callie's throat closed. "Gone? How can it be gone? How do we get back?"

Rowan held out a hand and helped Callie out of the frigid pond. Her dress dripped stagnant water over her feet and soaked the bottom of Rowan's pants. He kept her hand tucked in his as he pulled her into the park. Callie dug in her feet until he stopped. His face was unreadable when he turned back to her, his eyes black. Despite everything, she wanted to touch his wings, to let her fingers slide into their inky depths.

"They took the cauldron. *Eirensae* no longer has magical protection."

Callie digested what that meant with horror tearing at her chest. Without magic, nobody could get in or out of the city.

"Where are we going?" she repeated, forcing herself to meet Rowan's gaze.

Rowan stared at Callie for a long moment. She felt pinned, a moth beneath a needle.

"California," he said eventually.

"What's in California?" Another entrance to *Eirensae*, she hoped. She could still see the flames blazing through the buildings.

"The portal to *Fraeburdh*," Rowan said, expression strangely blank. "My home."

About the Author

Kacey Vanderkarr is a young adult author. She dabbles in fantasy, romance, and sci-fi, complete with faeries, alternate realities, and the occasional plasma gun. She's known to be annoyingly optimistic and listen to music at the highest decibel. Kacey is the president of the Flint Area Writers and the Social Media Director for Sucker Literary. When she's not writing, she coaches winterguard and works as a sonographer. Kacey lives in Michigan, with her husband, son, and crazy cats. Check out *Antithesis*, available from InkSpell Publishing.

www.KaceyVanderkarr.com

Acknowledgments

Reflection Pond is a labor of love, emphasis on the labor.

Authors will tell you that there's nothing more to writing a novel than sitting down and getting the words on paper. What they don't tell you is that you also must lose sleep, cancel plans, drink oceans of coffee, cry, and not quit until every iota of your being has found its way into your words.

They're just words, right?

Callie and Rowan's story isn't just about magic, it's about picking up your life when the pieces are scattered, it's about finding the strength to move on, even when you're paralyzed with fear. Callie and Rowan are you and me. They're teenagers and adults and children. They give me hope.

I'd like to thank my writing group, the Flint Area Writers. This story was the very first thing I read to them, and they have supported me along the entire journey—and it has truly been a journey. Mart, Kelly, Ashley, Holly, Chris, John, Tiffanie, and especially Nancy, who edited Reflection Pond, thank you.

MB. Look how far we've come. I'm so glad to call you my partner in crime.

RLL. Where would my writing be without you? Probably still stuck in the depths of my hard drive. Thank you for having my back and giving me a not so subtle shove when I need it.
Here's to rhubarb and biscuits.

My family, especially my husband and son, who suffer through living with a writer, thank you. I know it's not easy and sometimes (I mean, hardly ever!) my demands are difficult to meet.

To my readers. Thank you for your support. Hearing from you is the best thing that happens to me. Please email me: Kacey.Vanderkarr@gmail.com, visit me on Twitter: @kacimari, or stop by my blog: www.KaceyVanderkarr.com.

Like what you read? Consider leaving a review on Goodreads and Amazon. Reviews sell books!

For everyone out there who has a dream: Yes. Yes, you can.

Turn the page for a sneak peek of Poison Tree,

where Callie and Rowan's story continues…

Poison Tree

BOOK 2 IN THE REFLECTION POND SERIES

KACEY VANDERKARR

ഇ One ര

THE HUMAN WORLD felt wrong. Rowan scarcely remembered the last time he'd been here—not in a shoddy hotel room, but amongst humans, with the scent of decay clinging to every surface. No wonder they always seemed so desperate, the stink of their impending death clouded every breath.

Rowan watched Callie from across the room. She had her head laid back and her feet tucked underneath her. Her emotions had flipped from horrified to determined, to quiet and pensive. Beneath her closed lids, her eyes moved, but Rowan knew she wasn't asleep. He'd let the glamour fade from their clothes and bodies. Blood, pond water, and mud stained Callie's dress. He didn't look much better. His wings hovered above him, an ominous portent of things to come.

Rowan sighed and Callie's eyes opened.

"How long do we have to stay here?" she asked.

"Until we figure out how to get to California. It's not like we can walk two thousand miles." Rowan wasn't proud of how they'd acquired the hotel room. The wad of cash he'd plucked off a stranger lay on the dresser, a testament to their situation. They may be fae, blessed with magic and power beneath their skin, but they had no money, and in the human world, only money would suffice.

He was scared, but he couldn't tell Callie that. She'd put on her brave face after Hawthorne and Coal stole the cauldron and the portal disappeared. She hadn't mentioned the inferno they'd escaped in *Eirensae,* but Rowan knew it was heavy on her mind just as it weighed on his. Ash, Sapphire, Cypress, Willow, Jack. They were all in the city when it caught fire.

Callie's mouth tightened as though she read his thoughts. "Can't you just glamour us some money?"

Rowan pushed off of the sagging bed and paced to the window. It overlooked a cracked parking lot filled with decrepit cars. It reminded Rowan of his life.

"It doesn't work that way," he said, pressing a palm to the foggy glass. "We need identification if we're going to fly. Money if we're going to get a car the legal way." He felt Callie beside him. She'd moved with silent steps.

"I'll do it if you don't want to," she offered. "I don't know why we care about human laws, anyway."

Rowan shook his head, turning to her. His failure burned inside of him, hot as coals, bitter as acid. He'd promised to keep Callie safe, keep her in *Eirensae* where the Fallen couldn't find her. Yet, here she was, out in the human world. *Vulnerable.*

"You need to stay hidden," he said. He lifted a hand to brush a wave of blond hair from her forehead, thought better of it, and let it fall back to his side. He swallowed hard. "If anyone is going to steal a car, it's me. The last thing we need is for you to become a fugitive. The Fallen—"

"If it's what I have to do, then I'll do it. I need to know that Sapphire—"

"Your sister is fine. They'll all be fine."

"How can you know?" A frown tugged at her lips. She stared hard at him before moving her gaze out the window. "Hazel won't protect them, not if it means risking her own life." Callie fitted her palm to the print Rowan's hand had left on the glass. "I knew I wouldn't be able to keep my sister safe when we left, but now we know nothing." Her words grew quiet. "We don't even know if they're alive."

"We've made a real mess of things, haven't we?" Rowan muttered.

When he'd told Callie that they were going to *Fraeburdh,* it'd sounded like a good idea. Now Rowan wasn't so sure. Aside from the logistics of actually getting to California and through the portal into the City of War, it would be dangerous. Uneasiness prickled at his shoulder blades.

"When Coal called you his brother, you don't think he literally meant *brother,* do you?" She angled toward Rowan again, hopeful.

So she'd caught that, too. Rowan rolled his shoulders, but the sticky feeling didn't ease. "I told you I don't belong to *Eirensae.*" No, his home was somewhere worse. Somewhere that fed on hatred.

Callie nodded. He wished he could read the thoughts behind her blue eyes. He knew they must be terrible things. Seeing Coal had confirmed it for Rowan. He belonged to *Fraeburdh. Eirensae's* enemy. *Callie's* enemy.

She was quiet for so long that the sun had time to peek over the horizon, bringing a new day. "I might know a way to get us to California. You won't like it, though."

৪০◆୯৪

The house looked just as Callie remembered. Tan siding, the color of broken dreams, faded blue shutters, patchy lawn, bald in some places, overgrown in others. The porch drooped in the middle. The scent of pot lingered from the driveway.

"Paradise," Rowan said from behind her.

She tossed him a dirty look and held a finger to her lips. At least they had clean clothes. They'd spent the remainder of the stolen money on two pairs of jeans and sweatshirts. Rowan looked like a typical bad boy in the artfully frayed black jeans and a tightfitting black sweater. Callie felt like a hobo in her baggy hoodie, especially after months of wearing skirts and dresses.

Rowan had healed the aching bruises at her throat and the scrapes on her knees and elbows. She looked average now, with glamour covering her faerie markings. Human. Inside was a different story. Blue energy pulsed beneath her skin. She felt like a lighthouse in storm, so bright and different that she could never belong here again. Part of her envied Rowan's ability to blend in.

She led Rowan around the side of the house, their steps making soft squelching sounds in the damp grass. How many times had she walked up the driveway, too disillusioned to know better? She'd wanted so badly to feel normal, but Nate had never made her feel anything. Not even special. Their entire relationship was based on an imaginary feeling Callie wished she could find or at least understand.

Nate's rusted truck sat in front of a rotting garage. The orange, dilapidated monster was his baby. He poured every penny into the truck getting it to run. Now, looking at it, Callie wondered if he shouldn't have just put it out of its misery. The thing was longing for a junkyard years before Nate "rescued" it.

"This is your master plan?" Rowan asked. "That piece of garbage won't get us five miles up the road before the engine blows."

"Do you have a better suggestion?" Callie hissed, feeling along the bottom of the door for the magnetic key Nate left there. He had a bad habit of losing his keys. Once, after they'd searched for half a day, Callie found them in the freezer next to his stash of weed. She found the tiny box and stood, brushing flakes of rust and mud from her hand, fingers clutching the ignition key.

She dropped it into Rowan's palm. "You drive."

His eyebrows shot up. "It's a stick shift."

"I assume you know how to drive those?"

"Of course I do," he said, palming the key. "I just don't want you yelling at me when it catches on fire and we waste even more time getting to *Fraeburdh*."

Callie stared at Rowan, the sharp angles of his face, the stubborn set of his chin, the way his hair curled at the base of his neck. So much like Coal, and yet, Rowan could circle his hands around her throat and she would never be afraid. She remembered the hard steel of Rowan's body pressed against hers when he'd emerged from the Reflection Pond and how she never wanted that one moment of uninhibited relief to end. Rowan swallowed, and for the briefest moment, his exterior fell away and she saw something soft underneath, something terrified.

Callie turned away and wrenched the door open. The twisted metal groaned and left a line of rust on the ground. She climbed into the cab, ignoring the warmth of Rowan's hand on her back, and slid across the seat. "Come on," she said, patting the ruined leather. "Two thousand miles is a long way to go."

As they backed out of Nate's driveway, Callie let her gaze move to the house next door. Only a handful of weeks had passed since she'd been there, but somehow it looked worse in the pink and violet morning light, as though someone had put a dingy filter over her camera lens. The windows were dark and empty, even the broken blinds were gone. Plywood covered the cracked kitchen window and enterprising grass choked the sidewalk. The paint continued to peel and a shutter lay useless next to the porch.

She almost asked Rowan to stop just to be certain, but Callie knew from the empty feeling in her gut that her foster family was gone. Packed up, moved on. They'd probably forgotten about her by now. It shouldn't hurt, but the ache in her chest refused to be ignored. She'd expected to find missing person signs lining the telephone poles or a collection of candles in the last place she was seen.

She should've known there'd be nothing.

It was as if she'd never existed in this town.

Callie thought about the Fallen and *Fraeburdh,* and Elm, now free to wander around the human world. Maybe it was better that she had no connections. Fewer people would get hurt because of her.

Callie laid her head against the window and let the rumble of Nate's truck drown out her thoughts. It wasn't until she felt tears dripping from her chin that she realized it hadn't worked. She missed Sapphire. She missed her friends. She missed *home.*

₧♦ℚ

Across from Rowan, Callie slept against the door, her cheek pressed to the tiny ball of her fist. Strands of blond hair fell over her shoulders and hid one side of her face. He'd heard her cry and pretended he hadn't, not because he didn't want to comfort her, but because she would see the tears as weakness.

The sunrise bloomed into a warm fall day as the truck's tires ate up the distance to *Fraeburdh*—Rowan's home. The knowledge of where he came from was razor wire in his mind. It didn't feel real, and yet, it made sense. He'd always known darkness lingered beneath the surface. It was why he'd killed his foster mother. It was what forced him to push Callie away over and over again. He wasn't good. He didn't need confirmation to know this, though it certainly didn't help his positive attitude at all.

He glanced at Callie. Sunlight turned her hair golden and her cheeks pink. If only he could take her out of this. She refused to tell him what happened to her, but the memory crawled beneath his skin. He dreamed about it, nightmares that left him gasping and terrified. He just wanted to make things easier for her, smooth the path, but it seemed life had other plans.

Rowan waited as long as he could before he pulled into a gas station. The truck clunked along on fumes by the time Rowan reached the pump. He cut the engine and turned to Callie. She hadn't stirred in the sudden quiet and he didn't have the heart to wake her. He climbed from the seat, careful to shut the door quietly. A suburban pulled in to the opposite pump, driven by a pretty girl in dark sunglasses. She nodded at Rowan and he tilted his head in her direction. *Human interactions are so superficial,* he thought.

Inside the gas station, Rowan was assaulted by the scent of metal and poison and death. A greasy attendant sat behind the counter, blond head ducked over his cell phone. Every few minutes a loud cheer rang from the tinny speakers. He didn't look up when Rowan asked for a map, just pointed to a stand to his left. Rowan picked the one that showed all major highways across the country and then stood in front of the beverages, wondering which Callie liked.

Tea. Energy drinks. Flavored water. Coffee?

For a girl he cared deeply for, he knew little about her.

Who was Callie before she fell through the pond? She held her past tight and her secrets tighter. Rowan supposed not a whole lot had changed for him when he'd transitioned from human to faerie. He still preferred silence and didn't make a habit of making new friends. He couldn't blame Callie when he acted much the same way she did.

Rowan palmed a bottle of water and glanced out the front of the store. Callie's blond head was just visible through the truck's window. He reached for a second bottle and carried them to the register. He'd found a few crumpled twenties in Nate's console, along with a handful of change. He dumped the whole lot of it onto the countertop and waited for the clerk to count it out.

"Forty-seven fifty-three, man," the guy said, scraping the change into his hand and dropping it into the drawer. "That monster must run through gas."

Rowan nodded. "Something like that."

The clerk jumped at the opportunity to talk. "What's it got in there, a big block?"

He nodded again. Rowan knew little about cars. When he lived in the human world, he never had enough money for one. He spent his time in the training gym which was within walking distance of his house, cleaning after the place closed to pay for his lessons, and eventually teaching his own classes.

The guy closed the register and glanced out the window as if to appreciate Nate's rusted truck. His eyes widened. "Is your girl drunk or something? It's like ten a.m. on a Monday."

Dread sluiced between Rowan's shoulder blades as he followed the clerk's gaze. The dark-haired girl from the suburban had Callie's limp form cradled in her arms. Callie's head hung back, throat exposed. Her hair dragged the dirty cement.

The Fallen, he thought, recognizing something distinctly fae about how the girl held herself, shoulders back, chin high and proud.

Rowan was out the door half a second later, heart in his throat, fingers itching for a fight. He never should've left Callie alone, not even when he was ten feet away. His breath squeezed from his lungs in short gasps, panic a vise on his chest.

The girl in the sunglasses didn't look his way as he approached.

"Callie," he yelled, hoping to wake her. They would've knocked her unconscious, not killed her. The Immortality ritual was too specific for a quick death. *She's sleeping,* he told himself. *Not dead. Oh god, please not dead.*

Just before he reached Callie, there was a high-pitched sound of dispersing air and a thunk of something hard on flesh. Rowan felt himself falling forward long before he felt the blow to the back of his head. He saw a flash of silvery blond hair and then nothing at all.

⨷ Two ⨷

CALLIE'S BRAIN FELT stuffed with wet sand. Something cool and damp pressed against her cheek, and for a moment, she thought she'd fallen asleep against the window of Nate's truck.

Waves of agony slammed into her, battering the back of her head, each one more brutal than the last. She retched. Her stomach was empty and nothing came up but a sour taste. She kept her eyes squeezed shut until the nausea receded and even then it was a chore to slit her eyelids. The pounding resumed against her skull and she swallowed. Her throat was dry.

She lay on a cold stone floor in a shadowy room. A bit of light seeped from above, the window slatted with metal bars. When she tried to push herself up, pain lanced through her arms, which were trapped behind her. Tight, searing bindings secured her wrists. With a groan, Callie scooted her legs underneath her until she could sit. She leaned gratefully against the gritty wall. The bindings on her wrists clanked.

Metal, she thought.

Her brain worked in slow circles, thoughts nothing more than wisps in a hurricane. She remembered being in the truck with Rowan…and then nothing. Her stomach churned.

Drawing a deep metal and decay scented breath, Callie took in her surroundings. The cell was small enough to be a closet. It had a single window at the top of a metal door, where dim, flickering light filtered through. Beyond the door was silent except for the faint sound of trickling water, difficult to hear over her breaths.

She swallowed again, trying to force realization down. Rowan had warned her. The Fallen.

Callie bit her lip. Blood trickled against her tongue, the warm wetness surprisingly welcome. She shut her eyes and forced herself to think.

Why did her wrists feel like they were on fire? She rolled her shoulders but the movement was stunted and didn't make her feel any better.

Do not panic, she ordered herself. She was more powerful than any other faerie she'd met. The Fallen were nothing more than human—they didn't stand a chance against her.

Then why are you in this cell?

She shoved the thought away and focused on the energy. It was a candle burning bright blue at her core. She inhaled slowly.

Heat rose from the metal surrounding her wrists, hotter and hotter until Callie cried out. Trapped between her back and the wall, her flesh sizzled. The acrid scent of burnt flowers reached her nose.

"Is somebody there?" Her voice bounced off the walls and echoed back to her like a thousand ghosts. Callie winced. This couldn't be happening. This wasn't real.

A shadow crossed over the light and Callie heard the sound of a metal key creaking in the lock. The door crept open.

"She wakes," a warm female voice said. "And for a minute I'd thought I'd clobbered you too hard."

"Let me go," Callie said, her voice a raspy whisper.

The dark-haired woman carried a cheery yellow flame. It turned her pale skin gold and made her brown eyes flicker. She set the candle on the floor and knelt before Callie, brushing her long hair over her shoulders.

"My name is Tanna."

"I don't care what your name is. Let me go."

Tanna's teeth flashed in the dim light. She had a pretty, angular face, with a hard mouth, and sharp, watchful eyes. "Gildas would be unhappy with me if I did that. Since Elm claimed the other child as his own, we were left with you. Happy chance that you were chased out of your city."

"Who is Gildas?" Callie pressed. Though in the darkest part of her soul, she knew. Gildas was the Fallen who would kill her. She was so stupid, marching into the human world like she was strong, like she could take on anyone.

"Gildas is our leader. He'll be home in a couple of days. Until then, I'll keep you company."

"I'm powerful," Callie said. "I can give you anything you want."

Tanna grinned. "The only thing you have to give is your life." She patted Callie's knee. "The Fallen are rising, growing stronger each day. With Immortals on our side, it will be nothing for us to destroy the faerie cities and take back what is rightfully ours."

Callie lapsed into silence while Tanna fussed over her.

"Do your wrists hurt? I'm sorry about that. It's enchanted metal, nasty for the fae. Steals your powers. Painful, too." Tanna pulled Callie away from the wall to inspect the bindings.

Callie's head swam.

When Sapphire told her that the fate of *Eirensae* rested in her hands, Callie was certain Sapphire hadn't intended for her to die as soon as she made it outside. She needed a plan.

Tanna eased Callie back. "Are you familiar with the ceremony?" She scraped a fingernail down Callie's cheek. "Gildas has been practicing, carving up humans like pigs."

Callie thought of the scars that traversed Rowan's back and chest, thick, jagged marks from when his foster father had tried to become Immortal. That was Callie's future if she didn't find a way out. She met the other girl's gaze. "I'm not a human," she said, fighting to keep her voice strong.

Tanna's lips twisted into a cruel smile. "No, you're not. And that makes it so much better." Tanna licked her fingers and extinguished the flame, pitching them into darkness.

Callie's throat closed. She held her breath so Tanna wouldn't hear how frightened she was and listened to the soft scrape of Tanna's footsteps across the wet floor.

"Sleep well," Tanna said.

For a while, Callie could hear the soft sounds of someone breathing, but eventually footsteps followed and all went quiet, save the maddening drip of water. *This is what torture feels like*, Callie thought, adjusting her arms so the metal circlets around her wrists pressed against the outside. It'd gone on like this for hours at least, with Callie moving the burning metal from inside to outside, outside to inside whenever the pain became unbearable. Below the cuffs, her fingers were numb. Her shoulders ached. Her mouth tasted like rust and dirt.

She was tempted to feel sorry for herself, to let tears well and fall, but even when she closed her eyes, none came. She'd tried screaming. The shrill wail still echoed in her ears. No one answered.

Callie cracked her neck and rolled her shoulders, unable to get comfortable. The damp soaked through her clothes and the temperature dropped.

Without Tanna's candle, the room was completely black. Callie leaned her head back and closed her eyes. She couldn't see any better with them open anyway.

This is what hopelessness feels like.

❧ ✦ ❧

Sometime later, Callie woke to the scrape of a key in the lock. Candlelight flitted through the barred window as the door creaked open. She expected another cryptic conversation with Tanna, but the boy who stepped into the room was the complete opposite of the girl. Where Tanna was tall and dark, this boy was shorter, slim as a switch, and with pale gold hair that just brushed the tops of his shoulders.

Callie's heart lurched. Was this Gildas? Had he come to kill her? She shrank away, pressing her spine into the wall. Her wrists ignited with new waves of anguish.

He knelt before her, setting down the candle and a tray he carried in the opposite hand. Bright blue eyes roved over her face. His mouth dipped into a frown that grew deeper and deeper, until finally, he sighed.

Callie swallowed. She hated the terror burning the back of her tongue and the quiver of dread in her stomach. She didn't want to be afraid but what else was there to feel when she was waiting to die?

The boy tucked his hair behind his ears and rocked back on his heels. "Tanna has not been very nice to you," he whispered.

"What do you want?" Callie asked. She searched the tray he'd brought. It contained lengths of fabric, a small bowl of liquid that smelled of flowers and astringent, and a pair of leather gloves, but no sharp objects she could see.

His gaze met hers. The lines beside his mouth deepened. "My name is Gunner." He withdrew a key dangling from a chain from beneath his tunic.

Callie caught the scent of him as he leaned closer. It was earthy and rich. "You're fae," she said.

Gunner fingered the chain. "I was, yes, for a short time. Now I've had the unfortunate joy of joining the Fallen. I'm human," he said. "A cruel sentence, if you ask me." He lifted the key to eye level. "This is for the cuffs. If I promise not to hurt you, will you promise me the same?"

"Why should I?"

Gunner's mouth quirked. She found herself inspecting the gaunt angles of his face. He was painfully thin, but he held himself with an elegance that spoke of his faerie past.

"I can't lie. That's one truth that never fades, even when powers go, even when life dims."

"I don't believe you," Callie said. But she wanted to. The key would set her free.

"I came to tend your wounds." He gestured to the tray. "I don't want to hurt you."

"You're one of them. Of course you want to hurt me. You want me dead." Callie couldn't remember how she'd gotten here. She remembered stealing Nate's truck and falling asleep beside Rowan.

Rowan.

Did they have him, too?

"Gildas wants you dead. I'm simply part of a plan that will have no effect on me. This was never what I wanted. I was meant to join the fae, not be cast aside like a stranger. I had a *destiny* and it was taken from me." His harsh whisper cut off. When he spoke again, his words were calm. "They have my amulet. I've seen it. They told me if I helped them get you, they would give it to me. Yet, here you are, and here I am. Still."

Callie fought to think around the ache in her skull. She was tired, *so tired,* but his words filtered through like sand in an hourglass. "What city?"

"Fraeburdh."

"I can help you," Callie said, leaning forward. "I'm powerful, Gunner. Let me help you get out of here. I can get your amulet back. I can get you to *Fraeburdh.*"

Though Callie's voice was hardly a whisper, Gunner flinched. "It's allegiance or death, Calla Lily. I do not value many things, but my life is one of the last things I have. I came to help you, yes, but only to ease your suffering. I'm sorry." He swallowed. "Your promise, and I will take the cuffs off."

Callie bit her tongue. She couldn't lie to him. If she made it, she'd have to keep it. "I promise I won't hurt you," she said.

"Good." His smile was beatific. Gunner slid on gloves before helping her lean forward.

It was torture. Though Gunner's fingers were deft and gentle as he eased the enchanted metal from her flesh, it throbbed like the hottest fire. Finally, they rattled to the floor and Callie released her breath. Her arms felt like noodles when she brought them in front of her. The sweet agony of the muscles in her shoulders brought tears to Callie's eyes. Black, oozing flesh surrounded her wrists.

Callie detached from the wounds, as if she were seeing them on someone else's body. Now that the metal was gone, the pain hardly registered.

Gunner slid the cuffs to the other side of the tiny room. "Enchanted metal is the worst kind of cruelty," he said, shuddering and peeling off the gloves. He lifted a length of the gauzy fabric from the tray and dipped it in the bowl.

While he worked, Callie focused on the energy inside of her. She was weak, not just physically, but also magically. The burning, normally an inferno, was just a spark. Her arms were dead weight, the muscles exhausted from holding the awkward position for so long. She didn't have the drive to fight even if she wanted to.

"What do you know of Gildas?" she asked, inspecting the bandage on her arm. The searing ache was gone.

Gunner's gentle fingers started on her other wrist. "He has been in exile for twenty years. He lived in *Macántacht* for nearly two hundred. Then he tried to kill his brother and he's been out here ever since, just waiting to become Immortal so he can finally finish his revenge."

"I thought the fae of *Macántacht* were peaceful."

Gunner snorted. "I don't think you can classify them so easily. I come from the City of War. Do I fit what you expect of them?"

His blue eyes rose to hers and Callie found herself thinking of Rowan. She wanted to ask Gunner if they had Rowan, but what if they thought she was alone? If she asked, she might ruin any chance of being rescued.

"I don't know what to think anymore," she said eventually.

"Maybe I'm a poor example. I only spent one day inside the city. They didn't have time to mold me into a warrior."

"What's it like there?"

Gunner's hands stilled. "Dark," he said, as though this was the only quality that mattered. He resumed wrapping the cloth. "And *Eirensae?*"

"It's beautiful," Callie said. "It's exactly like you'd imagine a fairytale. Flowers and trees everywhere. Gorgeous faeries." She lifted a shoulder and winced. "It's home. Or it was. When I left, it was burning."

Gunner nodded. "Gildas talked about that. I don't know where he gets his information. It's like he's in all three cities at the same time." He returned her hand gently to her lap. "All done."

"Won't Tanna be angry that you've unbound me?" She eyed the manacles in the corner. Even at rest they were menacing, the black metal cuffs at least three inches wide. Callie imagined bits of her skin still stuck to the insides.

"I don't care what Tanna thinks. You're not here to be tortured, no matter how strong you are."

Callie lifted an eyebrow and then lowered it before Gunner noticed. "Please," she said. "Please help me get out of here. I appreciate this," she said, lifting her arms. "But a few bits of gauze won't save my life. Gildas will kill me."

Gunner eased backwards until he sat across from her, long legs folded in front of him. "I…" he hesitated, drawing a deep breath. His gaze wouldn't meet hers. "I want to, truly. Maybe if I'd never gone to *Fraeburdh*, maybe if I'd never known." He shook his head as though dislodging the memories. "What kind of power do you have?"

Callie frowned and didn't answer.

Gunner glanced up. "Of course. I'm sorry. It's none of my business. I just thought maybe you could understand…but that's stupid. I'm being selfish, aren't I?"

"I'm willing to listen if you want to explain yourself." The more he talked, the better her chances of escape. Even if Gunner wouldn't help her, she could overpower him if she gained her strength back. Overpower, but not hurt. Uneasiness crept into her throat followed by a deep longing for Rowan.

"I control wind. It's such a small thing really, but it was *mine*. It was humiliating, standing before King Arol and being told that there was no place for me. How could they not have my amulet?"

"Wait," Callie interrupted. "You said you were only there a day. In *Eirensae* you have two years to find your amulet."

Gunner's eyebrows furrowed. "The cities are different in that. King Arol has all the amulets stashed and ready for when children return. Warrior training begins immediately. He needs you imprinted and bound. Or at least that's what he told me when he had his guards kick me out. He took my powers. Sucked it right out of me." He opened his hands, palms up. "Now I'm this."

Callie felt a pang of pity for the boy. She shifted her weight. The movement made her wrists sting and stole her breath. She'd never felt this weak, not even after training for hours with Rowan. "How did you end up with Tanna?"

"They were waiting for me outside."

"With your amulet? Isn't that strange to you?"

"Of course it's strange, but all I want to do is belong. This isn't exactly what I had in mind, but it's better than being alone. *Anything* is better than being alone."

A few months ago, she might've agreed with him. She searched her mind for anything she could offer, any way to convince him to help her but came up empty. Closing her eyes, she laid her head against the stone wall. Distantly, she was hungry.

She came alert when Gunner picked up the gloves and eyed the manacles.

Callie's insides froze. "I thought—" she said.

"If I don't put them back on, Tanna will come up with something worse. Don't underestimate her. She's ruthless."

Callie glanced at the fabric wrapping her wrists. Muddy fluid had soaked through them. She bit back a gag. "Please," she begged. "If I'd known they were going back on, I never would've let you take them off."

Gunner bit his lip, his eyes skittering away from hers. "I *have* to," he said, his fingers already unwinding the gauze.

She swallowed a scream at the first kiss of the searing metal. Her energy, bright blue, slithered from her skin in wisps like smoke.

"I'm sorry," Gunner whispered, tears collecting in his eyes. Then he was gone, taking the cheery yellow flame, the tray, and Callie's hope with him.

৪০ ♦ ୯୪

The only thing Callie had to mark the passage of time was the erratic pounding of her heart and the sharp, searing ache in her wrists. She'd tried to doze, drifting just to the edge of sleep before an angry grumble from her stomach or a new pain startled her awake. Dozens of times she imagined a key grinding in the lock. How long did she have before Gildas returned?

A numb sense of detachment settled over her mind, heavy and viscous as oil. She thought of Sapphire, radiant as she accepted her markings as prophetess, Jack, holding Callie as she cried, and Ash, jaw bruised from Rowan's fist.

Rowan, his mouth crashing into hers just before they'd escaped the city. Time had been a whirlwind since. She hadn't even had a chance to process it. A raw sob erupted from her mouth. *Eirensae* had been everything she'd ever wanted and yet, still cruel and unfair. What would happen now that Callie couldn't save the city as Sapphire had foreseen? Would they be enslaved by *Fraeburdh?* Slaughtered?

Callie swallowed hard, forcing the emotions back into her chest. If she let them all out, they'd consume her, and she didn't know if she could handle that and Gildas at the same time.

The sound of a key broke through her thoughts, and this time, she hadn't made it up. Gunner slipped into the room, carrying a flickering taper candle, his hands gloved.

"Back so soon?" she quipped.

Gunner frowned. "Tanna's gone out. I thought you might like to use the bathroom and eat something."

"What's the point?" she said.

Gunner knelt to remove her cuffs. "The point is that I'm not a savage. I'm not Tanna, and I'm certainly not Gildas."

Callie glowered at him before looking away. She couldn't maintain the nice act she'd had earlier. He might lessen her pain, but he had no intention of helping her escape. With the cuffs safely moved to the corner along with the candle, he slid his hands beneath her arms and pulled her upright. She had to lean all her weight against him. Her legs were putty.

Gunner half-carried, half-dragged her into the hallway beyond the door. It looked a lot like her cell, windowless, with damp stone walls.

"Where are we, anyway?" she muttered as he led her to a rickety staircase. Pale light bled from the upper floor though it hardly chased away the shadows.

"This house is abandoned. We've been living off-grid, mostly."

"Squatting," Callie said.

Gunner nodded. "We use whatever Tanna can steal, which is a lot. That girl is—" he broke off. "Never mind. You don't want to hear all this."

Callie didn't bother agreeing. The trek upstairs, though Gunner had done most of the work, left her weak and gasping for air. He deposited her in an unstable chair at an equally unstable table, taking the seat across from her. Sweat beaded on his forehead.

Callie laid her cheek on the scarred wood and closed her eyes. She couldn't catch her breath. Her fingers tingled.

"I think we have some soup," Gunner said. "I know it's not much."

Callie groaned.

"I'll heat it up."

She listened to his footsteps retreat and lifted her head. Before the house became decrepit, this had probably been the family room, she decided. Aside from a rickety rocking chair in the corner and the table, the room was empty. How long had they been camped out here, she wondered, looking over her shoulder.

Hope sprang into her chest. There was a door, and through the dingy, barred windows, she could see outside. A yellow moon filled the glass, the brightness dimming the surrounding stars.

She'd never seen something more beautiful.

Steeling herself, Callie forced her legs to move. They didn't want to obey, and the effort left her head swimming and her back drenched with sweat. Callie took a breath and held it. She could do this.

She moved one foot, watching it slide from beneath the table. The other one followed, slowly, *too* slowly. *Hurry,* she urged herself.

She braced her hands on the table, ignoring the protesting wounds at her wrists and the shaking of her muscles. She would crawl. She would slither like a worm. She would get through the damn door.

Gunner emerged from the back of the house carrying a bowl and spoon. "I didn't heat it up. I figured it'd take too long."

Callie felt her hope snap like a kite string in a tornado. She slumped against the back of the chair while Gunner, oblivious to her escape attempt, set the soup in front of her.

"It's vegetable," he said, pushing the spoon across the table.

Callie stared at the cold meal, mind working. She had to eat it, and then she had to make Gunner go away again. Maybe it wouldn't replenish the strength the enchanted metal had stolen but it would help. She forced her shaking hand to move. It was like swimming through sludge, getting her brain and muscles to connect.

"Here," Gunner said, watching her attempt with sadness pulling at his mouth. "Let me."

Tears burned the back of her eyes as she opened her mouth to accept the first bite. The texture made her throat spasm. She chewed and swallowed, ignoring the nausea. It went on like this, open, chew, swallow, until finally the spoon scraped the bottom of the empty bowl.

"Can I have more?" she asked, avoiding Gunner's gaze. From the corner of her eye, she watched indecision flit across his face. She wanted to puke.

"I think we have another can," he said.

"Please," she said, letting tears of shame fall.

The second he was gone, Callie slid from the chair onto the floor, not bothering with her useless legs. She tucked her arms and used her elbows to drag herself across the dirty wood, teeth gritted, eyes squeezed shut. Every inch was agony. She wanted to weep when she finally reached the door. Tears streamed her face. Her arms and legs were slick with blood and ragged with splinters.

Cool air drifted beneath the rotten doorframe. On it, she scented grass and rusted metal. *Freedom.*

She propped her back against the wall and used her knee as a ledge for her arm. She could just reach the handle. Her fingers fumbled the knob before finding purchase. *Please,* she thought, *please.*

It was locked.

Callie's arm gave out and flopped to the floor beside her. She glared at it. She had to try again. She had to get out.

"I think it's time to get you back downstairs," Gunner said.

Callie's gaze moved to the doorway across the room. "Just open the door and I'll go."

Gunner swallowed hard. He moved across the room slowly, the bowl of soup shaking in his hands. It clattered to the table. "You can't even walk. How far would you get?"

A sob built in her chest. "I can do it. Just open the door." She licked her lips, tasted salt and metal. "Please."

Abandoning the soup, he came toward her, slowly, as though weighing his options. He was wavering.

"Please," she repeated.

His hands slid beneath her. Despite his waiflike appearance, he lifted her easily. "I can't," he said, voice breaking. "I can't."

"No," Callie said against his chest. In her head, it was a scream, but it came out as a whisper. She beat her hands against him, kicked her legs, lashed out with everything she had, but Gunner's grip never faltered, and why would it? She was too weak, too tired.

It was over.

Want more Callie and Rowan?
Order your copy of Poison Tree today!